Books by S. Kodejs:
The Manitou, Book One
The Manitou, Book Two
Eternity (Eternity Series)
Dance For The Devil
The Spirit Seeker Society
Better Off Dead

THE MANITOU: BOOK ONE

A NOVEL OF
HORROR AND SUSPENSE

Copyright 2013 by S. KODEJS

*Dedicated to my good friend, Jim Drake,
Who has spent most of his life in the forest
And, occasionally, tries to beat me at Scrabble*

PART ONE

... into the Stein

PROLOGUE

They never saw the skeleton. It fell in front of them, the decayed skull almost striking the younger man on the head before glancing off a tree trunk, disintegrating into a million specks of fine, grey dust. *"Jesus!"* Jerry yelled, leaping backwards. *"Jesus Christ!"*

The older man chuckled. "You should see the look on your face, Hackett. Very theatrical. Wish I'd brought my camera. Could've shown the crew what a chicken-shit you are."

"Very funny," Jerry said, his face twisted with disgust. He stooped to examine the remains, his heart pumping wildly. "Think its Native?"

"Gotta be. Who else but a chug would bury a goddamn carcass in a tree?"

"This is it, then. There's no doubt now."

"Nope."

"Bloodsworth isn't going to like it."

"Nope." The older man coughed a little, flexed his shoulder muscles and lit a cigarette. He took a long, deep drag and stood there, holding the cigarette in his right hand, the butane lighter in his left.

"Well, what should we do, Wendall? Should we pack the remains and take them to Bloodsworth, or should we mark the trail so the crew can make their way here?"

"Whaddya think we should do?"

Jerry looked at his boss with consternation. He didn't like the older man, found him rough and abrasive, but knew as a scout Wendall was tops. Wendall Scott had twenty-five years of forestry experience compared to

Jerry's six months. It surprised Jerry the older man would solicit his opinion and he cleared his throat nervously. "I think... the proper protocol is to *not* disturb the body – at least, not disturb it further. We should mark the trail with reflector ribbons and bring the team here."

Wendall took another drag on his cigarette, the smoke curling in fine tendrils around his lined face. "You do that, kid."

"Okay. I'll get the stuff from my backpack."

"Yeah."

Jerry turned away feeling proud. He knew he just passed an important test. Finally the crew was starting to treat him with a modicum of respect – it was tough being low man on the totem pole, even if he did have more education than the rest of the crew put together.

When he returned less than five minutes later, holding the ribbon in one hand and a plastic tarp in the other, two thoughts occurred to Jerry simultaneously. The first was perhaps he would earn a promotion. A discovery of this kind was significant to say the least, his name would be in the newspapers for sure, maybe even the nationals. The second thought was that he smelled smoke. Not the acrid, chemical scent of tobacco, but the moist, thick, woodsy scent of moss and damp earth, of decay. And of accelerant.

Then he saw it.

"Christ, Wendall! What the hell are you doing?" Jerry moved to stomp the smouldering fire, tried to save the bone fragments and skull from catching flame but Wendall held him back. The two men watched silently as the flames licked higher, consuming the bones before encompassing the base of the tree from which they fell. "Jesus, Wendall, you'll start a forest fire."

"Nah. Never happen – too wet. It'll burn itself out. Now if it was summer, say August..." His voice trailed, the dancing flames reflected in his eyes as he thought about the damage of a high season fire.

"Jesus." Jerry shook his head. "You're crazy, Wendall."

Wendall looked at the younger man, noting the handsome, eager face, now a portrait in dismay. "You don't get it, do you, Hackett? Six months with the company and you still don't have one iota of the agenda, do you?"

"I know we're searching for Native Indian remains so we can avoid logging in their ancient burial grounds."

"Shit, Hackett, you gotta read between the lines. This whole valley is ancient burial grounds, or if you care to look at it that way, you could even say all of goddamned North America is burial grounds.

"Those chug carcasses are everywhere. Why, when my daddy was a boy, he watched them bury a chug in a crab-apple tree out in Garry Point. Know where that it? Richmond. Goddamned Richmond! Didn't stop anyone from building there, did it? Now look at the place – a concrete jungle. Shopping malls on every corner. Not a green-assed acre anywhere. Same goes for Vancouver and Toronto and probably even New-Fucking-York. This whole country was crawling with chug trash at one time and if they'd've buried their dead in the ground like civilized people instead of hauling them up trees like goddamned chimpanzees, we wouldn't be faced with this problem, now would we?"

Jerry shifted uncomfortably. The fire had died down a bit, still crackling and hissing with a morbid sound that reminded Jerry of knee sockets being wrenched from their joints. "I guess not," he mumbled, finally. "But it still doesn't seem right."

"Right? Ha!" The older man spat the word, his spittle spraying the orange flames. "What do you know about *right*, you smart-assed, punk-faced college kid with so many degrees shoved up your ass you can barely sit straight? I'll tell you about right, Hackett, and that's a cold hard fact of life. *Right* is that forestry is this province's number one industry, an industry that employs thousands of people, people like you and me, people with hungry kids to feed and clothe. *Right* is that this province is running out of accessible places to log, quality timber is becoming scarce. Timber that pays *your* wages, I might add. The Stein Valley is the last major unlogged watershed in southwestern British Columbia, prime timber just aching to be cut, timber that'll keep Canadians in the world market and out of recession. You see the picture, Hackett? Are we gonna give up all that for a couple of dead Indians who've been that way for centuries? Waste millions of dollars on a pile of bones that should've been buried six-feet-under in the first place?"

"I guess I hadn't thought of it that way. But what if someone finds out?"

Wendall laughed derisively and kicked some dirt onto the burning bones. "Who's gonna tell? Him? No, sir, his speaking days are long over."

The axe seemed to come from nowhere, falling unhampered from the darkening sky, its dull blade imbedding itself deep into Wendall Scott's skull, sluicing his cranium with blood spattering precision, dividing grey matter from bone with such alarming accuracy that Wendall Scott was dead before his body hit the ground, falling, falling until it finally came to rest in the smouldering fire.

"*JesusChristJesusChristJesusJesusJesus!*" Jerry Hackett fell backwards, his boot catching briefly on the dead man before he scrambled away, running into the forest, slashing through underbrush that scratched and clawed his face, stinging his cheeks and poking his eyes. *"JesusJesusJesus,"* he cried, incoherent in thought and action, running in no particular direction, just away from the fire and the burning bones and his backpack with red ribbon and other vital supplies and from his dead boss with the hatchet sticking from his skull.

He didn't know how long he ran, for three minutes or ten or forty. He stopped when winded, feeling his chest would explode as he gulped deep breaths of cool mountain air, blood pulsating in his veins and coursing from his scratched cheeks like so many tributaries of a vast, ruby river. He didn't know exactly when reason returned, the precise moment he realized the axe must've been interred with the Indian, laid to rest high in the branches of the great Douglas fir with its master, jostled loose by time and the elements along with the ancient bones. Not hurled by some malevolent Native warrior with a thirst for revenge.

If reasoning didn't come all at once, the laughter did; great, gut wrenching spates of laughter that tore his insides and bordered on hysteria. Here he was, a highly educated man of twenty-eight running through the forest like a spooked fifth grader. The hatchet was an accident. A bizarre, spurious freak of nature – nothing more, nothing less. He had nothing to be afraid of.

Still, Jerry didn't feel like going back to collect his belongings. Not yet – and not alone. He would locate the rest of the crew and return with the others.

Yeah. That's what he would do.

Jerry squinted, trying to catch his bearings in the dense forest, his breathing still labored. Darkness was falling... soon it would be blacker than slate. He didn't know where he was and there was no point wandering through the night in this vast forest. He would make camp here and set out at dawn's first light. All his supplies – his compass, matches, food, bedding – were back with Wendall, lying there with an axe sticking out of his... *God no, don't think of that, Jerry-old-boy, don't even think about it.*

His hunting knife was strapped to his belt, lying snugly against his left hip and that's all he really needed. It would be freezing when the sun went down; the temperature was dropping rapidly. Already he could see his breath coming in panicked wisps. He would build a lean-to, use branches and leaves to keep him warm through the encroaching night. Yes sir, that's what he'd do. His education was coming in handy already.

What was that? A noise? Not a noise really, just a rustling. Probably a chipmunk or a squirrel or a small bird. Jerry cocked his head to the left, standing stock still with every muscle attuned, straining, struggling to hear even the faintest sound. *Definitely a small animal*, he decided. The preternatural quiet hung like a heavy, dank cloak.

If only he had some matches he could light a small fire to ward off the encroaching gloom, but he didn't. The matches were still in his backpack and the other fire and his dead boss... *oh, Jesus, change the subject.*

Food. That was it, Jerry-old-boy, *think about food*. No, not the three tins of pork'n beans and Puritan beef stew back where he wasn't going to think about, but of early berries and mushrooms and, oh hell, what was that other stuff he learned about in school? The stuff that looked like fungus but was really quite delicious... *Shit! There it was again!*

Another sound. Louder. Closer.

A specific, bloodcurdling, spine-tingling, rip out your toenails and stuff 'em down your throat sound –

definitely not the type of sound made by an animal. A whirling, whispering, whooshing sound that grew and grew until it surrounded him, enveloped him, a sound so intense Jerry could feel it explode outwards and grip him.

And the smell. An awful, putrid scent that swirled up his nostrils and down his throat, into his lungs and beyond... an odor that reeked of stagnant fecal matter, decayed and rotten like dead bloated fish and oily maggots and... and... smoke? Yes, smoke, and something else.... Jerry began to gag as he identified the scent of burning flesh, flesh he recognized as his own.

Jesus, he was on fire! Impossible but true. Flames sprang from his jacket, from his shoes, from the webbed flesh between his fingers. He could feel the melting skin under his nostrils, the burning pain in his ears, taste the fire inside his mouth coming from within and he crumpled in an ungainly heap, writhing and twisting and shouting, unconscious of everything but the fire and the pain and of the ringed wall of faces, peering down at him, chanting.... chanting.....*"We will not let it happen again."*

CHAPTER ONE

July never really made it to the rainforest. Sure, it was summertime elsewhere in the country: the balmy saltiness of the Atlantic, the endless dry heat of the Prairies, the laid-back sunshine of the West Coast – those places knew the joy of a Canadian summer. But here, in the magnificent Stein Valley, the heat couldn't quite filter through the century-old evergreens, through the lichens and mosses and damp earth which covered the forest floor. Only half-hearted warmth remained, easily sheltered from the overhead wind and outside world.

In some places the lush valleys gave way to craggy cliffs or alpine meadows and here the heat soared, blazing with fierce intensity that could quickly burn unprotected flesh. To step from the coolness of the forest into the open was like entering a furnace blast, the heat welcome at first yet quickly unbearable, leaving the recipient longing to return to the cool protection of the forest.

It was precisely this paradox that governed Dean Stockton's deliberations as he filled the backpacks – a large Rip-Stop Nylon model for himself and a smaller Pack Cloth sack for the boy. Theoretically he shouldn't be taking backpacks at all – this was, after all, supposed to be an authentic Native ritual. Ancient Indians didn't sport hoodies and blue jeans, nor did they take rain gear and pup tents and dried food. Dean chuckled as he tossed in a box of Starbuck's Via Columbia. Natives of yore definitely didn't take instant coffee.

"Ready yet, Uncle Dean?"

"Almost, Sport. Did you roll up our sleeping bags like I asked you?"

"You bet! See? Over there by the front door, just waiting for us. I can't believe we're really going."

"Me neither, Jess. Me neither." Dean looked at the boy and smiled, holding up his hand for a high five. The 'uncle' part was a misnomer, but anyone could see that with one glance at the pair, the nine-year-old Native Indian boy, small for his age but sturdily built, dark hair and dark skin and jet black eyes that saw far more than a young child should; standing next to a green-eyed, fair-haired giant of a man.

"Think we'll see any grizzlies?"

"Maybe. If we're lucky."

"Then I'll zap 'em with my laser gun."

"No, Jesse, you have it all wrong. Indians don't hunt with laser guns."

"Then I'll zing 'em with my bow and arrow."

"That's the spirit. Here, try this pack on. Too heavy?"

Jesse slipped an arm into each side and hoisted the little red pack. "Nope, it's perfect."

"Are you sure? You have to carry this backpack for seven days and seven nights, and I don't want you complaining that it's too heavy halfway through."

"I won't complain, Uncle Dean."

Dean bent and placed a hand on the small head. "I know, Sport. You never do. Whaddya say we head for Injun country?"

"Yes, sir!"

The drive wasn't long. A little over three hours from Vancouver, a city Dean tolerated and hated and somehow let become home. Three hours drive north through farmland and canyons and semi-desert until he came to the valley he was born in, the valley he loved. The valley he hadn't seen for almost a decade. The valley he'd sworn never to set foot in again.

The Stein.

Even the name sent shivers of anticipation down Dean's spine. Such a proud name, noble and strong.

The Stein held a lot of memories for Dean Stockton and not all of them good. Some were downright terrifying, and if it wasn't for a promise given at his best friend's deathbed nine years before, Dean Stockton wouldn't be coming back.

**

Samuel Hudson looked at the group surrounding him and stifled a chuckle. Two young Asian men, a German girl, an American, and two Canadians – coupled with himself, an African American. They looked like a sampling from the United Nations.

A more mixed bag he never had, but that wasn't an issue. He'd been guiding tours into the Stein for over six years and neither color nor creed mattered, nor did gender. What counted was stamina and common sense. Backpacking through the Stein wasn't a stroll in the park – it was an intensive lesson in wilderness survival. These six had to function as a unit or they'd all be in jeopardy.

What brought them here? The reasons were probably as mixed as the six eager faces before him. Who knew what drew a person into the wilderness? What impelled solid citizens to leave their warm beds to explore a distant, uncivilized world? Ignorance? Challenge? A primal need to conquer the earth and thus find oneself? Escape or conquest? Hell, Samuel reckoned he'd about heard them all.

He scanned the group and began his orientation speech. He had delivered this same monologue so often he could spout it backwards, in his sleep, standing upside down with a mouthful of pebbles. It was standard script, written by some faceless entity eons ago, avowing to the perils of the wilds. Basic stuff:

respect the forest, beware of wildlife, don't drop cigarette butts on the forest floor lest you start a fire, stick together, blah, blah, blah. Samuel added a few comedic lines of his own and this group, as all others, laughed in the appropriate places. Well, except for the Asians – they just smiled eagerly and looked a little confused. Samuel guessed they didn't speak a word of English and he was right. Then again, Samuel Hudson was correct about most things.

He couldn't spot any obvious trouble makers but it was always a safe bet to anticipate at least one. Expect the worse was Sam's motto. That way, if you were right you were prepared and if you were wrong, you were pleasantly surprised.

Before long one of these six would emerge as a natural leader and the other five would follow. They would make friendships – cliques if you will – probably by the end of the day, but the natural leader would draw them together. The natural leader could make or break the tour... which one would it be? Impossible to guess, only time would tell. Samuel smiled broadly, his alabaster teeth shining brightly against his ebony skin. Whatever the outcome, these six were in for an adventure of a lifetime.

**

Jaclyn Hackett Hart studied Don Blume carefully. They were standing outside the Totem Motel in downtown Lytton – a dusty, hot town with more rattlesnakes than people, just her and Don and four others who were listening to Samuel Hudson, their tour guide. The rest of the town seemed in hibernation, hiding from the intense morning sun, staying protected from temperatures that would reach sweltering proportions by noon. It was not unusual for Lytton to be the hot spot in Canada and today looked like a record breaker. Jackie noticed many homes had satellite dishes – she supposed there wasn't much else to do if you lived in Lytton.

She smiled as she acknowledged the mental put down – Lytton was nothing like the large, impersonal city she grew up in, where you could live next to someone for years and never learn his name. Lytton might be small and dusty and remote, but there was something innately appealing about it. There was a cosiness and sense of unity. The houses were freshly painted with sun-baked yards. Probably mostly retired folk, people who enjoyed how the dry heat relaxed their arthritic bones. There was pride of ownership that kept Lytton from fading into oblivion.

Jackie pushed a strand of coffee-colored hair from her eyes and turned her attention to the small, fidgety man standing beside her. During group introductions he'd stated his name, Don Blume, but nothing else. He was sweating profusely and bouncing around like a jackrabbit, looking everywhere but at the tour guide. His movement was sending up a cloud of dirt and the good-looking American man next to him, Bob Vance, frowned slightly and moved away, making a show of brushing the dust from his pant legs.

"Footwear," Samuel Hudson was saying, "is vital. The wrong footwear can be the difference between life and death in the wilderness. Let's say we come across a grizzly, you're gonna need to be able to run."

Don Blume looked at the guide in alarm. "Outrun a grizzly? That's impossible! They can run sixty kilometres per hour!"

"No need to outrun the bear," Samuel deadpanned. "Just be faster than the guy next to you." He grinned widely and the group laughed. Everyone except Blume. "Just pulling your leg, folks. Haven't had any grizzly attacks for over a week." Another wide, teasing grin. "Oh, relax," he said, looking at Don Blume directly. "Never had a grizzly attack nor issues with bears at all. Mosquitoes will be your only problem, but do keep in mind, this is the wilderness so keep your head up and your stupidity down and you'll be fine."

Samuel moved onto other dangers, sprinkled with a few more lame jokes and Jackie listened idly while focusing her attention on Don Blume. Blume was nervous. *Very nervous.* Sure, he tried to hide it, camouflaging his tension behind a bland facade, but the telltale signs were there: the stiffness of his bearing, the constant shuffling, his halting responses to the guide's questions, and most of all, his refusal to look anyone in the eye. This last one was the real cruncher. Jackie learned early on from teaching children that if someone wouldn't – or couldn't – meet your gaze, he had an awful lot to hide.

No one else seemed to notice Don Blume's nervousness but that didn't surprise her. Most people weren't particularly observant, usually too caught up in their own existence to pay attention to the world around them, a situation that was clearly occurring in this group. The two young Asian men were busy clicking photos at everything that moved and some that didn't; the German woman was taking notes of Samuel Hudson's speech with a penmanship as beautiful and fluid as her own magnificent Arian body. The American was rocking back and forth on his heels, a sure sign he was itching to go. But then, why shouldn't he be excited? A one week, fully guided tour of the breathtakingly beautiful Stein Valley was pretty powerful stuff, a nature lover's paradise, an environmental dream. If Jackie was going under different circumstances she'd be jumping up and down with joy, too.

But she wasn't. She was looking for her brother, a forestry technician who'd been missing since spring. These past three months taught Jackie more than just the pain of losing a sibling – it had shown her the futility of corporate bureaucracy, the frustration of unreturned phone calls and dead ends, the hopelessness of red tape indoctrinated into every step of her search. When Jerry first disappeared, his coworkers seemed helpful and eager to locate the two missing workers who'd been marking a proposed logging route. They searched the area Jerry and his boss were last seen, to no avail.

Then a strange thing happened. Her inquiries, once met with helpful consideration, were ignored. Everyone connected with the Jerry Hackett case was transferred to another division, so scattered that Jackie couldn't begin to locate them. The new men were brusque and cold, even vaguely threatening. It was as if her brother and his boss, Wendall Scott, never existed.

This tour was Jackie's last resort, a desperate final attempt to locate her brother. In her heart she knew it was unlikely that Jerry had survived. Had he been lost, surely he would have found his way to civilization by now. The Stein was large – but not that large. A man couldn't wander indefinitely without finding his way out, especially a man as knowledgeable about the wilderness as Jerry. And if her brother had been injured, dazed and unable to move, surely he would have succumbed to the elements by now.

That was the most likely scenario. The Stein posed any number of potential threats: steep cliffs and fjords, avalanche hazards, grizzly bears and mountain lions, a vicious spring runoff that could quickly swell a creek five times its usual capacity. Anything could have happened to Jerry – he was well versed in wilderness danger.

But to lose both men at once? Without a single trace of their whereabouts – no tracks, no equipment, no sign of struggle? And why hadn't they marked their location so others could find them? That was the biggest mystery of all. Jerry knew the value of trail markers and he was stickler for doing things right. Jackie just couldn't figure it out.

Maybe she would uncover something the others missed. Maybe she could finally lay her brother to rest. And maybe, only then, could she get on with her life.

**

Jackie was right about one thing – Don Blume *was* nervous. He didn't like talking to people, didn't like high temperatures, and definitely didn't like the idea of venturing into the Stein. Maybe his mother was right – maybe he should have become an accountant.

Of course that shouldn't surprise him – Mother was right about everything and it was his one act of defiance, his refusal to have her choose his career that landed him in this mess in the first place. But who could foresee that a desk job as a forestry engineer would have him tracking all over Hell's half-acre on this wild goose chase?

It was Arne and Ben's fault. They were to blame for this... this fall from grace. Those two fat, lying bastards spent all *their* time lazing around the office while *he* did all the work. They told him he had more experience, which was hog shit. They called it a promotion. A promotion! But Don knew the truth. He'd seen the pictures of Jerry Hackett and Wendall Scott's remains, what little remains there'd been, all black and charred and mutilated, especially Wendall's with the axe protruding from his skull – the whole thing was disgusting.

If it really was a promotion then it should be one of them joining this so called tour – this elaborate charade to get this Jackie Hart bitch off the department's back, for once and for all. Arne and Ben both had more seniority, so they should get the – ha ha – promotion. But Don knew the truth. Arne and Ben had gotten together secretly, probably when he was off taking a leak or something, and they nominated him when his back was turned and his pants were down. Literally.

And he knew why. Arne and Ben were just as goddamned scared as he was. They didn't buy the murder-suicide story the company first supplied, an employee gone bush-crazy on an abusive boss. Hell, everyone knew that Wendall Scott was a jerk and by all accounts deserved to die, everyone here felt like killing the son of bitch at one time or another, so at first the theory made sense.

Except that it didn't account for the savage manner in which Hackett's burned body was found. It was physically impossible for a man to do that to himself – sure, if they said he'd lit himself on fire and then been torn apart by a bear afterwards, then maybe the story would fly. But the corporate bigwigs, not adept at covering up bizarre murders (but why should they be – this is a *forestry* company, not a goddamned morgue, after all) panicked and issued a second, more plausible story to anyone who didn't know the real facts. Next they said the bodies were simply missing... that's what they told the families. No bodies, no questions. They transferred everyone involved to different units to eliminate speculation between the crew, leaving only Arne and Ben and himself, three guys who were so deeply involved in the company stock-wise they wouldn't dare say anything for fear of damaging their investments. Clean and simple, right? Yes, except for one snoopy sister acting like a dog in heat – she wouldn't give up. Stupid bitch.

She was staring at him, making him nervous and twitchy. And now she was smiling at him, all fake and insincere. Oh, he'd like to tell her the truth all right, he'd like to take the truth and shove it up the snotty bitch's nose.

Only he didn't know the truth. Not exactly. At first he couldn't figure out why Empire fabricated a story at all. Why not just tell the truth and show the bodies – mangled and burnt – as found?

Don didn't know for sure, but he figured something big had happened, obviously something large enough to threaten the entire company. The man in charge, Reginald K. Bloodsworth, wasn't an idiot. He must have figured out something with all that secretive research he'd been doing lately. That wily old fox had something up his sleeve. Don would bet his last nickel on it.

Empire Forest Products' bid to log the Stein was tenuous as best – a multi-million dollar deal that had environmentalists and Native rights groups opposed and screaming. The balance was currently not in the logging company's favor, but this delicate balance might ultimately be swayed and the right to log this valuable old-growth timber would be gained. And something had happened out here that threatened to tip that balance negatively, something he had to cover up. Whatever happened to Wendall Scott and Jerry Hackett had the company running scared. Real scared.

But what could it be? That was anyone's guess. Maybe that crazy old Indian who came barging into the office with his spooky, creepy predictions *was* right. That's what Arne and Ben believed. Personally, Don thought the two had come across some psychotic mountain man, a social deviant who got his jollies killing loggers. Who knew for sure? No one, probably, and if he could convince Jackie Hart that her brother was truly dead and gone, without her suspecting that he knew who she really was, then he could get the hell out of this forest and back home, where it was safe.

And if couldn't convince her, then he'd shut her up for good.

Look at the way the bitch was staring at him, eyes probing and demanding, like she was trying to see straight through to his soul. Don wished she would stop – it was really starting to make him feel jittery. Not that she was unattractive or anything. Far from it, actually, with that unusual color of hair and those clear blue eyes. Jackie Hart was really quite pretty, beautiful even, although certainly not his type. Now, the other broad, the German one, what was her name again? He knew he'd heard it... oh, yes, Benta Sturm... a photographer from some Kraut magazine with a name he couldn't pronounce; now *she* was a knockout! A real piece of work, that one. *Oh, fuck!* That stupid son-of-a-bitch tour guide was asking him a question, asking him why he was here. What was this, a fucking game show? Now they were all looking at him, waiting, demanding. Even the German girl. Oh, crap. Don mumbled something appropriate, some bullshit about getting away from city-life stress and now they were all laughing at him, taunting him.

Then the German girl smiled and everyone looked away. Don felt elation. She was interested in him, actually interested in what he had to say! It made Don feel better, bigger even and he puffed his chest a little, hoping she'd notice his muscles, newly acquired from working in the gym. Good god, he even felt less nervous.

**

Benta Sturm paused in her note taking and listened to Don Blume's answer. She could tell he had been staring at her but that didn't surprise her. Men always stared at Benta and had since the summer she turned eleven and her breasts developed almost overnight. One day she'd been as flat-chested as all the other little girls her age and then suddenly she looked like a woman, a fact her male playmates noticed and the female ones seemed to resent. Her legs decided to follow suit, growing impossibly long and shapely, and her waist seemed to narrow while her young hips flared. All in all, it had been a very frightening summer for Benta, who still wanted to play dolls with her girlfriends and not *doctor* with their older brothers.

Benta wished the tour guide would stop talking gibberish and get back to the ancient Native pictographs. These rock etchings, done in red ochre, were some of the most extensive in Canada – perhaps even the world. They were several thousand years old, a fascinating insight to ancient life. It was a discovery that ranked with the Egyptian hieroglyphics, yet an archaeological treasure Canadians seemed completely indifferent to. The Canadian government had taken no steps to preserve the ancient paintings and few Canadians knew anything about them. The ones that did know didn't seem to appreciate the true cultural and historical value, or perhaps they just didn't care.

This baffled and intrigued Benta, and when her editor suggested a photo shoot of the paintings, Benta jumped at the offer. This was exactly the kind of story that would be picked up and reprinted in a wide variety of publications: travel, archaeological, scientific, outdoor, even fashion magazines. She could envision skinny models in couture posing in front of the ancient etchings. Benta was certain that adventurers and scholars and archeological students worldwide would clamor to visit the Stein. If done right, her photographs would open the Stein to a large and varied influx of people, eager to see something new.

She just hoped that Mr. Samuel Hudson would spend more time showing her the paintings than he did talking about them. She would need a good half day to properly photograph the pictographs, and that was if the weather cooperated and her lighting was good. If not... well, if not she would stay behind while the rest of the group forged ahead. It wouldn't pose a problem: she was an experienced hiker and rock climber. In fact, she had hiked mountains and climbed peaks far more challenging than the Stein. This would be a piece of cake.

Don Blume was looking at her again and Benta smiled at him, noticing how he instantly puffed up like a stuffed pheasant. Poor thing – he probably thought he had a nice physique, when he really resembled a... what did they call it in English? *A scarecrow.* Certainly not what she envisioned a Canadian male to look like... goodness, were all men in this country so puny? She'd imagined Canadians to be somehow larger than life. What a disappointment. Now, the other man standing beside her, Benta believed he was American, he was more like it. Nicely built, strong features, intelligent looking eyes... too bad he was jostling back and forth as though his pants were on fire. A definite turn off.

**

Bob Vance couldn't *wait* to get started. He could smell money in the air, deals to be made, properties to be developed. *Why* was this Hudson fellow still talking? Couldn't he tell that no one was listening? Sheesh.

What a wretched little town this was. How could anyone live in a place like this? God, it was worse than living under a bridge – no action at all. Now Los Angeles – there was a city. L.A. was everything: a hedonistic playground, free enterprise at its very best, where hustlers had it made and losers didn't bother anyone. Why leave L.A. for a godforsaken hellhole like this?

Money. That's why. Pure and simple: money.

The Stein was a developer's paradise. Pristine valleys, unlimited fishing, big game hunting; the place was a biological jewel. Slam a thousand room resort in – luxury, mind you, everything had to be first class, Americans wouldn't travel to substandard facilities – and you had a gold mine. Have a couple of choppers fly people in and out, perhaps a float plane.... they'd love it.

Fishermen, hunters, nature lovers, boaters – yes, he'd build a dock, bring in decent sand like they do at Waikiki. Maybe film a reality show to get it on the map...*hmmm, he should jot that down.* Bob pulled out his Blackberry and started typing. What else? Ah, honeymooners would eat this shit right up. He would entice them all – then perhaps he might finally earn an award or two, plus the respect of his peers.

Say, he should give his business card to the Chinamen over there. Or were they Japs? He never could tell the difference, but what did it really matter? Chinks, Nips, Hongkers – they had all the bucks. Everyone knew the emerging economy of the Far East was the place to seek investors. Chicken Chow Mein and Hong Kong Dick didn't look loaded, but their parents probably were...

Actually, he'd give the whole group business cards – these other patsies didn't look wealthy but you never could tell. Money lurked everywhere. Bob learned early on to never judge a book by its cover. This group of misfits didn't look ripe but one might be hiding a bundle...or have a dear, old auntie ready to kick the bucket. It didn't pay to alienate anyone. It was all about networking.

**

Dean had forgotten how beautiful the surrounding countryside was. Well, maybe not forgotten – tucked the memory away, perhaps. Stored it in the deep recesses of his brain where he hoped to never recall it – psychologists might use the term repression, a mechanism designed to help humans withstand pain. Nature was kind – it allowed time to heal emotional wounds.

That was the theory, anyway. As Dean crested the hill that would take him back to his old home town, the raw agony of Emily Ann's death rushed over him, overwhelmingly intense, unbelievably fresh as if the tragic accident that took her life happened moments ago instead of nine years. He bit back the cry that threatened to escape so as not to frighten the boy – Jesse had suffered enough. The same accident which took Dean's wife also killed Jesse's parents.

Had it really been nine years? Hard to believe – Emily Ann's face was as vividly etched into his brain as if the image was stored yesterday. Still hard to accept he would never hear her laughter, nor feel her body against his as they made love... never again run his fingers through her baby fine hair.

This was the spot where it happened. If he looked hard enough he could see skid marks – no surely not. Not after nine years. These marks must be fresh – just one more accident on this nasty stretch of highway.

They had been such good friends, Dean and Eddy and Lyn. The trio had grown up together, one tow-haired boy and two Native youths. Inseparable, they were the three musketeers, squabbling good-naturedly and camping out and watching the same movie again and again until the only theatre in town played a new one. No one was the least bit surprised when Eddy and Lyn married, right out of high school. Then Emily Ann moved to town, a fresh face in a close knit society and suddenly she fit in too, like they'd always been four. And finally, Dean and Emily Ann fell in love and the circle was complete.

They'd been married only two months on that lazy Sunday afternoon. Everyone decided to see a movie, except for Dean who needed to study if he wanted to keep his scholarship – that was the only way he could afford law school – money was awfully tight, and besides, he'd seen the damn movie three times anyway. Hey, he had an idea, why didn't the three of them go, Just Em and Eddy and Lyn, and he would stay home and watch the baby.

Was he sure? Of course, Lyn, you go, I'll watch Jesse. He won't interfere with my studies one bit – look at him: a better baby was never born. Hardly ever fussed, quiet as can be, and besides, you and Eddy haven't been out without him. Not once in two months. Wasn't it about time?

Well, Lyn said, *he had just been fed, and he probably would sleep the whole time, but we could take him in the Snuggly so you can study uninterrupted.*

Go, Lyn, go. All of you – get out of here! I can watch my own godson for two hours without you mother hens clucking over me... and you too, Em, you're just as bad. He could see Emily Ann was hurt, she never did take criticism well, so he smiled to ease the sting, shooing them out, thinking: *I've got three chapters to memorize and two blessed hours of peace!*

Little did Dean know the two hours would stretch into nine long years, an existence so quiet and peaceful that it almost drove him insane.

The inquest showed the overloaded logging truck's cargo shifted as it came around the hairpin corner, causing it to spin wildly out of control. The backend fishtailed, then overturned, spilling giant logs like pickup sticks, crushing everything in their path. Death had been instantaneous for the women; Eddy and the trucker managed to hang on for a while but the end result was the same. Four lives wasted. Many more shattered, including one grieving young widower and an infant boy.

Eddy regained consciousness for a short while before he succumbed to internal injuries and Dean was there, at his side. "Jesse must grow up Native," Eddy whispered, each word a labored struggle. "Too much a white man's world. Don't let my boy lose his culture... his heritage. Don't let Jesse sacrifice his rightful path. Promise me, my brother." Brothers in spirit, never of the flesh. And so Dean made his oath. He would do his best.

Had he done enough? In retrospect, it was difficult to measure. Jesse remained in Lytton with his extended family, the wonderful Penny Littlefoot plus a plethora of aunts, uncles and cousins. Dean moved away, pursing his law degree, graduating in the top five percentile of his class and practising criminal law – not specialising in Native land claims as originally intended – that path was too painful. He never returned to Lytton but sent for Jesse often, school holidays and long weekends and summer breaks. Jesse would catch the train to Vancouver and Dean would meet him at the station, always arriving early so the boy wouldn't have to wait, and they would spend time together.

Dean tried to fulfil his promise. He took Jesse to see Native speakers and traditional ceremonies, like potlatches. He taught the boy to feel proud of his ancient culture, not disillusioned as so many Native children become. Together they learned all there was to know, and sometimes, like today, they applied their knowledge to practical use.

On this visit, they would learn to hunt, an age-old tradition for a boy Jesse's age. In the past, the Native warriors would leave the young brave alone in the forest; if he survived he was a hunter, if not – he was forgotten. As much as Dean tried to emulate the culture with accuracy, this was far too harsh for modern sensibilities, so he compromised by accompanying the boy.

They could have chosen a different place but the Stein was Jesse's ancestral grounds and another forest wouldn't suffice. The entire Native ideology was based on its spiritual attachment to the land and to compromise here would amount to blasphemy.

As well, Dean could have passed this rite onto one of the other members of the Lytton Band, but he had promised Eddy, and Jesse, and himself. They had been working towards this hunt for over a year, studying Indian weaponry, ancient customs and tribal rituals, and to bow out now just because he didn't want to visit the valley again was a cowardly betrayal.

Besides, he did want to see the Stein again. The admission shocked him even as he knew it to be true. Dean could feel the call of the valley, the way it reached for him, beckoned him. All at once the past slipped away, the torment of losing Emily Ann and his two best friends, and all the bitter memories between.

Dean knew only one thing for sure. He was coming home.

CHAPTER TWO

From Lytton, the tour group boarded a two-car cable ferry across the Fraser River, all seven of them squeezed into Samuel Hudson's battered, old blue jeep.

The ride was uncomfortable, yet mercifully short. Samuel drove, Don Blume perched in the middle, and Bob Vance sat in the front passenger seat, legs crunched awkwardly on top of his new four-hundred-dollar backpack. Benta, Jackie and the two Asians, who made a heartfelt attempt to speak in broken textbook English, were relegated to the back seat. All pretense of preserving one's personal space vanished. To Jackie, it seemed no part of her body wasn't pressed against someone else. Half her buttocks rested on top of the young Asian closest to her. She turned her head to apologize and poked into Benta's elbow. It was safer to remain still.

Jackie suspected why Samuel was doing this. Oh, she didn't buy the *'best to take one car'* excuse, that cars left unattended at the mouth of the Stein were subject to vandalism and bear attacks. Bear attacks? C'mon! No bear in his right mind would attack a vacant car unless there was a couple pounds of bacon inside.

No, Samuel's motives were basic psychology. Subject a bunch of strangers to intense proximity and they'll emerge as a group – social barriers broken. An artificial closeness was attained, a sense of camaraderie. Terrorists knew this, so did kidnappers. Jackie reflected that it really was true: how can you stay strangers when your ass was spread on some guy's lap? Instant icebreaker, even if the guy didn't speak English. Jackie smiled. She'd probably do the same thing in Samuel's place. She liked the black man instantly and already she could tell they thought along the same lines.

They were passing over the Fraser River, now, although Jackie couldn't see much, only a vague reflection of the muddy green water raging turbulently below. Presumably the cable car was safe, but it was still a sickly feeling to imagine the overhead wires snapping, twisted steel and shattered bodies plummeting into the river, and she swallowed hard, vanquishing the images as she looked away. Once again, Jackie realized, her vivid imagination was her own worst enemy.

She concentrated instead on the small Native Reservation they were passing through. It looked dilapidated and abandoned, but in the very center stood an old man, watching the Jeep intently. He had long grey hair and wore traditional native dress. She turned her head to get a better look but he was gone, and she blinked her eyes, wondering if she'd imagined him. As they drove along the dirt road, a feeling of malevolence took hold, and at the far end of the Reservation, Jackie did a double take. An pile of refuse lay on the side of the road, spelling the words: *GET OUT.* The letters were comprised of rocks and twigs and branches.

How strange. Was she seeing things? Jackie blinked, looking again, but already the image was past, two feet behind, now five, now out of view. Had the others noticed?

"Hey, did you guys see that?" she asked nobody in general.

"See what?" Samuel glanced out the side window.

"The warning sign, on the side of the road. It said '*get out*'."

"Huh," the tour guided answered. "Nope, didn't see it."

Bob Vance laughed, waving his fingers and affecting an eerie voice: "Ohhh, get out, get out while you still can."

A few other snickers and she felt decidedly silly.

"Where was it?" Don Blume asked. He was the only one who seemed to be taking her seriously. His eyes met her in the rear-view mirror and she felt uncomfortable as they connected.

"Ah, I guess it was nothing," she mumbled. "Just a quirk of light."

Conversation moved on, with Bob Vance asking the guide what kind of wildlife they could expect to see. Jackie tuned it out, thinking about her missing brother. *GET OUT.* An omen? Words to heed or childish prank? The unease in her belly, ever present since Jerry went missing, grew slightly. Uncomfortably.

Jerry. Where was he now? What really happened in this forest? Would these mountains and valleys ever relinquish their secret?

Get Out. GET OUT! The words looped through her brain. Relax, Jackie told herself, get a grip. Nonetheless, a series of chills prickled her spine.

**

Samuel began to sing. He started quietly, his voice deep and melodious. The others were quiet, not sure what to make of this new development. Samuel suppressed a grin – they never were.

When he was certain he had their full attention, he let his voice grow louder, filling the cramped Jeep with the rich, soulful sound of *'Born Under A Bad Sign'*, Hudson style. A little blues with a twist of Sammy-soul... that usually got their juices going. By the end of this tour, they'd all be singing the blues. Singing and lovin' it.

Jackie joined in and Samuel caught her eye in the rear-view mirror and winked. Thatta girl! Where'd she learn to sing the blues? She winked back and he sang louder. Maybe this group wouldn't be so bad after all. Things were looking up.

"Okay, gang. Here we are," Samuel said, pulling the Jeep to a sudden halt. "This is it, time to hit the trail. Last chance to back out."

"This is it?" Benta asked, her German voice cutting the pure mountain silence. She took out a camera and clicked a few shots. "For posterity."

"Grab your gear," Samuel said, tossing everything on the ground. He removed the last backpack, shut the gate and began wedging stones under the Jeep's rear wheels. Then he strode to the front, lifted the hood and removed some wires.

"What are you doing?" Don Blume asked, his voice rising nervously.

"Taking out a little insurance. No spark pluggy – no engine runny, get my drift?"

"Uh, no, I'm not sure I do."

"No engine runny – no stealah the Jeep."

"Ah." Don Blume shifted uncomfortably and Samuel studied him. The man was not a happy camper. Why the hell was he here? He didn't fit the profile of the average Stein trekker, but then, everyone had his own agenda, and Samuel didn't much care for probing into other people's business. He knew one thing, though – the natural leader hadn't yet emerged. He suspected Jackie Hart might fill that position nicely or perhaps the Yankee. And, he'd bet his bottom dollar that Mr. Don Blume was going to be a royal pain in the ass.

**

The hiking was steady but not difficult. The trail was narrow enough that they were forced to walk single file. As they penetrated deeper into the forest, the temperature cooled. Gone was the soaring heat felt in

Lytton, replaced by fresh, almost chilly temperatures. The breeze gently stirred the trees and the forest echoed with birdsong and the chatter of small creatures. Lacy patterns filtered through the tall branches and dappled the trail. Fungi and lichens grew on the trees and rocky out-jets. Ants and beetles industriously crossed the earthen trail, and the group stepped back with a collective yelp when they came across a large bull snake sunning itself on a boulder, earning a good-natured chuckle from Samuel. The forest was alive.

Midway through the afternoon, as shadows stretched like long grasping fingers, Samuel diverted off the trail to a large rock boulder to show them the first pictograph. "Careful not to touch it," he cautioned, as Benta reached over to stroke it. "The oil from your fingertips is damaging."

Benta knew that. She should be ashamed, she thought, giddily. But she hadn't been able to stop herself. There was an attraction, an allure pulling her fingers forward of their own violation.

"This is it?" Don Blume asked incredulously. "This chicken scratching is what the fuss is about? Why, it's nothing more than a few red lines. Looks like a five-year-old drew it."

"These chicken scratches, as you call them, have great cultural significance. They provide an insight into early Native life. See this? This represents a two-headed snake and probably was a warning of some kind. The Nlaka'pamux were great believers of guardian spirits and often left messages for protective purposes. Ancient legends tell of supernatural beings known as 'transformers' who traveled the land when the earth was new, accomplishing great feats of heroism. Whoever left this message was trying to tell us something."

Jackie felt shivers run down her spine. A message? Like the lettering she saw on the Reservation?

"Does anyone have any idea what this message might be?" Samuel continued.

"Yeah," Don Blume muttered. "Obviously someone failed ancient art class. A two-headed snake, indeed."

Bob Vance tittered appreciatively. He didn't much like this Blume fellow, but the guy was right: it did look like chicken scratches.

Benta pressed forward. "I believe paintings like this indicate evil. The artist was probably asking his guardian spirits to protect him."

Samuel was impressed. "Someone has done her homework. This would be considered a 'power spot' – where the Spirits resided. Someone, indeed, was telling others of his dreams, or his experiences, or perhaps trying to ward off his enemies or evil spirits. What else can you tell us, Benta?"

"Only that the paintings predate two hundred years. Some are dated older, perhaps two thousand years ago. And, some of the pictographs are believed to be made not by humans but by the spirit world."

"Hogwash," Don Blume muttered. "How can a Spirit make a picture?"

Benta ignored him. She was already unloading her camera and taking pictures. "Okay, let me set up."

"No time for that today, Benta. We've fallen behind schedule as is. Don't worry, we'll catch it at the end of the tour – we'll loop back this way; I'll make sure you get another crack."

"What's the point if you're just going to rush me through it?" Her disappointment was ripe.

"Sorry," Samuel said. "We have a lot of ground to cover so we can't stay in any one spot too long, but don't worry, I'll be taking you to see other pictograph sites – there are thirteen sites discovered so far."

Benta looked longingly at the etchings. That sounded promising, but there was something about these particular pictographs. She could barely tear herself away. "It said in your brochure that we would be camping at the pictographs."

"We'll be near them, but not right at the site. The closest camp will be about a kilometre away."

"But the brochure –"

"We need to carry on now. Folks, grab your belongings, we have a few more kilometres to put in before we bed down for the night."

"No, wait!" Benta was growing agitated, her accent becoming stronger. "I need more time, at least an hour. The lighting is still good; I mustn't waste it."

"Listen, Benta. I've got a lot of folks here who aren't in the best of shape and they're tired. That's when accidents happen. I have a reputation for being a safe guide and I want to keep it that way. The trail to the campsite is steep and with cliffs surrounding it – if we leave any later, we risk running into nightfall. Someone could lose their footing and then where would we be? You'll just have to wait."

"I'll remain here, by myself," Benta's voice was adamant, arrogant. "I'll catch up with you. Just mark my trail map where you'll be."

Samuel focused his full attention on Benta, and Jackie was amazed the pretty blonde wasn't withering in her footsteps at the fierceness of his glare. "That is not possible. The group stays together at all times. You are bound by the waiver you signed, it is a safety issue and a legal issue. Grab your stuff – now. If you are unhappy, make sure to note it in my review. You'll all get a chance to fill out a comment card at the end of the tour."

**

It was almost eight when Samuel told them they could stop for the evening and set camp. Jackie slipped off her backpack and stretched, enjoying the sensation of her tired muscles, aching pleasantly from the day's exertion. She was in good shape, kept fit with aerobic dance and an active lifestyle, but still, a full day's hike in the wilderness placed strain on muscles not regularly used. She yawned heartily, not bothering to hide it.

She reached into her pack and pulled out an emergency Snickers bar and broke it in half, passing it to Benta. The other woman had remained sullen and angry-looking for the remainder of the hike, keeping to herself. "Sorry you didn't get more time at the pictograph site," Jackie began hesitantly. "I could tell it was really important to you."

Benta accepted the chocolate and smiled gratefully, and the two women shared a quiet moment of euphoric sugar high.

"Thanks," Benta said, licking the last vestiges of chocolate from her sensuous, full lips. How was it, Jackie wondered, that the German woman's lips were rosy even without lipstick? She herself felt sweaty and unkempt. She reached into her backpack and fumbled for some Chapstick and then swatted a mosquito. Better look for the bug spray while she was at it.

"C'mon, ladies, stop your primping," Samuel called jokingly, his deep voice melodic in the quiet forest. "We've got work to do."

He wasn't kidding, Jackie thought ruefully. Samuel kept them so busy pitching tents and cooking they didn't have time to talk. Open campfires were prohibited, but as a registered tour guide, he had a special permit. Still, he kept the fire small and the flames low. Afterwards, as they sat around the wavering firelight, he regaled them with campy ghost stories, holding the flashlight to his face so his head appeared to float above his body. It was like being at summer camp again, like being thirteen, and even though you knew the stories were hopelessly false, the shivers still crept up your spine.

"I've got one, I've got one," Bob Vance volunteered. "One dark and stormy night in L.A., a young couple were making out in a parked car. The radio was playing love songs, and the boy had just taken the chick's top off, enjoying her double D's, when a newsflash blared." He made his voice spooky, emulating the newscaster: *"There is an escaped murderer on the loose."*

"In L.A.?" asked Jackie. "How unusual."

Bob ignored her. "The chick got scared and wanted to go home. The boy didn't want to but she insisted, so he sat up and tried to start his car. Nothing happened. The car was out of gas."

"Oh, puh-lease," groaned Benta. Her good humor seemed to be restored. Nothing like a decent meal to put a smile back on your face, Jackie reflected.

"No, no, this is good. I'm almost at the end. So, the boy goes for gas, tells the girl to stay put, to keep the door locked and not open it for any reason, no matter what. No sooner has he left when she hears a desperate scraping on the roof and an eerie, otherworld moaning: *'Let me in, let me in'.* She freaks out and crouches down on the floor –"

"Obviously wasn't driving a compact," Samuel quipped and the women giggled.

"And all night long, she stays there, whimpering between news bulletins and the constant scratching. And when morning finally comes –"

"Her dead boyfriend is hanging over the car with his fingernails scraping the paint." Jackie and Samuel finished the story in unison.

Bob Vance looked slightly dejected. "Oh. You heard that one."

"Back in grade school," Jackie laughed. "Only it wasn't L.A., it took place in Stanley Park."

"My version occurred in my college parking lot," Samuel stated, with mock severity.

"Outside a bar in Dusseldorf," Benta added, smiling. "Looks like that story has been around the world."

"Too bad it never gets better," Samuel added.

"Thanks a lot," Bob said. "Anyone else got one?"

"This whole thing is stupid," Don Blume said, standing abruptly. "I'm going to bed."

The guide stood. "Don's right. We have a full day ahead of us. Better catch some shut eye."

They disassembled. Samuel had earlier assigned them sleeping groups. The division was natural: the two women would share one tent, the Asian men in another, and finally Don Blume and Bob Vance. Only Samuel had a tent to himself.

At first Jackie felt uncomfortable sharing a tent with a virtual stranger, but now, after the earlier warning and silly ghost stories, she was suddenly glad she wouldn't be sleeping alone. The message kept reappearing in her mind, and she shivered as she visualised the twig and stone letters. *GET OUT.*

As they prepared for bed, she decided to approach the other woman about it. "Benta, I can't stop thinking about the sign I saw on the Reservation."

Benta looked at her curiously. "What do you mean by *'reservation'*? I am not familiar with this word."

"It means Native village, like the one we passed coming here. I'm certain I saw a sign that said 'get out'.

It felt like a warning, kind of like the pictographs – like how they warn evil away?"

At the mention of the pictographs, the German woman stiffened, and Jackie was sorry she brought it up. She hurried to change the subject. "You mentioned you didn't see the sign, but did anything else strike you as being strange?"

"Ja, the whole group is strange. Especially our guide. I don't trust him."

"Really? I kind of like him, actually," Jackie said. "Samuel seems really competent – I feel like we are in good hands."

"I would like to learn more about your aboriginal people," Benta said, frowning. "Such poverty. It's very sad the way those people live. Why are they so poor? Why does everyone ignore them?"

Jackie debated her answer. "It's a contentious issue. Status Indians are entitled to free housing, post-secondary tuition, different tax rules, so in theory, they should have more money than the average Joe. Despite that, Reservations are sometimes no better than ghettos. There is still wide-spread alcohol and drug use. Not every Reservation, mind you, but still, far too many. The children grow up to believe this behavior is the norm and the cycle self perpetuates."

"Hmm," Benta said, considering. "Perhaps when you are given things for free it removes the incentive to try?"

"No," Jackie said, searching for a way to explain. "It's more complicated than that. It's a cultural difference. A different way of life, a different value system. The Natives relate more to the land, don't recognize white man rules and boundaries." They were getting off topic. She slipped into her sleeping bag and tried one last time. "So, you didn't see anything strange today?"

"Just the men." Benta turned to look directly at her, and Jackie could tell by the widening of her eyes and the teasing tone in her accented voice that this had become a game. "The question is: which man is strangest?"

"Don Blume." The name slipped out immediately, without thought. "He gives me the creeps."

"Yes. A little man with a small brain and a big ego. What do you call it? Little man syndrome? Big ego and tiny penis. Dangerous combination."

"Benta!"

"Is true, ja? The more – how do you say... pompous, yes, that's the word... the more pompous a man is, the smaller his penis size. No, don't look at me like that," she said, laughing. "Is absolutely true. Scientific fact. Pompous men have small penis."

"Scientific fact? From what, '*Penis Quarterly*?'"

"Ja, very important magazine. Now the other guy, the American, his penis is maybe little bigger, but not much, you understand? Still small." She spread her fingers apart about four inches. "About this long, ja?"

"Oh, no." Jackie was laughing.

"Fully erect."

"Stop it! They'll hear us!"

"So what? Is true... now the Asians –"

"No more, please, I can't take it!"

"The Asians have incredibly long penises." Benta spread her hands apart to an eighteen inch span.

Peals of laughter. "You're making this up."

"No, is absolutely true. Why do you think there are so many Asians in the world? Incredibly long, powerful penises. Best kept Oriental secret."

"You do realize I won't be able to look any one of those men in the face tomorrow, don't you?"

"Of course not. You'll be too busy looking at their pants."

"Stop it!" Jackie threw her pillow at Benta, hitting the other woman squarely in the face. But the truth was, Jackie was having fun. More fun than she'd had in ages, certainly since Jerry went missing. It felt good to laugh again. "Are you ready for bed? Shall I switch off the flashlight?"

Benta's voice was thoughtful, definitely more serious. "I'm thinking of going back to the pictograph site, to take more photos."

"What? It's pitch black out there."

"No, there is a partial moon, we just can't see it because of the tree cover. It's more open at the site and it's such a clear night. The effect of moonlight illuminating the red ochre would be magnificent. Very primitive. Ja, I think this is how the drawings were meant to be seen."

"You're serious, aren't you?"

"Ja." Already Benta was packing her photographic equipment, adding batteries.

"But you can't go! It's a couple of kilometres away and the path is so steep... it's dangerous, Benta. You could slip, or get lost, or run into wild animals."

"Don't worry. I've done this kind of thing before. You know, last summer I went to Nepal. It was breathtaking. Much higher than this. This," she waved her hand dismissively, "is a walk in the countryside."

"Benta, no," Jackie said growing serious. She thought about Jerry, also an experienced outdoorsman. "Remember what Samuel said: we must stay together at all times. No one leaves the group. I'm sure if you ask him, tell him the importance, he'll make sure you get the pictures you need. He seems like a reasonable man."

Benta's expression turned tight. There was no point arguing about this. If she wanted to go, she would go, regardless of the rules. She hadn't gotten this far in her career without taking risks. The way the other woman was yawning, she'd be asleep in minutes. Benta decided to bide her time and wait for the camp to fall asleep and then she'd quietly slip out. By her calculations, it would take her less than an hour to return to the site, she'd spend a few hours taking pictures and return before anyone one was the wiser. Lack of sleep didn't bother her: her adrenaline was racing enough to keep her up for days.

**

"Whoa! Look at that silhouette – must be the German babe. That's what I call a rack and a half. My, isn't this an unexpected bonus?" Bob Vance cleared his throat, emitting a long, low wolf whistle.

Don Blume nervously looked over, saw the curve of the Benta's breast illuminated against the thin tent wall, felt the heat rise in his loins. Bob was right: Benta was stacked. And smart, too. Plus, she liked him, Don could tell. His hand ached to caress himself but he checked his impulse just in time, remembering he wasn't alone. Besides, he chastised himself, it wasn't seemly in any case. Remember what Mother said.

Mother. His phallus deflated immediately. Don knew darn well what Mother would say.

Benta waited one hour. As expected, Jackie was asleep within fifteen minutes. She quietly stuffed her flashlight, the GPS and a can of bear spray into her pocket. The photography equipment lay by the tent door and she collected it quietly. As an afterthought, she arranged her sleeping bag so it looked occupied. She finished buttoning her red plaid shirt and slowly unzipped the tent flap, looking like a pretty barmaid with her rosy cheeks and braided blonde hair, exactly the kind of fraulein pictured on travel posters for

Oktoberfest. The kind of girl who hadn't a care in the world except getting her milk to the cooler before it churned. Perfectly innocent.

**

Bob Vance was having trouble sleeping. It was too quiet here, he missed the city noises. Nothing like the distant roar of an ambulance or the muted blare of a traffic horn: the classic city lullaby. "Ho! I think one of 'em is leaving. Yup. There goes the tent flap."

Don kept his eyes squeezed shut. Would this idiot never settle down? It was all rustling, throat clearing and the occasional sarcastic observation. If this is what summer camp was like, he was glad Mother never agreed to let him go. He should have insisted on a private tent.

"You gotta see this, man. Wow, she looks like X-rated Heidi."

"Bob, I think you should turn in now. It's getting late." Obviously the subtle hint of extinguishing the light an hour ago went unheeded. The American ignored him, continuing his vigil by the tent door, covertly peeking through the corner. "Bob?"

Bob shot a disappointed glance over his shoulder. This guy was a wet blanket. "Don't you want to know what she's doing?"

"No." It was an effort, but Mother would be proud.

"But...."

"Bob," Don repeated, more firmly now. "I think we should allow the ladies their privacy."

A heavy sigh. "Yeah, I guess you're right. Probably not much to see anyway." Bob let the tent flap fall and he slid into his brand new goose-down sleeping bag, a top of the line beauty in cobalt blue which cost him four c-notes, but what the hell, it would keep an icicle warm at minus forty, with a wind chill factor of... oh, hell, he couldn't remember what the salesman said, but he did remember that you didn't know what to expect with Canadian weather. You never could tell this far north – it might be summer, but there were glaciers here. "She's probably just taking a leak or something. Yeah," he continued, smacking his lips at the thought of her shapely bottom gently spread open, legs apart, the hot stream flowing down. "The golden shower." Bob Vance closed his eyes, visualising it.

Man, he was tired. He felt like he could sleep forever.

**

"Warm enough, Sport?"

"Yes. Uncle Dean? Is this how ancient Indians sleep?"

Dean smiled, his green eyes crinkling gently at the corners. "Not exactly. Ancient Indians didn't have sleeping bags and pajamas, and definitely no Ninja figurines, but I think we're close enough." He glanced at the sky. "Weather looks clear, so I think we made the right decision to skip the tent and sleep out in the open, just like the aboriginals."

"Our fire is all wrong."

Dean glanced at the Primus camp stove. Another negative. "Well, we're not allowed to have an open fire in the summertime, it's against the rules. Could start a forest fire."

"Do you think they know we're here?"

"Not a chance, Sport. We've been real quiet. We covered our tracks just like real Indians and our bug lights are too dim to notice. No one would be able to find us unless he stumbled right into us, and by then, we'd be long gone."

Jesse nodded and yawned, his eyes closing. Dean noticed he seemed appeased. That was good – the boy had been so disappointed in learning that others were in the valley. Somewhere along the line, Jesse got the idea they would have the forest to themselves. It was an unrealistic expectation. At over a thousand square kilometres, the Stein was a big chunk of real estate. Yes, it was secluded and they might not see another living soul, but then again, they just might. Dean tried to explain this to Jesse, that just because the Stein was ancient Indian land didn't mean that only Natives were allowed to visit, but still the boy seemed upset. He kept gazing at the empty Jeep in the parking lot like it was the enemy.

Since Jesse couldn't grasp the concept, Dean changed tactics. "Why don't we pretend to track down the *pale faces*? Like ancient warriors, tracking our quarry. Real hunters." Jesse loved the idea and the game was on. They knew little about their subjects except it appeared to be a party of seven. All adults by the look of their shoe prints, one large man and six smaller. They crept close enough to see four tents, heard snatches of conversations, Asian by the sound of it, and then retraced their steps to camp here.

Dean looked at Jess. The boy was sleeping soundly, dead to the world. Once upon a time, Dean slept like that, but too many miles and too many memories contributed to a habit of wakeful, restless nights.

Dean reached over and clicked off the gas flame. The moon cast unearthly shadows across their campsite. As always, he thought of Emily Ann. It was going to be a long night.

**

Benta swung her flashlight, looking for the trailhead as she reached the plateau. It wasn't difficult; the moon hung in the night sky like a carved lantern and the trail was well marked. The stars overhead shone brilliantly. She located the easy ones first: the two Dippers, Orion's Belt, the Milky Way. Spectacular. She took a moment to scan the sky, looking for Gemini, her astrological sign. It wasn't as visible this time of year, but there it was, faintly – the twin stars of Castor and Pollux, which the ancients believed influenced favorable navigation. She could use that influence tonight, she thought, smiling a little. As she was getting ready to carry on, she noticed Draco the Dragon from the corner of her eye. The ancients believed this to be the gateway between the mortal world and eternity. It seemed unusually vibrant tonight, shimmering in the night sky.

She was glad she decided to come tonight, despite the guide's wrath. She did her best work in solitude. The others would be distracting and she wouldn't get to spend as long as she needed to capture the pictographs. She hadn't travelled all this way to do a rush job, and from the look of things, Samuel kept a rigid timetable.

Daylight shots would be acceptable – certainly good enough for her editor's picky taste. But something would be missing. There was no spark, nothing to make the photos come alive. She wanted to make the images leap from the cold pages into the reader's living room.

The subject matter was fascinating, all Benta dared to hope for. The primitive shapes seethed with mystical life. Benta revisited the feeling she got earlier, almost orgasmic, when she'd traced her fingertips over the ancient etchings, knowing it was forbidden to touch them, enjoying the sensual caress with skin that couldn't get enough, could never get enough. This was her art, her true lover. A mere human male could never compete with this.

The trail was not difficult to negotiate but still she took extra care. The steep cliffs Samuel mentioned earlier lay to her back but there was still danger. A wrong placed foot, an unseen tree root snagging her shoe could be disastrous. With this in mind, she hiked with extra caution, picking her way along the trail, focusing on her footsteps. She was gone for less than thirty minutes when she got the distinct feeling someone was watching her. She couldn't see anyone, or hear anything, but she knew someone – or something – was out there, keeping pace with her in the forest. Call it a sixth sense.

The wind whipped suddenly, then died as abruptly as it begun, a mini-maelstrom. Odd, considering how calm the night was – and how dense the forest was. With foliage this thick, one could usually hear the wind rustling the treetops long before it filtered through, and by that time it was a weak, gentle breeze – not a gust like this.

And icy cold. The temperature dropped abruptly, as if she'd walked into a freezer. Her exposed skin developed goose bumps and she wondered if she should stop long enough to retrieve a sweater from her backpack. Weird that she should feel so cold: her pace, although slower than a daytime hike, was still brisk enough to work up a slight sweat, especially carrying all this equipment. If her heart rate was any indication, she should be removing clothing instead of layering up.

She paused momentarily to get her bearings. Was she even on the right path? It was difficult to be certain in the dark. She fumbled in her pocket for her GPS and confirmed her direction. Yes, she was going the right way. *Why then, this inexplicable urge to hurry?*

According to the GPS and her trail map, she was almost at the point where the path forked. There she would connect with the descending trail that led to the pictographs.

Snap!

Benta brought her head up sharply. There *was* something behind her.

A twig breaking? An animal?

Perhaps.

Why couldn't she shake the sensation something was watching her? She steadied her pace and controlled her breathing, forcing herself not to panic, and began working out a strategy. Once she reached the trail, she might be able to outpace whoever – or whatever – was following her. She was surefooted and she was fast. For comfort, she curled her fingers around the canister of bear spray in her pocket.

Damn these heavy cameras. The tripod weighed ten pounds alone. She would definitely invest in a newer, lighter aluminum model when she got back home. Not as sturdy, perhaps, but easier to lug around than this dinosaur.

Steady, girl. Don't lose your nerve. You're almost there and you've had to put up with much worse in the past. Remember that time in the Andes? The avalanche? Or the train ride in Pakistan when she'd awoken to find men groping her? She was a master at getting out of difficult situations.

The snapping sound again. This time, closer and louder. Something was definitely there.

Could it be Jackie, following her? No. The other woman was totally zonked when Benta snuck out. Besides, Jackie might be in good shape but wasn't as fit as Benta, who worked out religiously and competed annually in the Frankfurt Iron Man competition. The other girl was worn out, yawning repeatedly during their camp dinner. The only thing Jackie would accomplish tonight was a solid eight hours of sleep.

Who then?

One of the men? Benta had seen the tent rustle as she left camp, knew someone was watching her. Had someone followed her, hoping for a little nocturnal action in the woods?

That seemed the most likely scenario.

Then why this impeding feeling of danger? Her fight or flight impulse was activated and screaming code red.

She could call out – her follower was very close now. If she called out she could end this charade. Call out and demand an explanation. Demand to be left alone.

"I know you're there." Her voice came out in a series of puffy squeaks and she knew immediately she'd made the wrong decision. Now her pursuant knew exactly where she was and she felt a blinding flash of pure terror clawing at her like hot, grasping fingers upon her neck.

Benta lunged into a full-fledged run.

**

Dean stood, stretched, and paced the perimeter of the campsite. The gentlest of breezes wafted over him and he looked up, searching for a hint of rain in the night sky. Not a cloud in sight, only a hundred million stars twinkling brightly above. This far from civilization, without city lights and pollutants, the stars shone with amazing clarity. It was beautiful yet humbling.

He heard something, a long way off, almost like a human cry. Dean strained to hear more but the forest was silent.

He gave up listening after a few minutes. *Probably one of the tourists trying to locate an outside biffy*, he thought with a chuckle, and settled back to watch the beautiful glaze of the Milky Way.

**

For a moment, Benta thought she had shaken her pursuant. The crackling decreased behind her and now the only noise was her own labored breathing. *Probably one of those loser guys after all, looking for some midnight fun.* Benta decided to give them a piece of her mind when she returned to camp. Life was too short to put up with jerks like that.

She slowed her pace slightly, taking more care with her footing, and redistributed the weight of her equipment. *There! The trail – there it was.* The path forked just as the map indicated.

Suddenly the sounds returned, only this time a thousand times stronger, coming at her like countless heartbeats, clamoring with deafening thuds, closing in, stifling her, surrounding her from every angle.

**

Jackie sat bolt up, bound uncomfortably in her sleeping bag, and screamed.

She was having the most awful nightmare – a dream so vivid and real, every nuance fleshed in numbing detail. Her brother Jerry was running through the forest, chased by unearthly beings, desperately trying to get away. In the background a warning chant sounded: *GET OUT GET OUT GET OUT.*

Jackie fumbled for her flashlight and checked her watch. 12:01. Just past midnight. She'd been asleep for barely two hours and she felt groggy and disorientated. The dream about Jerry was fading, but she felt the heart-pumping terror that only a good nightmare could induce.

She glanced at Benta's sleeping bag. It was still, the other girl remained asleep. Good, she hadn't woken her.

**

Bob Vance was also having a nightmare, but when he awoke at Jackie's scream, he couldn't recall it. Only an uncomfortable sense of doom. He was sweating profusely and the expensive sleeping bag was drenched. He flung open the zipper and let the cool night air wash over him. It never occurred to him that he'd be too warm in the Stein; he would definitely lodge a complaint at Dick's Sporting Goods. This pricey sucker was going back for a refund.

He lay back and listened to Don Blume's erratic snoring. Great.

He tried to recall his dream. It had seemed important, a warning of sorts. But the threads were gone. The harder he reached for them, the quicker they dissipated. *No matter*, he thought, fanning himself in an effort to cool down. He was burning hot, as if his body was on fire. *No point worrying over a silly nightmare.* In his line of business – real estate development – nightmares were a common occurrence.

**

Faster, faster. It was gaining on her. Benta quelled the urge to scream, saving her energy for running. She lost her footing, almost stumbled, then regained it, losing a precious millisecond. Just like the Olympics. Just like running a high school race through the pretty German landscape, careful not to glance at your opponent because you might lose time. But this time, she couldn't help it. This time, she had to look, was compelled to look, and she almost fainted as she saw...

**

Don Blume wasn't awakened by the scream. He was already awake, keeping his eyes squeezed tightly in the darkened tent. When Bob stirred and began unzipping his sleeping bag, cursing a blue streak, Don faked sleep – keeping his breathing deep and even, throwing in some snoring for authenticity. It was a skill he'd perfected long ago, pretending to be asleep when Mother checked in on him.

Damn Arne and Ben. They should be here, not him. His Adam's apple bobbed convulsively and he willed it to still. Something was happening. *Something bad.* Don knew it.... he could feel it. He wanted to be home in his own warm bed, hunched under the red floral spread, safe with Mother. Yes, even with Mother.

Because something was happening to someone, somewhere. And sooner or later it might be happening to him.

**

... a ringed wall of faces. Not human faces, but animals. Of bears and birds and fish and wolves, oh yes, definitely wolves. Some half-animal and half-man, mutilated faces and long, hairy legs like twisted Centaurs. The wolves had huge, salivating mouths, and they began to nip at her, tearing her clothing, slicing her flesh, inflicting pain Benta hadn't imagined possible.

A great, winged raven with claws and feet and arms and a black curved beak, flew close and grinned at her, its beak spreading apart to reveal shiny rows of sharp teeth. Benta flung her arms wide, striking it with the steel tripod, and it fell back, cawing and crying, but not before it ripped off a large chunk of blonde hair, still attached to a piece of Benta's scalp.

This time, she did fall, and the mass was upon her, writhing and chanting and singing, and ripping her apart in pieces.

**

The five men exited their tents, Bob and Don appearing last, when the noise of the others made it clear they were the only ones still inside. "Wake up, you pussy," Bob said, landing a less than gentle punch on Don's prone form.

"What's going on?" Don asked, making his voice heavy with sleep.

"Dunno," Bob answered, whipping off his damp shirt and searching blindly in the dark for another. "Turn on the goddamned flashlight, will you? This fucking backpack is locked up tighter than Houdini."

They emerged to see Samuel fully dressed and the Asians in pajamas and flip flops, looking ridiculously out of place. They were waving flashlights and chattering excitedly, exchanging worried glances and jabbering their fingers repeatedly at the girls' tent.

Bob spoke first, addressing the Asian men, his voice managing to convey both amusement and disgust. "Please tell me that *is not* 'Hello Kitty' pajamas you're wearing. For the love of Christ."

Don peeked nervously as he cleared his throat. He didn't know who *Hello Kitty* was but he did see a cowboy print on the other guy's. What was wrong with that? It seemed more sensible to sleep in pajamas than boxers and t-shirt like Vance. He thought about pointing that out but found he couldn't speak. *Calm*, he thought, *Mother would expect you to remain calm.*

Samuel spoke first. "Ladies, are you all right?"

Jackie crawled over Benta, poking her head through the tent, looking embarrassed. "I'm sorry," she whispered. "I didn't mean to wake you. I'm fine – just a nightmare."

"And the other lady? Ms. Sturm?"

"Benta, no she's ok, still asleep..." Jackie stopped, frowning. "Hold on." She flicked on the flashlight and took a closer look at Benta's bedding, then touched it tentatively. As she feared, the bag was empty. "Oh, shit, she's gone."

"Gone?" Samuel barked. "Where?"

"I don't know. Uh, maybe to the pictograph site... she was talking about going earlier but I talked her out of it. Or, least, I thought I had."

"Alone? In the dark? Is she crazy? I thought I was very clear: the group stays together. No matter what." He was shouting now.

Jackie's shoulders sagged. "She wanted moonlight pictures."

Samuel grimaced. He'd had some dumb-assed tourists before but this took the cake. "I'd better find her."

"No!" Don Blume almost shouted the word, his panic evident. He realized everyone was looking at him oddly and lowered his voice. "I mean, you should stay here with us. We need you. What if something happened here, like a bear attack? Your responsibility is to us."

"My obligation is to everyone," Samuel said, angrily. The muscle in his jaw was working furiously; he was beyond pissed off.

Don said, "She broke that obligation when she went off on her own. Besides, you have no idea where she went. Jackie's just guessing she went to the pictographs, she could be anywhere. It'd be like finding a needle in a haystack, a very large haystack. What if something happened to you? Where would we be, then? There was nothing in the brochure that stated we would be left alone to fend for ourselves."

"He's right," Bob Vance added, feeling chilled. It *was* scary out here. So dark. So isolated. He felt homesick for the congestion of Los Angeles. In L.A., you might be surrounded by four million weirdos, but at least you were surrounded.

Samuel looked at Jackie. "What do you think?"

"I don't know. I hate to think of her all alone but the guys are right, you would be putting yourself in danger. I'm not sure we could find our way out if something happened to you."

Samuel drummed his fingertips, considering. He should go after her, he knew. But some inner sense urged him to stay with the group. Don Blume was an idiot but he did raise a valid point: it was total supposition that Benta went to the pictographs. She could be anywhere. It would difficult, if not impossible, to track her in the dark, and it did mean leaving the rest of the group alone. They didn't know it, but he was armed in case of animal attack. It was rare, but it did happen. Leaving them alone would like be leaving lambs to the slaughter. Especially the guy in the Hello Kitty pajamas. Seriously? That kind of dress might be acceptable in the Orient, but it didn't fly here. "I suppose," he said slowly, "of everyone here, Benta is the most experienced hiker. She listed on her registration that she's hiked the Andes and the Himalayas. It's idiocy to hike this valley at night – even assuming she's got a decent flashlight and GPS. I guess she knows what she's doing, but when she gets back, I'm gonna rip a strip off her. And if any of you other wing nuts gets the brilliant idea of sauntering off, day or night, you're off the tour. Got it?"

Everyone nodded.

"Okay," Samuel said heavily, "it's settled. Go back to bed. I'll stay up and wait for her."

They returned reluctantly to their tents.

Jackie crawled across the empty sleeping bag, feeling guilty. If only she'd been more cautionary to Benta about going off, or had alerted Samuel about Benta's proposed plan, or even stayed awake longer, then Benta might be here. She hadn't realized how serious the German was.

She switched off her flashlight, hunkering into her sleeping bag. It still held her body warmth. She started to think about her nightmare, of Jerry running through the woods. The look on his face – pure terror.... she shivered and clicked the flashlight back on, feeling foolish. Foolish, but also a little relieved. The batteries were dying down when she finally drifted back to sleep.

**

Bob Vance slipped into his sleeping bag thinking: too bad about Benta. What would happen if she didn't come back? Would they end the tour? He'd certainly miss her spectacular hooters. Too bad he didn't give her one of his cards – you never knew who was thinking about buying property. Sometimes buyers came from the strangest places.

Ah, well, there were still the Orientals. Everyone knows they have all the money these days. Tomorrow he'd concentrate on the Asians – give them a card before they disappeared too. Hell, he'd give them a bunch of cards – the one thing Orientals had more than money was contacts. There were millions of the slanty-eyed bastards running around and they all needed a place to live.

**

Don Blume could only think of one thing: *she won't be coming back.* He knew – he'd seen the pictures of Jerry Hackett and Wendall Scott.

Don wished his mother was here.

It was all Arne and Ben's fault.

**

The Asians returned to their tent looking worried and confused, chattering quietly. The one in cowboy pajamas zipped the flap closed and they disappeared inside.

**

Samuel sank into his cot chair and sighed.

This group was beginning to smell like trouble. People leaving in the middle of the night... It didn't bode well. Not well at all.

He sighed again and shifted to get comfortable, failing miserably. He was getting too damned old for this crap.

**

Benta Sturm's last coherent thought was of her native land. She would never see her home again. She would die here in this country of small men and big trees. And her marvellous photos of the ancient pictographs would never be shared with the world.

**

Dean awoke with a start. He had dozed while sitting upright. As far as Dean could recall he had never done that. He glanced over at Jesse and his heart froze. Standing over the sleeping boy was a fully grown grey timber wolf with a distinguishing diamond-shaped white patch over its left eye. It was intent on the child, its salivating mouth close to Jesse's own, and it was doing something....

My God.

It was sucking the child's breath.

Dean locked eyes with the beast for a single moment before he sprang into action. He hurled himself at the creature, intending to knock it away from the boy.

Contact was never made. The wolf leapt back, howled once – a low, primal sound that shattered the silence, and then it turned and fled, vanishing into the night.

CHAPTER THREE

Morning came abruptly, arriving in the manner of rolling dark clouds that hung ominously low, shrouding the valley in an ethereal mist. It was unseasonably chilly and Dean shivered as he quietly moved to start the Primus stove. He was cold and stiff from sleeping on the ground. He would sell his soul for a cup of Starbucks, the morning newspaper, and at least four more hours in a real bed.

He flexed his shoulders, hearing the muscles and tendons pop. Well, the coffee he could make happen.

City life was making him soft. If someone told him ten years ago he'd feel this lousy after a sleep in the forest he would have laughed aloud. Yeah, he noticed the occasional grey hair lately, sticking out like wiry mavericks announcing to the world he was no longer in his twenties, but that never bothered him. Yet this! This betrayal of flesh. He was going to have to rethink his workout plan.

Ten years since he'd camped the Stein, slept on the ground, breathed pure mountain air. Ten years could really change a person and not always for the best. *Maybe it was time to change back*. Time to stop living in the past. Time to allow a little joy in again. Emily Ann wouldn't want him to spend the rest of his days in this unhappy limbo, would she? No.

There. Even the thought of Em didn't hurt as much as it used to. Didn't hurt hardly at all – only left a warm aching memory at the thought of her sweet smile.

He felt the healing magic of the forest seep through him. Or, maybe it was the magic of coffee, he thought, lips quirking, taking his first blessed sip. A beam of sunshine broke through the cloud cover, illuminating him momentarily, bathing him in sudden warmth, and

Dean turned his face upwards, soaking it in. The simple things made the fabric of life bearable. Perhaps this trip would prove as beneficial to Dean as it would the boy. It might be a catharsis for them all.

The sunbeam disappeared as suddenly as it came; the campsite darkened. Jesse stirred and Dean glanced over. That wolf business had scared the bejesus out of him last night, but Jesse hadn't even woken. Wolf attacks were rare, almost non-existent. It was not normal behaviour for a healthy wolf to pursue humans. They should have used the tent – but that went against the authentic experience he was hoping to create.

Should he tell Jesse? No. Jesse would no doubt get a kick out of hearing the story, maybe even think Dean made it up, but some deep instinct cautioned Dean to keep quiet. At least for now. He would tell Jesse later, when they were back in the city.

"How did you sleep, Sport?"

"Fine."

"Hungry? I have a big breakfast planned – a real man-handler's special: pancakes, ham, oranges.... Jess? You feeling okay?"

"Yeah."

But the boy didn't look well. His skin was sallow and his eyes underscored with puffy circles. Dean crossed over and felt his forehead, searching for a fever, but the flesh was cool, normal. Still, Dean was unconvinced. "Are you sure, Sport? Does your stomach ache? How about your throat? No? Let's see, are your glands swollen? Hmm. Everything looks okay. Maybe we should go home, Jess. Don't want you getting sick out here."

"No! I'm good, really I am, Uncle Dean. See?" He leapt from his sleeping bag and hopped around. "If I was sick, could I do this?"

"Well...." He did look better. Already his skin was resuming color and his dark eyes becoming alert. "All right, then. But put some clothes on – running around in your pj's will make you sick for sure. Aren't you cold?"

"Nope."

"Now I do feel old," Dean muttered. Kids were so damn resilient. Jesse didn't seem to feel this weather at all – he was running around like a maniac, climbing on a rock then jumping down. "Jesse – Come on! Clothes!"

Reluctantly Jesse dressed and they began making breakfast. Dean kept watching the boy for signs of illness – at first indication he was prepared to pack up and return home, but none was forthcoming. Indeed, Jesse seemed more active than normal – if that was possible. Ah, to be nine years old again without a care in the world.

They ate quickly, then packed up and made their plans. They would follow the group of seven, see how close they could get without being spotted, then maybe take some time this afternoon to practise hunting techniques. All in all, it promised to be an entertaining day. Dean glanced at the swollen sky – hopefully the rain would hold off. Then everything would be perfect.

**

There was a fair amount of dissention. Benta hadn't returned and everyone was debating what they should do in the event Samuel didn't find her. The guide left at dawn to track the missing woman, telling the group to stay put. Bob wanted to continue with the tour, with or without Benta. Don wanted to leave the Stein immediately, before whatever happened to Benta happened to him. Jackie wanted to wait and decide when Samuel returned. She was worried about Benta, of course, but also wanted to continue the search for clues to her brother's disappearance, which was the whole point of this expedition. To abort after only one day would set her search back, again. It was unclear exactly what the Asians wanted. They kept gesturing wildly and talking fast, occasionally exchanging unreadable glances.

"She chose to leave, did she not?" Bob Vance looked at Don with annoyance when the other man refused to answer. Although silent, Don's Adam's apple bobbed convulsively. He looked like he was ready to explode.

"Look," Jackie said, trying to diffuse the situation. "I'd hate for this to end, too, but Don's right. Benta's safety comes first. What if she's hurt? What if she fell and can't get up, or got lost, or –"

"That was the risk she took when she chose to go alone. In the middle of the night," Bob stated disgustedly. "Dumb blonde."

It started to rain, lightly. "Great," Bob mumbled, hurrying to the cover of his tent.

Don looked around the thick forest. Even in daylight it looked foreboding to him. "How long do you think Samuel will be?"

"A couple of hours," Jackie answered. "It was about two kilometres to the site, assuming she's there. If she's not, he'll probably look around a bit."

"This is really putting us in arrears," Bob grumbled from his tent. He pulled out his Blackberry. No cell service, of course. When he built the hotel that would have to change. Customers would demand Internet and cell service with their wilderness experience.

**

It was hours before the steady drizzle let up and Don hunched his damp shoulders together, staring at the forest apprehensively. The others had retreated to their tents and he wished he could too, but he was loathing spending time with Bob Vance.

The longer Samuel was gone, the more Don grew convinced that evil had befallen the missing woman. When Samuel found her, her remains would resemble those of his coworkers. Then it would be game over. This Hart bitch would see the mutilated body, possibly make the connection to her brother, and blow her mouth all over town. His mandate had been to oversee this tour, get the Hart woman off the company's back. He will have failed miserably. Mother would be furious.

No one would believe Jackie, of course, who could? The idea was unfathomable but it would cause a public spectacle. An inquiry would be made, certainly reporters would arrive, swarming like filthy flies, all manner of crazies and looky-loos would descend, loitering and searching, and perhaps even... finding?

Then what?

More deaths, more mutilated bodies. Publicity would be a game changer; already the moratorium balance was precarious. Each side had a valid position – Natives intent on preserving their aboriginal grounds versus loggers trying to boost the flailing forestry industry. A tough judicial call, so complex the committee was deadlocked. Anything, especially a situation like this, could swing the scale to the other side. Did he say swing? Don ground his teeth. Hell no, it would *blast* it out of existence.

If Empire failed to secure this logging contract, his company would go out of business. He'd be out of a job. Unemployed. A failure.

Mother would kill him.

If he didn't keep a lid on this, the Hart bitch would finish him. He had to convince her all was normal, that the Stein was just another forest, where men might go missing but certainly not attacked by.... well, he wasn't sure what.

As if reading his mind, Jackie emerged from the tent. She walked a moderate distance into the forest, without stating her intention, and Don realized she was probably relieving herself. He envied her: his bladder was aching with fullness but he was too intimated to venture into the forest alone. Too late, he realized his mistake. He should have taken a piss when everyone was in their tents.

She returned shortly. "You okay, Don?" she asked warily.

"Why wouldn't I be?" he snapped, harsher than intended. His voice sounded overly loud even to his own ears.

"No reason, you just look... " Jackie let her voice trail off. She wasn't sure how he looked. Scared maybe? Angry? Unhinged?

"What's the ruckus about?" Bob asked, emerging from his tent. The Asians followed suit and they all stood around, looking at each other.

"I'm hungry," Bob stated. "It's way past lunch time. Christ, Samuel's been gone for hours, do you think he's ever coming back? Let's get some grub started."

"Good idea, Bob," Jackie said, "I'm kind of hungry myself. I'm sure Samuel wouldn't mind. What do you think, Don?"

Don glared at her. It was her fault he was here. If she had just accepted Empire's explanation about her brother, as Wendall Scott's wife had, then he wouldn't be here, like a sitting duck.

Look at her standing there, all coy and sweetness, but Don knew the truth – could feel the truth – could see it in her unblinking blue eyes and by the way she stood, feet planted squarely in the earth and hands securely across her chest. Her determination was flashing like a neon light headlining in Vegas.

She was a fake. Don knew it. All this crap about caring for the German broad was a ploy to snoop around for her brother. She didn't give a rat's ass for the other girl, anymore than he did.

"Don?"

Jackie's voice startled him and Don repressed the urge to scream: *Don't you know what you'll find out there? Don't you know, you stupid, stubborn bitch? A goddamned mess, that's what. A mutilated pile of flesh so desecrated that it'll become your worst nightmare, the image seared into your fucking brain, forever changing the way you look at the world. Is that what you want?*

Ooh, the pressure. All eyes looking at him, demanding. Even the Asians stopped their infernal chatter and were staring, staring.

Mother.

Jackie.

Both women. Both bitches. Whom to please? Whom to please? What a fucking can of worms. Don fixed his eyes on Jackie for one brief moment before looking away. This was her fault. If she hadn't kept nosing around, he wouldn't be here. She was to blame for everything. Certainly for being stuck here, freezing and so scared he felt like crapping his pants. If they found the German's body it would be her fault – he'd lose his job and have to tell Mother...

No! One thing was apparent: if they found the dead girl, Jackie would have to be taken care of, just like the insects and rats, and later, the annoying neighborhood dogs he'd purged for Mother. He would fix it so she couldn't tell anyone, ever. Then everything would be all right.

For the first time in several days, Don smiled with true happiness. He'd found a way out of this impossible mess, all by himself. Everything would be okay. Mother would be so proud. Too bad he would never be able to tell her.

"Don?"

"Oh, all right," Don said, smiling happily. "Whatever the group decides is fine with me. Let's eat." He headed into the guide's tent without hesitation, calling, "What does everyone want? Ham and cheese sandwich okay? There's not much to choose from."

Bob Vance looked at Jackie and whispered, "I'd watch your step around Blume. I don't think his boat is on an even keel, if you know what I mean."

Jackie nodded. She'd been thinking the same thing.

**

"Whoa, Sport!" Dean stopped abruptly and dropped into a crouch position, motioning for Jesse to do the same. So much for authentic Native tracking – Dean, the teacher and essence of all wisdom in Jesse's eyes, had nearly stumbled into the very people he was tracking.

At their original campsite.

That was strange, Dean thought. Surely they should have moved on by now. Why were they just sitting there? Maybe it wasn't a tour group, just a random group of campers staying in one spot. That would be disappointing – no way to practise tracking skills on a motionless quarry.

"What was that? Did you hear that?" A man's voice came from the campsite, and Dean had only a moment to glance at him before flattening himself against the cold, hard ground. Jesse followed suit without being told, perfectly silent.

The man turned, gesticulating with alarm to the others. "There's something out there."

Dean lay still, feeling ridiculous. He hadn't meant to scare anyone. This game of cowboys and Indians was idiotic.

He looked at Jesse: the boy's face was simply euphoric. He looked like his father, and Dean had the uncanny feeling of being transported back twenty years. Eddy used to look exactly like that, same wide-assed grin, and Dean was forced to concede that while this lurking in the forest stuff might be idiotic, it was also fun.

Exactly like when he and Eddy were kids.

Ridiculously fun, Dean thought, feeling the dampness soak through his jacket, smelling the mossy dirt of the forest, seeing a broken twig laying inches from his left eye. He moved his head slowly, ever so carefully so as not to make a sound and smiled at Jesse. The boy looked back, a waif in copycat pose, eyes like small black saucers.

"Over there," the man was saying, pointing frantically. "In the woods. I heard it – a rustling noise. A huge, rustling noise. It sounded like a bear."

"Oh, sure, Blume," a second male voice said, and two more sets of denim clad legs stepped into view. "Like *you've* seen a bear before. You probably heard a squirrel or something."

"I know what I heard and it wasn't a squirrel. It was big. And it sounded like there was more than one – two, three... maybe a herd."

"A herd, you say? A herd of bears tramping thought the woods?" A little chuckling. "Listen to what you're saying, Blume."

"Oh, yeah, Mr. Big-City smarty pants? I suppose *you've* seen a bear before?"

"Only a bear market when I'm unlucky."

"Then shut the fuck up."

"Geez, Blume, take some Prozac."

Then a woman's voice: "Maybe both of you should relax. Here, come and sit down. If there are any bears out there, you two will have scared them off by now. Come on! Samuel will be back anytime now and then we'll go for good." Her voice was soft yet firm and Dean thought it was the loveliest sound he'd heard. Against better judgment he craned his neck to get a closer look. He felt a compelling urge to match a face with the voice, but it was too late. She had already turned and was walking away from his line of vision. The two men followed and soon he could see nothing. Dean tried to hear their conversation, strained to make sense of the soft, hushed tones but was rewarded only with a steady murmuring.

Dean motioned for Jesse to follow and they crept backwards a few metres, then turned and retreated stealthily until they had placed a half kilometre between them and their previous hiding spot.

He felt giddy, lighthearted. As if time peeled away and he was a boy again. He felt like running thought the forest with joyful abandon. Like beating on his chest like a modern day Tarzan and hollering into the wind. Like running back to the clearing and seeing what kind of face and personality went with that lovely, angelic voice.

Now, there's a thought. *Excuse me, Ma'am, but I was hiding in the bush, pretending to be a primitive Indian, stalking you and your friends, and I'd like to ask you on a date. Next time you're in the city, that is.* Yep, a real original pickup line. Smooth as silk.

She'd probably have him arrested.

Dean smiled a lopsided grin at Jesse, noting the rosy cheeks and glittering eyes. It was apparent the boy was enjoying himself, too. Jesse needed a good time, and hell, if he was honest, so did he. When was the last time either of them had any fun? And if running through the forest, pretending to be wild Indians in search of quarry constituted a good time, then so be it.

"How'ya feeling, Sport?"

"Fantabulous! Did you see 'em, Uncle Dean? A whole bunch of them, white settlers, just like on TV. And they didn't even know we were there. They thought we were bears."

"Or squirrels."

"That was awesome."

They shared a smile, comrades in arms. "Sure was, Sport, the best." *One thing was sure*, Dean thought, feeling the adrenaline pump through his veins, *no matter what came next, the kid was having one heck of a vacation.*

**

By six o'clock, the clouds parted long enough for the sun to shine and the day's bone chilling damp finally began to fade. Their lunch meal long digested, the group milled about, growing anxious and bored and hungry. Don Blume still hadn't the courage to venture into the forest to urinate, and while he contemplated standing at the edge of the campsite and just turning his back on the group to pee, he knew he wouldn't be able to. He never had been able to urinate with an audience. So he held it, well past the point of pain.

"Samuel should be back by now. He's been gone all day – it'll be dark soon. You said he'd be only an hour or two. He should be back by now. Back here. Here. Now. Don't you think? Don't you think he should be back by now? SOMEBODY ANSWER ME!"

"Calm down, Don. Samuel will be back, he's obviously having trouble finding Benta," Jackie answered, trying to keep her voice soothing. Truth was, she was concerned, too.

"No he won't! He won't be back. He's gone, gone forever. It's got him."

"What's got him?"

But Don wouldn't answer. His mouth clamped shut and his pale face (if it was possible) grew even paler, and his eyes bulged as if the words he was biting back wanted release so desperately they threatened to burst from his eye sockets.

"Why don't you sit for a moment, Don? Sit here on this log, beside us."

"Don't patronize me. I am not an idiot." The words came out in slow, stifled gasps, and Jackie apologized, relieved. At least he'd gotten control of himself.

"What do you mean by 'It', Blume? Another one of your imaginary bears?" Bob asked, and Jackie silenced him with a glance, whispering, "Don't antagonize him."

"It's clear Samuel isn't returning," Don stated, more composed. "He specifically said he'd be back in an hour or two, and it has been over ten hours. I think we should go."

"Go where, Blume? To the movies? The 7-11 for a Big Gulp? In case you haven't noticed we are way out here, in the middle of nowhere. We couldn't leave even if we wanted to."

Don looked at Bob Vance sharply. "What do you mean?" His bladder had long moved past simple pain: it was sheer agony. Stabbing pains spread through his abdomen. He was going to have to brave the forest. There was no hope for it. He glanced around apprehensively: everything *looked* calm. The sunshine helped: the shadows were less ominous.

"I mean, who's going to guide us out of here? I, for one, don't have the foggiest notion how to get back to the car. Do you? No? Didn't think so, and it's my guess Chicken Chow Mein and Hong Kong Dick over there don't either."

"I have a compass," Jackie said.

"That's a start."

"But I didn't think to check our position when we started."

"Great. Back to square one."

"Plus, there's the matter of the Jeep. Even if we had the keys, which we don't, Samuel removed the spark plugs."

Bob grimaced. "Well, aren't you the voice of little Miss Sunshine."

"Just saying."

Everyone was quiet. A few long minutes passed. "Look," Jackie began, "we are reasonably intelligent adults. I'm sure if we had to – which we won't, because Samuel will return any minute now – I'm sure we could find our way out. I know the trail was difficult to follow, but there has to be markers of some sort. They always mark trails –"

"Who does?" Don demanded.

"Well, I don't know – boy scouts or Parks Board employees or.... well, the point is, there are people paid to specifically mark trails so people like us can find our way out."

"I hate to burst your bubble, sweetheart," Bob said, "but I didn't notice a single marker on the way in, did you?"

"Well, no, but then I wasn't really looking."

Don Blume moaned and Jackie shot Bob a withering glance. "All right, so we're stuck here for a while. What's the worst that can happen? We don't turn up in a few days–"

"Six."

"Six days, and they'll send a search party for us. Simple as that. We have food, we have shelter, we can last for six days."

"Assuming we're not torn apart by Blume's so-called bears."

"Stop it, stop it, stop it!" Don yelled, one hand on either side of his head.

Jackie crossed over the campsite and placed an arm on Don's shoulders to calm him down but he shrugged her off and moved a few feet away, pacing. "Now are you happy?" she asked Bob. "Why are you such a pessimist?"

"Just a realist, babe. Why are you such a Mary-fucking-Poppins?"

"I hear it!" Don screamed. "I hear it again. It's coming!"

**

Dean heard it, too. "Ssh," he cautioned Jesse and they quietly slid under the apron of a large Douglas fir. The tree was growing off the slant of a small hill, leaning towards the south, and the north side offered a thick veil of protection, the large branches sweeping the ground. "Something's coming."

Whatever it was, it was making one hell of a noise.

**

"Do you hear it?" Don demanded.

Jackie nodded, listening carefully. It was a long way off, the same direction Samuel had gone. A definite thudding sound, irregular, with a crackling noise every so often.

"I hear it," Bob said. Even the Asians stopped talking and looked in the direction of the noise, heads cocked slightly to one side.

"Do you think it's Samuel?" Jackie asked.

"I hope so," Bob muttered.

Another noise, closer and more pressing, and they turned in time to see Don Blume stripping off his jacket.

"What in God's name are you doing, Blume?"

Don struggled out of the sleeves, letting his jacket fall as he feverishly began unbuttoning his shirt, tugging at the garment with such alacrity it began to tear.

The other noise, the large one, was coming closer, but the group's attention had shifted to the drama unfolding in front of them and they failed to notice.

Blume's shirt was completely off now, joining his jacket in a heap on the ground, and now he was lifting up his undershirt, pulling at it frenetically, trying to loosen its neat tuck from his trousers. His harried movements were slowing him down, making the simple task difficult. He finally succeeded, lifting his undershirt high to reveal soft ripe flesh, as pallid as his face, and grotesquely hairy. Jackie watched, wanting to turn away but unable to, and was the first to gasp when he lifted his shirt higher, higher, to reveal...

– *closer now. Even they couldn't ignore the crashing sounds* –

... a small handgun which Don Blume grappled and released with a flourish, brandishing wildly.

**

Jesse was staring with such intense concentration that Dean thought: *it's like he's in a trance.* Not a muscle twitched. The child never swallowed nor blinked. Not once. A highly unusual state for a nine-year-old boy, especially one as active as Jesse. Dean had the urge to shake the boy but didn't for fear Jesse might cry out.

That would be bad.

Especially with that thing crashing though the forest a few hundred metres or so in front of them.

What the hell was it? It was moving fast, smashing through the trees, a hollow thump-thump-thumping sound punctuated every few seconds.

Dean couldn't see anything. The same thick branches which hid them also obscured his vision. Besides, crouched as he was in this ungodly position, his leg muscles cramping uncomfortably, it was doubtful he'd have a clear line of sight even if the branches weren't there. This was an old growth forest and between him and the Noisy Thing there were at least a hundred trees.

The Noisy Thing stopped for a moment and the forest was silent.

Too silent.

There were no natural sounds – no cawing of birds, no clucking of chipmunks. It was as if all living animals sensed this ominous presence and simply vanished. Dean felt like grabbing Jesse and fleeing.

But to move now would be a hideous mistake. He knew this instinctively, knew they must remain perfectly still. Jesse seemed to realize this too. Although Dean dared not move his head the fraction of an inch necessary to see Jess, he could tell the boy was as motionless as before.

The Noisy Thing was still halted and Dean wondered if it was probing, searching for something. That was bad. He wasn't sure how much longer he could remain still – the pain in his cramped thigh was screaming for release.

He had to move, had to... had to... but then he would be exposed and so would Jesse. The pain was intense, a muscle spasm like no other, gripping his muscles, threatening to snap his leg in two... had to move, had to...

Abruptly, the Noisy Thing started again, in a different direction, moving away from him and Jesse but towards the campers.

He had to do something to help them. Judging by the way the Noisy Thing was moving, he'd better be pretty damn quick about it.

But what? What could he do when he didn't know what he was up against? *And Dean deeply suspected he really, really didn't want to find out – couldn't find out... it would irrevocably change his life forever.* But if he didn't help, if he didn't do *something*, if he stayed hidden under this tree like a goddamned coward, how could he live with himself? How could he rise every morning and look at his unshaven mug, knowing the fate of those innocent people rested in his hands and he blew it...

Like you blew it for Emily Ann. Where were you when that logging truck smashed into her and broke so many bones in her body she resembled a jigsaw puzzle?

He had to help them. He didn't know how but he would formulate a plan while he was running after it.

And Jesse?

Don't forget about Jesse. He couldn't very well go chasing after some unknown entity with the boy in tow. *Could it be a grizzly?* But no – who are you fooling? No grizzly would make a racket like that. No animal on God's green Earth made a racket like that.

He could leave Jesse here, under the tree, where he would be safe. Not the perfect solution, but from where he was standing – or rather crouching with spasming thighs bringing pain to a whole new level – it was the best solution.

But what Dean saw when he turned his head made his blood run cold. Jesse, still unnaturally still, had begun to grin. Not a nervous, silly schoolboy grin – the kind of smile when the school principal caught you throwing rotten eggs or pulling a BA; the sort of smile where you know you shouldn't but couldn't help it – that Dean would have understood. This grin wasn't silly nor boyish. It was an evil leer, growing and growing until it showed Jesse's molars, until it seemed his lips would split apart, stretched beyond capacity.

And he was laughing. Almost silently, but Dean could hear it. Barely. A demonic, possessed laughter that originated low in the child's throat and caught in his mouth, as if he was laughing mostly on the inside.

And his eyes. Always dark, the eyes of a pure-blooded Indian, Jesse's eyes were usually full of humor and love and mischief. Now they were jet black, fathomless and totally blank. The pupils were indistinguishable from the irises, the whites all but vanished.

Dean didn't know what this meant, but he knew it was bad. *Very bad.* Worse than the Noisy Thing. Worse than Em's death. Maybe worse than anything.

**

"My God, he has a gun!" Jackie said.

They all stared at Don Blume who was now circling, holding the handgun tightly. He would be still for a moment then lunge forward, his movements erratic and apparently senseless. The rest of the group stood silently, unsure what to do, until one of the Asians (Jackie thought it might be Hong Kong Dick – she wasn't sure, and she was annoyed how Bob's racist nicknames stuck in her mind, especially at a time like this *and why was she wasting thought on such trivial matters while a crisis situation loomed?*) took a photo of this crazed lunatic, and Don, hearing the shutter click, swung and pointed the gun at Hong Kong Dick. The Asian squealed and dropped to the ground, hands covering his head, and his countryman followed suit. Don squeezed the trigger and the bullet flew harmlessly through the air, imbedding itself in a tree across the clearing.

"Jesus Christ!" Bob said, gasping. "The man's a fucking lunatic!"

**

Grinning and grinning, and laughing that awful laugh. Dean couldn't bear it anymore and he reached forward and began to shake Jesse, gently at first then harder as the grinning continued. "Snap out of it," he commanded, and then, doing something he never dreamed he'd do, never in a million years, Dean slapped Jesse lightly across the face.

**

"What the fuck is going on?"

"Samuel! You're back. Oh, thank God!" Jackie said.

"I repeat – what is going on?"

"Isn't it obvious?" Bob asked dryly. "This wacko has gone bush crazy and is trying to rid the world of Chinamen."

"Oh shut up!" Don said. "I wasn't trying to hit him – I was trying to save us from that... that thing out there."

"Try telling that to Hong Kong Dick. I do believe our friend has shit his pants."

"Can you blame him?" Jackie asked. "I'm about ready to crap mine."

Samuel shook his head. "I leave you people alone for a little while and all hell breaks loose. Now, let's take it from the top – what's going on and why has Blume got a gun?" They all looked at Blume; he had his back towards them, near the edge of the campsite, and was facing the forest, nervously pacing and holding the gun squarely in front of him, arms stiffened as if rigor mortis had set in.

"It's out there... it's out there," Don ranted, maintaining his hysteria. "Don't you understand? It's out there and it's trying to get us. To kill us. Can't you see? Can't you hear it?"

"The only thing I hear is you, Blume," Samuel said.

And it was true. The Noisy Thing had stopped. Everyone was silent for a few seconds.

"It *was* there," Don stated, turning to face them and clutching his gun defensively. "I heard it. They heard it too. Ask them. They'll tell you."

Samuel looked at Jackie quizzically and she nodded. "He's right. Something was running through the forest, towards us. It was making a crackling sound and then a thumping sound. It was very loud."

"Which direction?"

Jackie pointed and Samuel frowned. "I just came from there and didn't hear anything. Could it have been a tree falling?"

"No, it lasted too long – several minutes, and it seemed to be getting closer. A lot closer."

Samuel scanned the sky. "Thunder?"

Jackie frowned. "No."

"An animal of some sort?"

Bob laughed and it startled them. "It'd have to be one hell of a loud animal!"

Samuel scratched his chin thoughtfully. "Animals can behave very strangely sometimes. Any number of things could cause – say a moose or bear – to charge. Territorial conflicts, injury, fear, protection of their young... all of these could make it act irrationally. About twenty years ago I saw a rabid bear tear through a forest pushing down trees. It was incredible. It took four of us to finally bring it down."

"Rabies?" Bob asked, looking worried. A rabid bear rumor wouldn't bode well for his hotel development. He didn't know much about rabies except that it was fatal. One hundred percent fatal. You got it – you died, no exception. When he was eight, he was bit by a stray dog – enough to break the skin and the grownups went nuts. Must have been a rabies scare in Southern California at the time. His mom rushed him to the hospital and the doctor stuck him what appeared to be a twelve-inch needle and it hurt like hell. Certainly a hell of a lot more than the dog bite.

"Relax – it's been ten years since a human tested positive for rabies in this province. Just a theory, that's all. Now Blume," Samuel said, approaching Don with an outstretched hand. "Why don't you give me the gun?"

"The hell you say."

"Come on. You're liable to hurt someone with it."

"I'm keeping it! You can't fool me with your bullshit bear story. I *know* what I heard and it was no goddamned bear. I know!"

"Then put it away – for now. There is no danger anymore."

"You're going to let that fruitcake keep the gun?" Bob asked and Jackie poked him. She knew where Samuel was going with this: diffuse the threat first and deal with the situation later – when everyone had calmed down.

Don looked at them, hesitating slightly before pointing the trigger at Bob Vance's chest. "You are such a fucking know-it-all. I should shoot you and shut you up for good. You think you're safe, you slick city shit, but I know better. I hope it gets you. That'll show you. That'll shut your smug face up for good."

"Don," Samuel said. "Put down the gun."

A look of disgust crossed Blume's face and he hesitated for a moment longer, taking one last long look into the forest before tucking the gun into his pants. Everyone collectively expelled a breath, especially Bob, who was muttering, "That fucking lunatic threatened me. Did you see that? He fucking threatened me."

"All right," Samuel said, breathing easier. "Now that's over, let me tell you what I found."

**

Dean noticed the exact instant the Noisy Thing ceased: it was the same moment Jesse snapped out of his trance. The forest grew silent and Jesse blinked his eyes and looked at Dean with bewilderment. "Uncle Dean?"

Thank God, the kid was okay. A little pale, but otherwise unscathed. Everything else was forgotten: the Noisy Thing, the other people, the woman with the beautiful voice. He would never find the face to match that sweet voice but it wasn't important. Not anymore. He wrapped the child in a bear hug, squeezing tightly. "We're going home, Sport. We're going home – now."

Jesse shifted immediately. "No! No! Please, Uncle Dean. I don't want to go home, I want to stay. Please, please!"

There was no mistaking the sincerity in the boy's pleading. More than sincerity: his tone was desperate. Dean never heard the boy plead like this. Indeed, Jesse was a fair-minded child who rarely asked for anything. His general placidness and non-materialistic nature was such an enigma that this sudden outburst, so intense, so fiery, was all the more surprising.

And confusing. Dean felt his insides twist. "Sorry, Jess, but we have to. You're not well. I want you to see a doctor."

"No, no! Please don't make me go back. Please. I'm not sick, really. I'll be good – I promise. Please don't make me go. I hate it there."

"You do? I thought you loved Aunt Penny."

Jesse began to cry in earnest, the tears springing from the corners of his black eyes and cascading down his cheeks. He looked pitiful.

"Jess? What is it? You can tell me."

"He made me promise not to tell anyone. He said if I told anyone... he'd...." Jesse swallowed, his voice trailing.

"Ah. Who did?"

"Uncle Harry.... Aunt Penny's boyfriend."

Dean gripped the child's shoulders gently. "You need to tell me, Jess. It's very important. I'll protect you, you can count on me. You've always known that, right?"

Jesse nodded. He wiped his eyes with the back of one dirty sleeve. "Sometimes... when Aunt Penny's not home... he does things... to me."

A sour feeling developed in Dean's stomach, the kind of feeling where you've eaten something a little off – bad enough to make your gut ache but not rotten enough to actually vomit. "Does he touch you?"

"In bad places."

"Show me."

Jesse pointed to the front of his pants. "Here." Then to his bottom. "And here. I don't like it when he does that. It... hurts."

"Oh, fuck." The foul feeling grew a whole lot worse, a hundredfold. Now Dean did feel like throwing up, like raging and going crazy and punching somebody's lights out, but he kept it together for the boy's sake, and he held the child again, this time more tenderly.

A muffled voice from against his chest: "Are you mad at me?"

"No, never."

"You won't make me go back?"

"Not a chance."

"Promise?"

"I promise." It was a promise he hoped he could keep. He wasn't familiar with child abuse laws but he did know the law protected a minor when an allegation was made. At least, that was white man's law – Native law might be another ball of wax. He felt the boy sob again and he held him a little closer. Damn the laws – all of them. Jesse was never going back. Not as long as Dean was living.

A few more minutes and Jesse's breathing relaxed considerably. "Then we can stay?"

Dean nodded. "For now." Until he figured out what to do.

Dean would have been shocked had he seen Jesse's face, still pressed tightly against his chest, split open in a wide, wicked grin.

**

"What did you find, Samuel?"

"Nothing at first. I ran all the way to the pictographs and scouted around. There was nothing there – no evidence of Benta at all. The soil is soft and I should have seen tracks, even ours from earlier, but there was nothing. Not a single track."

"Maybe the wind and rain covered them up?"

"Uh-uh. Too sheltered. It was as if no one was there, ever."

"Maybe Benta covered the tracks – you know, to make her photographs better?"

"That's what I was thinking. I found tracks at the trailhead which may have been Benta's but they disappeared and I couldn't pick them up again. But wait, there's more. Here – look at this."

They all peered closer, even the Asians, at the metal pipe held in Samuel's hand. Bob finally asked, "What is it?"

"Dunno. I was hoping you might be able to tell me. Anyone recognize this?"

No answer. "Are you certain? Think closely, especially you, Jackie. You shared a tent with her. Does it look like part of her photographic equipment?"

"I don't know – maybe. Could be part of a tripod. Whatever it is, it's broken beyond recognition. See how it's dented?"

"Yeah," Bob said, "and jagged. Like something ripped it apart."

Samuel titled his hand slightly, rolling the metal, exposing the underside.

Jackie gasped. "Is that...?"

"Blood? Maybe."

Bob took the metal from Samuel's hand, his face aglow with morbid fascination. "It's caked on. Like it was splattered. Where did you find it, Sam?"

"Where the trail forks, about a kilometre from here. It was off to the side, under the bushes, with only a little bit poking out. I almost missed it."

Jackie looked at it, grimacing. "Maybe it's not Benta's."

"What are you getting at?"

"The pipe – if it was so well protected, it could have been there longer." A horrible image occurred – the sight of her brother's hideously battered body laying under the bushes, only one swollen finger exposed on the path, while people continuously walking past him – right past, while he laid there, a decaying corpse rotting away to nothingness. Maybe this metal was Jerry's. Jackie felt the bile rise in her throat.

"It's possible, but I think it's fairly fresh. Old blood would have flaked away, grown darker."

"So what does that mean?"

Samuel raked his hand over his bald head. "Who knows? Maybe Benta bonked some animal on the skull, or maybe we're not alone."

"Not alone?" Don asked, suddenly. Until now, he'd kept his distance. "What do you mean, *not alone*? What do you know that we don't?"

Samuel shrugged. "It's a big forest and it's not closed to the public. There are probably all sorts of people walking around."

"So that loud noise –" Jackie began.

"Could have been someone playing a practical joke on you. And I'd say, judging from your terror stricken faces, they got you good."

Everyone laughed a little nervously. Everyone except Don, who maintained a closed-fisted grip on his gun.

Sam's voice turned serious. "On the small chance there is something dangerous out there, I suggest we remain close together. No one else ventures off alone, agreed?" The group nodded solemnly. "Okay. Now, regarding Benta's disappearance, I need to report it, organize a search party. I can hike out alone or we can go together. Either way, we will continue the tour, it'll just be altered."

"Surely you're not talking about hiking out today?" Jackie stated.

Samuel frowned. "Of course I am. The sooner I alert Search and Rescue, the sooner they'll locate Benta."

"But Sam," Bob spoke up. "That's a full day hike. It'll be dark in a few hours."

"What are you talking about? I've been gone only hour, maybe two. We have plenty of daylight."

The group exchanged glances. "Uh," Jackie said, "check your watch. It's seven o'clock in the evening."

Bob added, "You were gone almost twelve hours, man. We thought you weren't coming back."

Samuel looked at the group, slowly, and then looked at his watch. He shook it, staring at it, frowning. *He had lost ten hours.* When he looked back at the group, their faces reflected the confusion and terror he felt.

"Huh. Well," Sam stated finally, "I guess I spent more time searching than I thought. Okay, group, we'll head out first thing in the morning." Inside, he was a roiling mess, but he masked it. No use upsetting the group further. He scratched his head again, turning away.

There must be a logical explanation. He couldn't think of one right now, but there had to be.

"C'mon, people," he barked. "Let's get this campsite organized. "Vance and Blume, get a fire going – not too big, mind you, last thing we need is to start a forest fire. Keep it minimal. Jackie, grab the Asian guys and start prepping dinner. I'll get you the ingredients. Tonight, we are having Jambalaya, Hudson-style. Hope you like it spicy. Okay, people, what are you gawking at? Move it!"

CHAPTER FOUR

Dean watched the boy closely. He was looking for any abnormality, any behavioral discrepancy or physical oddity... anything at all to indicate Jesse was unwell.

But there was nothing.

Jesse was picture perfect, textbook normal. An average nine-year-old boy, enjoying a camping trip with his uncle. Cheeky sometimes, mischievous at others, but mostly just pleasant to be with.

The forest was calm. Stellar Jays and chipmunks filled the woods with happy sounds and the sunshine was a welcome relief after yesterday's chill. They slipped into easy banter, as comfortable as the flannel shirt Dean was wearing. Nothing at odds; everything at peace.

So why, then, this gut-wrenching, heart-stopping urge to grab Jesse and get the hell out of here?

Maybe because of the Noisy Thing, whatever the hell that was. Dean was certain there was a logical explanation – there had to be.

He just couldn't think of one.

Or maybe his urge to flee was caused by the girl with the beautiful voice and shapely legs. That was less logical – and absurd. But the fact remained: this unseen woman affected him more with her soft spoken tone that any woman since Em. *Pathetic, Stockton,* he chided himself. *You're fantasizing about someone you've never met, never even seen her face.*

His emotions were as unsettling as the Noisy Thing.

The Noisy Thing – whatever it was – was tangible and could be explained or fought (as need be) and he could continue on. To be involved with another woman the way he was with Em – and to lose her – that would surely finish him.

So, from a combination of need and desire, Dean and Jesse hung back, losing contact with the group. If he wanted, he could re-track them. If he wanted.

They spent the morning studying lichens and mosses found so abundantly on the forest floor. Dean pointed out which mushrooms were edible, which fungi to avoid, and even discovered some that would treat the consumer to one wild, hallucinogenic ride.

The morning lazily slipped into afternoon and they stopped by a small creek to eat some tuna and dried beans. Dean showed Jesse how to soak the beans in the pure, icy creek water, but Jesse decided he liked them crunchy instead. The day began to warm in earnest now, and Dean stripped off his flannel shirt, leaving on just his t-shirt. Still a little cold for bare chests and Indian war paint, but pleasant all the same.

Dean found some suitable tree branches which he stripped and fashioned into spears, but despite an hour spent searching, they couldn't locate any trout. Perhaps when they got to one of the many lakes their luck would change.

The wildlife so absent yesterday had returned in plenitude. They saw squirrels and grouse, heard an owl and even found a small lizard sunning itself on a rock. Seasonably correct, nothing abnormal. No signs of wolves, although there was plenty of bear scat – both grizzly and black bear – to prove the valley's healthy bear population existed. Dean hoped they wouldn't come in contact with any grizzlies and he patted his backpack. Secured against one side lay a good old Smith and Wesson .38 Special. Protection... just in case. Jesse didn't know. What kind of ancient Indian would go around packing?

Dean swept his gaze across the forest, noting the enormous Douglas firs and cedars – trees established long before Christopher Columbus ever dreamt about conquering a new world. And what a world it was.

No self-respecting, pure-blooded ancient Indian would carry a concealed weapon, but to venture into the wilderness without the means to defend himself, a man would have to be a fool or very, very naive.

Dean liked to think he was neither.

**

"Are you certain this is the right way?" Jackie asked.

"Of course I am," Samuel answered, testily.

"It's just... it looks so different. I don't remember any of this."

"Relax, I know this trail like the back of my hand."

"It's just... well, it seems like we're climbing a lot, shouldn't we be descending? And, we're going north, I can tell by the sun."

Samuel stopped. Her words made sense, but he knew this was the correct trail. Wasn't it? He rubbed his bald head in confusion, surreptitiously reaching into the pocket to find his GPS, coming up empty. It was gone. So was his compass.

He must have lost them yesterday, like he lost all those hours.

He had to keep it together, not let the group see how addled he was. "It's a short cut," he said. Sounded feeble even to his ears. "Now quit jabbering, you don't hear the men complaining, do you?"

The farther they hiked, the thicker the tension became. The forest grew denser and the terrain more difficult to travel. Jackie hung back slightly, stung by Samuel's criticism. But this put her back with Bob and Don, whose constant bickering made her grit her teeth. The arguing would stop for a few minutes, then flare again abruptly, as it did just now when Don fingered his gun again.

"For Christ's sake, Bloom! Would'ya quit waving that damned gun around?"

Don looked at Bob tightly, squinting into the realtor's face. "You'd like that, wouldn't you? You'd like me to drop this gun so *It* can get me. You're probably in on this whole thing, aren't you? You're in cahoots with *It*."

"You're a fucking lunatic, you know that Blume? Grade-A nutcase, certifiable. They should lock you up and throw away the key."

Don's grip on the gun tightened and he pointed it directly at Bob's face. "Oh, yeah, like *I'm* the lunatic. You're the one yelling at a man with a loaded gun. And it *is* loaded, Vance. Very loaded. I could pull this little trigger here and blow your tiny brain to bits."

"You haven't got the balls."

Don's face remained impassive save for one tiny neck muscle which seemed to be working overtime, twitching in a most fascinating and repulsive manner.

"Do something!" Jackie whispered to Samuel, but the black man remained transfixed. She looked helplessly at the Asians who stood quietly, watching the entire scenario with widening brown eyes. No help from that quarter.

Jackie began to move forward, intending to knock Don's arm away so if a shot did fire (and indeed, his finger was shaking so badly on the trigger she feared he might trip it accidentally) it would go high, harmlessly into the sky. An errant thought occurred as she moved forward (feeling sluggish and in slow motion, her feet impossibly heavy) and examined the thought momentarily before storing it away for further consideration.

Still, she couldn't push the thought away entirely – it was too big a revelation and her mind tumbled over it awkwardly, feeding the possibility, dismissing its strangeness and implausibility. As Jackie's hand came in contact with Don's shoulder, knocking his arm away an instant before the bullet was released, the idea exploded with alarming reality.

The men were becoming more primitive.

Somehow, someway as they trudged through this darkening forest, the men around her were reverting to a primal, less civilized state – each in a different manner. Don Blume and Bob Vance were becoming more aggressive – especially with each other. Their faces were animalistic, contorted with barely suppressed rage. Jackie had no doubt either would happily harm the other – the spent bullet casing lying on the forest floor was proof of that.

And Samuel? He was going the other way – becoming less aggressive, less in charge. Unsure of himself. Lost. Yesterday the guide showed strength and leadership yet today he stood passively alone. What was happening here?

She'd heard about these male *'find the inner man'* retreats where participants unburied their primitive selves. Was this it? Some male bonding ritual?

No. *It was stranger than that.*

This was more like their true personalities were emerging, the parts kept hidden from society, from themselves. Then, like an alcoholic with too much drink, these traits were becoming unveiled for all to see.

And the Asians? Were they different? Jackie didn't know enough about their personalities to judge, but they seemed unchanged. Maybe warier. Like herself. And a whole lot more confused.

"You tried to shoot me, you slimy little bastard. Why, I'll kill you –"

"I should've shot you while I had the chance, before this bitch –"

"Gentlemen! I think that's quite enough." Jackie's voice was sharp. "Get control of yourselves."

This took them back a little, and they stood silently. Bob had the grace to look ashamed; Don just looked angry. "Samuel?" Jackie prodded. The black man stood perfectly still, eyes glassy and inattentive. Jackie touched his hand slightly, surprised to find the flesh hot and dry. "Sam?"

Samuel blinked twice and looked at the small group, surprise registering on his face. Jackie felt a chill run up her back, felt her skin tighten, felt the fine hairs at the base of her neck stand up. "Samuel? Do you know who we are?"

Samuel stared blankly for a moment longer, and then his face broke out in a sheepish smile. "'Course I know who you are."

"Good. Sam? What should we do now?"

"Why, Miz Jackie, I believe we should set camp for the night right here," Samuel looked at Don Blume – who was still holding the gun with tightly clenched fingers – expectantly. "That all right with you, Mastah?"

Miz Jackie? Mastah? *MASTER?* There was no sign of joking here. Samuel appeared to be genuinely serious. Jackie looked from one to the other, surprised to see Don's face relax, his countenance assume a cocky, self-assured stance.

"That'd be fine, boy. Just set the tents up here."

"Yes, Mastah."

What the *hell* was going on here? Jackie fought the urge to run.

**

At nine o'clock the sun fell behind the mountain ridge to the west, and by nine-fifteen it was surprisingly dark. The heavy cloud obscured not only the stars but also the moon, so the night was doubly black. The only light came from the fire: a warm, golden light that cast dancing shadows on the surrounding trees.

No one mentioned the fact they were obviously deeper into the Stein. No one mentioned Benta. On several occasions, Jackie attempted to bring it up, but stopped. Afraid. Instead, she played along.

The men made a joint decision to conserve batteries, only using flashlights when absolutely necessary – one of the few decisions of the day that made sense to Jackie. Everything seemed off kilter; way off center, but Jackie was reluctant to trust her senses. To do so would result in hysteria. Perhaps the oddity of the day could be chalked up to an average day in the wilderness. What did she know? She was a city girl – born and bred.

Unlike last evening's small cook fire, this one was large and raging, the crackles and pops soaring high in the night sky like miniature fireworks. Everyone was sitting quietly, except for Samuel, who was busy cleaning up the evening meal. Jackie had offered to help – insisted, actually – but Samuel pushed her away, albeit good-naturedly. There was no more slave/master talk, for which Jackie was eternally grateful.

Don had finally put his gun away, although Jackie noticed he kept it close by. He and Bob steadfastly ignored each other, a situation not easy to maintain in so small a group. Even now they sat on opposite sides of the fire. They were aware of each other, Jackie noticed. When Don stood and turned his back on the group, proceeding to urinate on the closest tree, Bob covertly watched. Jackie turned her eyes away, disgusted.

That was another thing they had started to do: urinate and defecate whenever – and wherever – the urge arrived. Jackie understood the need to conserve the flashlights, and she sympathised with the men's reluctance to venture into the darkened forest, but really! Even a dog had the good sense to attend his needs away from camp.

She, for one, was not about to expose herself among these men. Jackie had been putting off the inevitable for as long as she could, but now she rose and reached for one of the pooled flashlights.

"What do you think you're doing with that?" Don snapped.

"I have to go to the bathroom. I'll just use it for a moment."

"Forget it. We might need it later – when It comes back."

"Oh, for goodness sake, Don! Be reasonable."

"You be reasonable. Go at the edge of the campsite like the rest of us."

"Oh forget it. I'll go without the damn flashlight. If I'm not back in twenty minutes, send a Saint Bernard."

"If you're not back in twenty minutes, it means you're not coming back."

She sighed. "Lighten up. It was a joke."

Bob poked the fire with a stick, sending more sparks flying. "You're not going out there alone, are you?"

"Yes I am."

"Out there? Can't you hear those howling noises? Sounds like a pack of wolves in the distance."

"Yes."

"Whew-ee," Bob whistled. "Idiot-boy is right, you're a goner."

"We're not coming to get you if you get lost," Don said. "Understand?"

"Yes," Jackie snapped sarcastically. "Thank you for your support. Very chivalric."

She turned and walked about a hundred feet into the forest.

**

"C'mon, Jesse. It's time for bed."

"Just one more story, Uncle Dean. Please?"

"You've already had three. I don't know anymore."

"How about the one where you and my Dad tried to make a parachute?"

"You want that one again? Aren't you tired of hearing that old yarn?"

"Nope."

"All right, but this is the last one. If it gets any later, you'll have to start telling me stories." Dean staged a theatrical yawn that fooled no one.

"Okay."

"Promise?"

"Cross my heart until I die."

"Well, that's a bit of overkill. Okay, here goes," Dean settled back comfortably. They had taken great pains to make a mattress from leaves and moss, and it was surprisingly comfy. No need for the tent tonight, although Dean had it close by in case the weather turned foul. After the other night's wolf incident, he wasn't keen on sleeping alfresco, but Jesse insisted. "Okay, here goes: When your Dad and I were a little younger than you – about eight years old – we decided to make a parachute. So we took one of my mother's big white bed sheets from the clothesline –"

"Was she mad?"

"Boy, was she ever. Mom didn't have an electric washing machine, just this old wringer washer that took forever to use. Anyway, we got this nice clean sheet and chopped it up with scissors, then tied rope to the ends and attached an old milk crate to the bottom.

"Next, we snuck down to the Trading Post, which sold everything under the sun, and climbed onto the roof."

"Because it was the highest building in town!"

"Right. Three stories. We climbed the fire escape –"

"You carried the parachute and Dad carried Mrs. Parry's cat."

"That's right," Dean chuckled. "You know this story better than I do. So, we got Mrs. Parry's cat, a big old grey Tom with scary yellow eyes – as scary as Mrs. Parry's – and we carried him all the way to the roof. The cat was none too pleased, which led to a permanent scar on your Dad's arm. He was yowling away, and we waited for a big gust of wind, spread out the parachute and stuck the cat inside the milk cart and tossed it over the side."

"But it didn't work."

"Nope. Boy, did we get in trouble. I got a spanking so hard I couldn't sit for a week, got my allowance suspended for months *and* had to apologize to Mrs. Parry. And the cat –"

"Didn't come back for three days."

"And walked kind of funny ever since. The end. Goodnight, Jesse."

"Goodnight. Uncle Dean?"

"Yes, Jess?"

"I love you."

"I love you, too. Now go to sleep. We have a lot of hiking to do tomorrow." A lot of hiking tomorrow and a lot of thinking tonight.

The boy finally fell asleep, warm and content and peaceful looking. His early sickness had disappeared completely, and as Dean poured himself another cup of coffee he tried to decide what to do.

So much to think about.

Could the allegations of abuse be true? Dean knew Penny Littlefoot well; she was a fine, wonderful woman. She raised Eddy, Jesse's father, from a young age. Penny was warm and maternal, the perfect embodiment of motherhood. She kept a meticulously clean house, baked cookies and cakes like there was no tomorrow, and always had an overabundance of affection for Jesse – or so it seemed. Was she aware of Jesse's torment?

And Harry? Dean only had passing acquaintance with Harry, but he seemed decent. Hard working, loyal... he had been part of the Littlefoot household for several years. It was hard to imagine Harry abusing a child, but Dean understood many abusers were the most unlikely suspects.

Could it really be true?

Jesse had no reason to lie. Kids didn't make these things up.

Had he?

No – why would he?

Dean's mind flicked through the possibilities in rapid succession.

What would he do now? Ah, that was the million dollar question.

Finish the holiday, so as not to further upset the boy. Keep things on an even keel. Return to the city with Jesse in tow. Take the boy to a child psychologist for evaluation (and confirmation?). Notify the authorities. Contact Penny Littlefoot. File a petition for temporary custody.

It wasn't going to be easy.

Dean sighed. Nothing worthwhile ever was.

**

Jackie took her time. She was far enough from the group to feel a comfortable distance, yet close enough to see the campfire. It was very dark here and Jackie was surprised to find she liked it.

She understood suddenly why her brother enjoyed the outdoors so much. It was peaceful here. Away from the group, she was alone with her thoughts and she liked that. One got a sense of smallness from being in the forest – standing next to these giant trees and surrounded by a myriad of wildlife helped put things in perspective. Jackie felt vulnerable, yes, but also realized a certain strength. She could survive out here alone if she had to.

And if things got any weirder back at camp she just might do that.

They were much deeper into the forest than yesterday. While it suited her personal agenda of finding Jerry, she wondered why no one else seemed bothered by it. She had taken care to watch for landmarks along the trail – the path seemed well defined, and she'd surreptitiously broken branches to mark the direction they'd taken whenever the trail forked. She was confident she could find her way back to the original site if she had to.

No one mentioned Benta. Or the need for a search party. It was as if Benta, in the eyes of the men, never existed.

Even more disturbing was the behavior of the men. Their personality changes were... alarming. Was this somehow linked to Jerry's disappearance? Jackie thought about her brother for a while. *Oh, Jerry. Where are you? What really happened? Will I ever find out?*

After a while she grew cold and tired, and reluctantly made her way back to the campsite. No one acknowledged her presence save for a tentative smile from the Asians. Jackie returned their smile, said goodnight and climbed into her tent. She didn't bother undressing. Tonight she felt safer sleeping clothed.

**

Jackie's absence signalled a kind of winding down for the rest of the group, and presently, they began to retire... the Asians first, then Samuel, Bob Vance and finally Don Blume. Don had decided earlier to switch tents, preferring to lodge with Samuel instead of Bob, a decision everyone regarded wise considering the animosity between the two men. When he finally settled in, Don was relieved to find Samuel asleep and he smiled slightly as he zipped his bag.

What would Mother think now, seeing him share a tent with a black man? Ho haw – Mother would have a royal fit!

Don's smile broadened and he felt stronger, more assured than he'd been in a long time. Hell, stronger than he'd felt *ever*. Oh, boy, Mother would *hate* that.

Mother.

He'd like to tell her a thing or two.

He'd like to walk into the kitchen with muddy feet! Oh, boy – that'd make her mad. Furious! Livid!

He'd like to throw a bunch of dirty dishes into the sink, mess up the tidy yellow afghan on the sofa... and... not make his bed. Ha!

He'd like to take Fluffers, Mother's prized Persian cat, and put it outside and lock the door. Or... drive Fluffers across town and take it to an animal shelter, saying it was stray. Or take the cat across town and throw it out the speeding car onto the highway, watching it splat all over the pavement.

How would Mother like that? Ha ha.

Better yet, Don would like to grab that stinking white cat, who Mother liked so much better than him, and shove that ugly furry white thing all the way up Mother's tight ass.

**

Bob Vance lay awake in his bed, fidgeting. Squirming. His mind wandered over the day's events and as always, when he couldn't sleep, he began to think about real estate. That always calmed him down. He remembered that he wanted to build something in this valley, some kind of building... what was it? Hotel. Oh, yes, that's what it was. A luxury hotel. He was quite excited about that. Or had been. It was hard now to understand exactly why he'd been excited. Why would he get so excited about a hotel?

Bob thought hard, really hard, trying to remember. Oh yes. *Money.* He could make money from building a hotel. Lots of money.

But who cared? He already had lots of money and what good was it? It was useless. After all, he couldn't *fuck* it.

Now the female in the other tent. He could fuck that. What was her name again? 'J' something. Jane? Judy? Jackie... that was it... Jackie. Yeah, he could really fuck her.

Bob thought about bending her over, taking her from behind, rutting and ramming, over and over until he got release. Oooh, that would be so good.

Bob could smell her now.

A part of him cried out that could not be true, that she was too far away, that it was physically impossible. But that part of him, deep inside and quickly fading, drifted away as he realized he really *could* smell her. The lightly perfumed hair, the faint sweet scent of her perspiration, the womanly juices running between her legs... oh, God, he had to have her.

But she would scream and others would stop him. J...J... what was her name? Bob couldn't remember and he realized it didn't matter. The female would scream and the others would come running, especially that fucking Blume asshole. And the guide would be on Blume's side – any idiot could see where *his* loyalties lay. They would stop him and he *wanted* the female... *needed* the female, *had to have* the female.

Oh, God, it was so hard to think.

His head was pounding, pounding. *How could he think with all this noise?* Bob began to rub his forehead but the pounding continued. He rubbed harder and harder until his fingers became like talons, scratching his flesh, ripping and clawing until blood ran solidly into his eyes, obscuring his vision but that didn't help. Only the female could help him now – only she could release this awful pressure. *Oh God, he had to find her.*

Could he still find her?

Bob threw back his head and sniffed the air. Her scent rang true and strong, and Bob grinned.

He could still find her.

**

Samuel lay motionless, trying desperately not to wake the sleeping man next to him.

No, suh. Mastah Blume would be most angry with Old Samuel if his sleep was disturbed. Mastah would wump him real good, yes suh, he surely would.

Oh, but he was hungry. Samuel had been so busy taking care of Mastah's needs he hadn't eaten his own dinner. Then, after he'd cleaned the dishes and tended the fire and laid out Mastah's bed, Samuel finally sat down to eat his own dinner. There'd been a bit of a commotion. Miz Jackie (such a kind, pretty lady) had gone into the forest and everyone stopped talking to watch her go and Mistuh Bob said: '*She's a goner'*, and then when everyone was watching her, Mastah Blume reached over and dumped Samuel's dinner into the fire.

Mastah Blume smiled so pleasantly as he did it.

Samuel sat, feeling terribly confused, watching his dinner spark and sizzle and burn. He didn't understand why Mastah wanted Old Samuel's dinner burnt, but Mastah must've had a good reason. And that was good enough for Old Samuel.

Still, Old Samuel's mind wandered and he found himself thinking of fried chicken and fluffy mashed potatoes and collard greens. With gravy. And corn bread. And apple dumplings. Old Samuel imagined putting a crispy piece of chicken into his mouth and tasting the tender, juicy meat, and his stomach growled. Loudly.

"You awake, Sam?"

"Yes, Mastah."

"Good. I've been thinking."

"'Bought what, Master?"

"Our friend, Mr. Bob Vance. He's become a problem."

"Yes, suh?"

"You understand that, don't you Samuel?"

"Yes, suh."

"We can't have a problem in the camp, can we now?"

"No, suh."

"It's bad for everyone. Harmful. A fellow like that is unpredictable. Could get us all killed when It comes back. Do you see what I'm getting at?"

Samuel was confused. He wasn't sure whether a 'yes, suh' or 'no, suh' was appropriate, and he sensed to answer wrongly would be a bad thing, so he grunted a noncommittal kind of sound and hoped it would suffice.

It did. Don had changed tracks. His voice was warm and cajoling and Samuel sensed his Master had something important to say. He was right.

"Will you protect me, Samuel?"

"Yes, suh."

"Even if it means your own life is in danger?"

"Yes, suh."

"And if someone was threatening me, planning to hurt me, would you stop him?"

"Yes, suh."

"Would you do anything to stop him?"

"Yes, suh."
"Even... kill him?"
"Yes, suh."
"Good. Excellent. I want you to listen very carefully to me, all right, Sam? All right?"
"Yes, suh?"
Don's voice was shot with urgency. "Someone is planning to hurt me, Sam. Hurt me badly – very, very badly. Maybe even kill me. Yes, I'm certain of it. He's planning to kill me. I need you to stop him, Samuel."
"Yes, suh."
"Stop him before it's too late."
"Yes, suh!"
"Do you know who it is, Samuel?"
"No, suh?"
"It's Bob. Bob Vance. He wants me dead. And you dead, too. All of us – he means to kill all of us."
"Even Miz Jackie?"
"Especially her. And the others, the Chinamen. He's going to kill us all. It'll hurt, he'll do it very slowly and painfully. Bob is very cruel. Bob is evil."
"Yes, suh!"
"Do it now, Sam. DO IT NOW!"
"Yes, suh!" Samuel leapt up, entangling himself in his sleeping bag momentarily before he broke free and he charged into the brisk night, his motions unplanned but urgent all the same. He didn't know what he would do to Bob when he found him, he didn't know how he would kill him, only that he must. Samuel had to kill Bob Vance –

Kill? He became confused again and his mind cleared. He wasn't a killer. Samuel T. Hudson could barely kill a spider, let alone a man. Why was Don Blume insisting on it? And why was Don in Sam's tent?"
"Kill him, Sam. Kill him now!"

"Mastah!" Samuel became focused again. He looked straight ahead and saw Bob's tent, illuminated by the embers of the dying fire. The tent was bulging as something tried desperately to emerge, through the flap – still zipped shut – and Samuel heard a ripping sound as the nylon tore apart, and out came Bob with blood pouring from his face, eyes flashing wildly.

Bob saw Samuel and lunged forward, whispering: *"Don't try to stop me... don't stop me... I need the female... I needneedneed...."* And Samuel knew it was true: Bob was coming to kill the Mastah.

Bob came at Samuel, bloody fingers outstretched, clawing the air and slashing at Sam's eyes.

It was over both quickly and quietly.

Samuel knocked the crazed man off balance and choked him. Strangled him hard enough to feel Bob's throat collapse and his neck snap. Bob never knew what hit him and he never made a sound, save for one, soft gurgling noise as his last breath left his body. Samuel felt as though he finished almost before he started and he stood there, in the cold dark night, wondering what to do next.

No answers came, so Samuel tenderly lifted the body – ever so gently – and returned Bob to his tent, tucking the dead man into his sleeping bag and closed the ripped tent flap as best he could.

Then, hearing the sound of a lonely owl hooting in the distance, Samuel rinsed the blood from his hands with icy water and went back to bed.

CHAPTER FIVE

The old Indian caught everyone off guard, just as he had the first time. Arne Johansson and Ben Hoight were taking a coffee break, playing a quick game of Five Card Stud at which Arne was rapidly becoming the loser. A half-empty box of Tim Horton's donuts stood temptingly on one side of Arne's desk and Ben's hand halted in mid-donut reach when the old Indian made his presence known. Timothy B. Rector (Timbee to everyone who knew him) sat motionless at Don Blume's desk, computer screen forgotten, his brown eyes bulging disbelievingly and his mouth hanging wide as he gaped at the intruder.

It was Timbee's first encounter with the old Indian.

It was Arne and Ben's second, and the old guy still startled the bejesus out of them. As with the first time, he seemed to appear from thin air. Sandie Lewis, the cute little redheaded receptionist, remembered neither admitting him *nor* seeing him.

The Indian had a face which looked older than time – dark-skinned and heavily wrinkled. Eyes shrunken so deeply it was difficult, nay impossible, to ever read them. Flowing grey hair that traced an oily path down his back, and more teeth missing than remaining. He was small – less than five feet, maybe four and a half, and he spoke with a hoarse cackle that seemed rusty with lack of use. His dress was traditional Native garb – full regalia. Everything – the feathered headdress, the leather thong and moccasins, the heavy beads and tribal war paint – looked textbook perfect, and therefore, somewhat fake.

If Timbee could be forgiven his astonishment (as Don Blume's temporary replacement, everything was new and vaguely surprising here at Empire Forest Products head office – a job he *still* couldn't believe he had the good luck to land, even if it was only a temp position) then Arne and Ben couldn't. They'd seen the Indian once before (Arne had seen him many times since – in his nightmares – a fact he would not now, nor ever, admit) and they'd remained polite but aloof.

The old man had jabbered predictions which sounded vaguely like threats and they brushed him off, giving him a bunch of forms to fill out and directed him to appropriate channels. This wasn't, as Ben pointed out, the correct department. They just did leg work for production services, implementing surveys to determine which areas were to be logged, along with occasional field work. Now this guy wanted Public Relations, one floor down and three doors across... Public Relations handled complaints. Go see them. This wasn't their jurisdiction. Not their department. Definitely not their job description. Fill out these forms and go see Public Relations. One floor down and three doors across.

"You are new here," the old Indian said, focusing on Timbee. "Leave now and this will not concern you."

Timbee sat transfixed in his chair – paralysed and unable to move. His computer began blinking demandingly, the monitor resplendent with blues and greens. The material he'd input into the computer – statistics about logging production in the upper Haida Gwaii – mysteriously began to self-destruct. Odd. This program had so far been virus free.

The rasping voice continued. "Your friend, the other one who sat here... dead."

Arne choked and spoke first, his voice rising with incredulity. "Don is dead?"

"Not... yet." The Indian's voice was painfully slow. Each man found himself leaning involuntarily closer, straining to catch the quiet words. "Soon. The destruction must stop. Leave our forests alone. The Elders are angry. They have nowhere else to go."

"Look, old timer," Ben said, standing up and surprising himself. "I told you last time: it's not our department. Go to Public Relations, one floor down and three doors across."

"It is too late for your friend. His time will soon come. He has sealed his own fate. But the destruction must stop or more will die. Many, many more. The Elders are angry."

"I told you –"

The Indian fixed him with one rheumy eye, and the three men were surprised to see that underneath the cloudiness the Indian's eyes were pale blue, beautiful in their strangeness and intensity.

Then he was gone.

"Well suck my cock and blow me to Heaven," Arne said.

"I didn't know Indians had blue eyes," Ben added.

Timbee looked around the small office, looked at the bemused wonderment of his coworkers, noticing the sudden blankness of the computer screen, thinking about how happy he'd been when he scored this coveted position. Unemployment was high – this job was a Godsend. A chance to leave his minimum wage job at the food court and finally use his university degree. A chance to pay his student loans and get out of debt. He thought about the Indian. He thought about what the old man said. And, Timbee picked up his belongings and said to no one in particular, "I quit."

**

Jesse woke first, climbed into Dean's sleeping bag and hugged his uncle tightly. Dean was caught between a smile and a groan. The child's affection pleased him greatly, but a more miserable night he'd never spent. He had tossed and turned constantly as if his bed was laid upon a pile of pointy rocks. Sleep had been elusive, and when sheer exhaustion finally claimed him, Dean's dreams were filled with horrific images.

Shattered bodies.

Dismemberment. Impalement. Decapitation. Even – God bless him – *scalping.*

He struggled to awaken, to end the torment, but now consciousness was as evasive as sleep had been.

He also had one hell of a headache. Felt as if someone belted him a good one, right over his left temple. He raised a hand to touch it, half expecting a bruised lump, but no, the skin was smooth. But throbbing.

"I'm hungry, Uncle Dean."

That made Dean smile. A hungry kid was a healthy kid, or so it stood to reason. "Feel like oatmeal?"

Jesse made a face. "How 'bout ham and pancakes?"

"Sorry, Sport. Ham ran out yesterday, we're on dry rations now... real camping food. The pancakes I can manage though."

"No, oatmeal's okay."

"Good. I have a little brown sugar to make it awesome. After today, we won't have any fresh stuff left. Why don't you set the bowls out and I'll get the food?"

"Deal. Can we hunt today?"

"Sure."

"Can we wear war paint, just like ancient Indians?"

Dean smiled. "Wouldn't have it any other way. Shall we make it as authentic as possible?"

"Yes, please. That'd be cool!"

"All right. After we finish here, we'll go by the creek and find berries to make a paste – that should made good war paint. Then, maybe we can carve spears from branches. Dead ones, though, a good Indian leaves the forest as untouched as possible."

"Don't forget bow and arrows. You promised."

"Of course, wouldn't be caught dead without bow and arrows." Dean smiled, his headache abating, and he squinted at the sky. "I just hope this weather holds out."

**

Had there been a body left to discover, Jackie would have been the one to find it. It was she who finally walked over to check the interior of Bob Vance's tent when it became apparent the realtor wasn't joining the rest of the group for breakfast.

"Maybe he's ill?" Jackie said, walking toward the tent, looking for the opening. Bob had positioned it away from camp, so it faced the forest. She rapped on the side of the tent as she passed. Did one knock on a tent? She wasn't sure of the proper protocol. "Bob?" she called, listening carefully. "Bob?" Then to the others: "I don't think he's in there."

Samuel looked confused, as if he was vainly trying to remember something. It was a struggle, and the black man gave up, his face becoming impassive. "Where else would he be?"

"I don't know. Bob?" she called again, rounding the far side. "My God, the tent flap is ripped to shreds!"

Everyone rushed over, crowding around. Jackie unzipped the torn nylon and looked inside. "It's empty. He's not – Oh! My God!" Jackie backed out of the tent, a rush of evil swirling around her head like poison gas – evil so strong she could almost taste it. Fear gripped her heart, squeezing the organ so tightly she had to gasp for breath and she expelled the air in tiny, painful spurts.

"Jackie? What is it?"

"I don't know," she said, shaken. "It was as if something was in there… something that wanted out."

"Did you see anything?" asked Samuel.

"No, I didn't have a chance to look before... well..." She hastened a look at Don Blume, hating to use his word but unable to find another, "before *It* came out." Then she added, rather defiantly, "I am not going back in there."

"Well, *I'm* not going in there, either," said Don Blume, his features pasty white. "I told you It would come back, and now it's got Bob."

"Don't be ridiculous," Samuel said, and Jackie was relieved to see the guide regain his leadership. "I've been working this forest for over six years now and there's nothing abnormal in these woods. I'll stake my life on it. Don has everyone scared with his nonsense talk. *I'll* go in the tent and check it out."

Don's face tightened. He didn't like the turn of conversation, felt vaguely like he should be in charge (although *why* he didn't know, he was never in charge of anything, Mother never allowed it) but he remained quiet, voicing no objection.

"Nope, nothing here." Samuel said, his voice slightly muffled from inside the tent. "Nothing at all, except... Good Lord!"

"Samuel?" Jackie asked. "What is it?"

"No... it can't be... it must be a mistake." Sam began to back out of the tent, and everyone, including the Asians who couldn't possibly have known what was going on, who could only feel the tension within the group, moved back a few feet, as if preparing for flight.

Samuel straightened, his face a study in disbelief, in shock, as he stared at his hand and the thing in it, and the group felt their eyes drawn toward it.

"What is it?" Don Blume asked, eyes squinting with keen fascination. He bent forward to get a closer look, carefully avoiding contact with the thing, with the bloody tissue that now stained Samuel's hand. "What is it?"

"It looks like... but it can't be... it's impossible..."

"Yes, I think it is –"

Alarmed Asian jabbering as they too decided it must be –

Jackie continued to stare at the repulsive thing, wanting to look away, desperately willing her eyes to pick another focal point to keep the pulpy, lacerated flesh from her view. She wanted to faint, she wanted to throw up, she wanted to scream and run away but instead she swallowed heavily, closed her eyes briefly (but still the image burned) and tried to compose herself. When at last she felt calm enough to speak she said, "It's part of a scalp."

"Bob's scalp?" Don Blume asked.

"I think so. See that patch of hair... what's left of it? It's the same color as Bob's."

Samuel shook his head. "I don't understand. I've trekked these woods for over six years and nothing like this as ever happened. Ever. Grizzlies, yes. The odd cougar, maybe. Snakes, sure. But this?" He scanned the forest, peering into the thick underbrush and heavy tree cover. "This doesn't make sense."

"Something must have hauled him from the tent," Don stated. "That's why the flap is damaged."

"But what?" Jackie asked. "What kind of animal could do that?"

"Cougar, maybe," Samuel said. "Bear. Even a wolf."

"But surely we would have heard something?"

"You'd think," Samuel agreed.

Don turned away in fear. He didn't think it was an animal. He thought It had slinked into the campsite stealthily in the night and snatched Bob Vance's sleeping body. And after It was finished with Bob, he thought the body probably resembled those of Jerry Hackett and Wendall Scott.

Jackie backed away. Had something taken Bob or had he left of his own accord, fleeing into the night as Jackie herself had felt like doing? And if he left, why was the tent in tatters, why was his stuff left behind? And most damning: what about the piece of scalp?

Was it an animal or some kind of psychopath? Is this what happened to her brother? What kind of danger was she in? She glanced at Don Blume, noting the twisted look on his face. That didn't surprise her; she knew he was completely unhinged. That left her, Samuel and the Asians. It was time to make decisions. She had to be strong.

**

Dean fashioned a bow from a young hemlock sapling – not the strongest bow ever made, but it would suit their purposes. For the bow string he used soft cedar bark, rolled together to form twine. He carved the arrow from a thick mountain birch branch he found near their campsite, and Jesse surprised him with a handful of golden eagle feathers. "That was a stroke of good luck," Dean murmured, fastening the feathers to the end of the arrows with mixture of cedar bark and tree sap. "Better than store bought," he proclaimed, and Jesse smiled, obviously pleased.

The clouds parted and glorious warmth descended over the valley, becoming temperate enough that Dean and Jesse felt comfortable removing their shirts. They found some reddish clay and a thatch of blackberries, and they ground them together to make a kind of dye. They helped each other apply the paint in various slashes on their foreheads and cheeks, and when Jesse began to smear some on his chest, Dean followed suit. What not? The kid was having a ball.

Feeling primitive (and very foolish if anyone but Jesse should see him) Dean chanted and danced a little as he cut down another dead branch, this one a birch, and he sharpened one end to make a crude spear. "Ready, Sport?"
"Ready."
"Then let's go hunting."

**

Jackie was wrong: she didn't have the Asians to count on. After witnessing what was debatably Bob Vance's bloody scalp, the two young men unceremoniously packed their belongings and left. Jackie tried to stop them (difficult with the language barrier) and momentarily thought about joining them, but they left in such a hurry she really didn't have a chance. She watched them go with a twinge of regret.

She noticed they never looked back.

"Can't say I blame them," Samuel offered, and she nodded. "Considering recent events, we need to abort this trip. I'm not sure what's going on here but the proper authorities should be notified."

Jackie startled. What about Benta? Had he completely forgotten about Benta? What about yesterday's assertions that they were leaving the Stein to alert Search and Rescue? It was as if Benta never existed – at least to the guide.

She was in over her head, had been from the moment she passed that warning sign, only she'd been too stubborn and stupid to realize it. It was time to get out before she ended up like Bob. But the question was: should she try to hike out herself or stick with Sam and Don Blume? Was she safer with or without them?

She studied the two men covertly. They *seemed* normal this morning. Don was cleaning up the breakfast mess and Samuel was packing the tents and supplies.

She watched as he left a tidy pile of items they weren't taking with them: Bob's belongings, the Asians' tent. When he caught her staring, he said, matter-of-factly, "No point lugging this stuff around, it'll slow us down. I'll send someone to salvage it when we get back to Lytton."

That moment, Jackie thought, couldn't come soon enough. She personally didn't care if she never stepped foot in this wretched forest again.

**

Don Blume listened unobtrusively as possible. Could what he was hearing be true? Were Samuel and Jackie planning to leave the Stein and tell everyone?

Shit. This was getting worse all the time.

What the hell was he to do?

Now there were four disappearances to look into. Jerry Hackett and Wendall Scott, Benta Sturm and now that asshole Bob Vance. This would mean a full scale investigation. The media would flock... lost tourists always generated lots of interest, especially when they were Internationals. It was as if Canadians were far too polite to misplace people from other countries. Somehow, he had fucked up.

Empire would be furious. He would be transferred to some meaningless department. No, Don amended, he would probably lose his job.

Mother would kill him. She relied on his income.

Don Blume rubbed his temples as the conflicting emotions overwhelmed and confused him. None of what happened was his fault. Nothing he could have done would have changed things (well, except to tell everyone about the grisly pictures at the outset, but that wasn't really the objective, was it?). How was he supposed to know the German bitch felt like wandering the forest at midnight, taking goddamned photographs?

Jesus. And people said Germans were supposed to be smart.

As for the realtor... was it Don's fault something got Bob Vance in the middle of the night? Don rubbed his temples some more, unsurprised to feel throbbing begin. Great. He was on the verge of a migraine. The throbbing intensified and Don felt he should remember something. A niggling idea surfaced that he knew something about Bob's disappearance, but it scared him so he pushed it to the back of his brain while the throbbing got stronger.

Four deaths. A whole lot of explaining to do.

Unless... unless he could get rid of these two. Yes, that would work. He could say an avalanche got them...*did avalanches happen in summer?* Sure, why not? Some of these peaks had glaciers and where there was snow there were avalanches. Yes, that would be plausible. The bodies would be virtually unsalvageable. And himself? *Why, he barely managed to outrun the dang thing.* Why not? He'd started working out a few months ago, he was in good shape, people would believe it. Hell, he would be a hero!

Except for the Asians. That was a kink in the plan. Already long gone... no chance of catching up with them now. Unless... unless... he killed the others now and ran like the devil through the forest to catch them and killed them too.

That would work.

Except for one problem.

Then he'd be alone in the Stein. By himself. *With It.*

The idea sent shivers down Don's spine. That was to be avoided at all costs. He would keep the group alive until they were safely out of Its range, say the parking lot. He needed them until then. Then, he would kill Jackie and the guide, take their bodies somewhere else, like... oh, maybe the Fraser Canyon and dump them over the side... and worry about the Chinamen later. Besides, Hong Kong Dick and Chicken Chow Mein didn't speak English. Maybe they wouldn't be an issue after all. Maybe they'd return to Japan or China or Mongolia or wherever the hell they were from and just disappear. Yes, that would be good.

The throbbing dimmed slightly and Don felt better. He had a plan. Not the most perfect plan, not the tidiest plan – after all, there were a few loose ends – but it was feasible. It would work. And he could worry about details later, after he'd gotten rid of the others, after he was out of this horrible place. Safe and sound. With Mother.

**

Dean was amazed at Jesse's agility with the spear. The kid was fantastic. Where had he learned to throw like that? Jesse's first throw had been a little wobbly, second a whole lot steadier, and on his third throw he speared a marmot. The kill was so clean the rodent hadn't a chance to utter one last shrill whistle.

Dean bent over the dead marmot and removed the spear. "Well, guess this is lunch."

Jesse's victory smile faded. "You mean we're going to cook it?"

"No, we're going to eat it raw."

"Eeew."

"Just kidding – of course we'll cook it. First history lesson: never let anything go to waste. Natives never hunted for pleasure or sport, not like the white man. Natives hunted for survival, and every bit of their kill was used. Nothing wasted. The skins were dried and cleaned and used for clothing or shelter, the flesh was consumed, the bones used for all sorts of things, like weapons and utensils. They were resourceful, never threw anything out. I guess you could say they were the first recyclers."

"Yeah, I know... but do we really have to eat it?"

Dean smiled. "Yes, and I want you to think about that the next time you kill something. You kill it – you eat it." He saw look on the boy's face and ruffled Jesse's hair affectionately. "Don't worry, it'll taste good. We'll cook it on a spit, just like your dad taught me. We did it all the time when we were kids." Dean picked the animal up and headed for the stream. "C'mon, I'll show you how to gut and clean it."

**

"That okay with you, Don?" Samuel asked, looking at his watch. "It's nearly ten o'clock, still early. If we get a move on, we can be out of the Stein by tomorrow afternoon."

"Sounds great," said Don, his smile wide.

"Samuel?" Jackie asked. "Do I have a few minutes before we leave? I'd like to go down to the creek and wash up."

"Sure – no problem. Just don't take too long."

"Twenty minutes, tops." She smiled gratefully as the guide nodded and gathered a change of clothing and a bar of soap. A bath would be wonderful – she had two days of grit and grime accumulated in her hair, under her fingernails, everywhere – but that wasn't her true reason for leaving. A little dirt was uncomfortable and it wouldn't kill her, but staying with these two might.

As much as she tried to convince herself that Samuel and Don were acting normal, she knew they weren't quite right. She sensed danger. Benta's disappearance could be rationalized: an experienced outdoorswoman and hiker, perhaps she'd decided to travel on her own to get the photographs she desired. Benta hadn't come across as a team player. It was weak, but plausible.

And now, Bob. His disappearance was not as easy to explain. Combined with the shredded tent and bloodied scalp, it appeared an animal might have gotten him. But surely the others would have heard the commotion? She'd slept lightly last night, yet heard nothing.

What should she do? What *could* she do? Surely it was more dangerous to go off half-cocked into the woods like the stereotypical hysterical female? *Even if she felt like doing just that.*

Be sensible, she cautioned herself. If she stayed with the men, at least she knew where the risk lay. Alone, she was vulnerable. She was a city girl, not adept at wilderness survival. Who knew what dangers lurked out here? Wild animals, exposure... the very real possibility of getting lost. And there *was* something dangerous here, she had no doubt about it. Whether it was linked to her brother's disappearance was debatable, but the threat was real. Just not tangible.

Jackie reached the creek. It was a pretty spot, not visible from the trail and almost deep enough to submerge oneself in. The water was clear and cold, but the sun was warm and there was a primitive sensual pleasure in exposing one's skin to the purity of it. She stripped hastily, allowing a quick look over her shoulder to make sure no one followed her and dipped in quickly.

Jackie gasped. The water wasn't cold – it was *freezing*.

She resisted her initial impulse to leap out, forcing herself to remain, and gradually she became accustomed to the temperature. Then it was lovely. Small rocks gave way to large flat stones perfect for sitting on. The water came to her shoulders and she let her feet float to the surface, studying her surroundings. The vegetation was lush and thick, with many shades of green merging together to create a magnificent backdrop. Above she could see the mountain peaks, jagged and snow-topped. The water swirled gently around her and she turned her attention to the creek itself. Fine sand had formed at the bottom, black and flecked with gold. Jackie reached to examine it, allowing the silt to sift through her fingers, noticing how the sunshine glittered off the specks, dazzling her with their brilliance. She knew it was only mica, fool's gold, but it was fun to pretend. And why not? It wasn't too far from this very spot that the country's largest gold rush was mined. And sitting here, with the cold, pure water swirling around her naked body, with the forest unspoiled and virtually untouched since the beginning of time, Jackie could almost believe she was in another era. A time where men rode mules through these woods, packing their belongings and searching for fortune, a time when computers didn't exist and television wouldn't be invented for many years to come. A simpler, happier time. *A time when her brother might still be alive.*

**

Dean unsheathed his hunting knife. "This is how you do it," he said, holding the marmot carcass for Jesse to see. "Pay attention – next time it's your turn." He proceeded to carefully de-skin the creature, remove its bones and filet the flesh. "Not a whole lot of meat here, but enough for a light lunch."

"I can't believe you plan to eat that."

"Stop grimacing," Dean said with a chuckle. "We're going to eat this, and we're going to like it. I promise. Marmot kebabs."

"Yuck."

"Now see these?" Dean asked, pointing to the innards. "These organs can be used to make all kinds of medicines and potions. Take the bladder here... any girls you want to get romantic with? We can make a love potion from this."

"Uncle Dean! That's gross!"

"I know, I was only teasing. But I wasn't kidding when I said the Natives used every part of their kill. I'm not certain what the bladder was used for but I'm sure they had something in mind. Maybe a necklace or pouch –"

"Eww, disgusting!"

"Since we don't need the entrails, we'll leave them lying on this stump. That way all of nature's little beasties can have a nice, free feast. Just you wait and see, Jess, by tomorrow all this stuff will be covered with bugs and maggots and stuff."

"That's disgusting too."

"Not really. It's the law of nature. Nothing goes to waste, everything has its use. Everything gets integrated back into the cycle."

"Uncle Dean?"

"Yes, Sport?"

"I don't feel so hungry anymore."

Dean laughed. "All right, I'll let up. Here, let's clean this skin. It'll make you a fine souvenir. Maybe we can make a cap or something, like Daniel Boone."

"Who?"

"Never mind. Come on, let's find a way down to the creek and wash this thing off. I could use a bit of a wash too, look – I'm covered in blood."

Jesse groaned and Dean smiled. Maybe he was laying it on a little thick.

The approach to the creek was easier than anticipated. The west slope was precipitous but he found a natural path, perhaps forged by animals. Jesse trailed behind, enthusiasm lagging, and Dean reached the creek before him.

Then he heard it.

A soft, lilting voice swept in a gentle melody. It was coming from upstream, carried by the wind. And Dean knew the voice belonged to the woman he heard earlier. The sound of her beautiful voice was etched into his memory.

He had to see her. Jesse finally caught up, head hung glumly, and Dean motioned for him to stay put. He passed Jesse the marmot skin and showed him how to wash it, then told him to wait here. Quickly and quietly, Dean made his way up the bank of the creek to the next level, and there he saw her.

Her back was toward him and she was kneeling in the water, washing her dark hair with a bar of soap. The bubbles traced a milky path down her slender back, exposed from the waist up.

She was naked and he stood mesmerised, listening to her gentle singing, unable to place the song, knowing he should turn his back or at the very least announce his presence, but unable to, fearing the spell would be broken.

It was. Jesse called out "I'm finished", and she turned around, eyes wide and mouth open in surprise, then fear. Her song turned to scream, and Dean moved forward to placate her, to show he wasn't a threat, but she began to back up, breasts bare for an instant before she grabbed her towel.

The screaming stopped and she looked around wildly for an escape. "Stay away," she warned. "I'm not alone, others are nearby and they'll be coming any moment."

"I know," he said, realising after he spoke how badly that sounded, as if he had been spying on her, which of course he had. Dean raised his hands in front, a universal gesture of goodwill, only to notice they were still covered with marmot blood. Belatedly he realized how he must look, stained with blood and war paint, chest bare and hair uncombed. He looked like a maniac. "Don't worry, I won't hurt you," Dean said.

Jesse arrived, holding the dripping skin, talking as he approached. "How does this look, Uncle Dean? I cleaned it just like you said... oh!"

"He's learning to hunt," Dean said. "We're, uh, camping," he finished lamely, uncharacteristically lost for words. His razor sharp mind, honed in the courtroom, was reduced to babble. "Uh, sorry for the intrusion. We'll leave now." He grabbed Jesse by the shoulder and hauled him backwards, feeling foolish, feeling like a dolt, feeling like a schoolboy. Worse, he realized he was blushing.

Jackie watched them go, towel clutched tightly to her front, mouth parted in astonishment. She stayed there for a few minutes until she was certain they were gone, then slowly made her way from the creek, careful not to turn her back on the direction the man had been. She dressed quickly, pulling her jeans over still wet skin. Her towel was soaking but she wrapped it turban-style around her head and carefully made her way up the steep bank.

All was quiet. Samuel and Don Blume either hadn't heard her screams or simply didn't care, for neither appeared. The man and the boy were gone and she breathed a sigh of relief, then smiled slightly. What a sight he had been! Like a wild mountain man, savage and well-muscled, primitive even, until his boyish shame made him human again. Jackie sensed he was no threat, not after the initial shock, but then again, one never knew. Some pretty strange things had been happening here.

The bloody bit of scalp came to mind and she sobered, thinking of how the man was covered in blood. Coincidence?

Now she felt frightened again and quickened her pace back to camp. Jackie shivered. Out of the frying pan, into the fire.

**

Don Blume and Samuel were packing the last of Bob's things. "Are we really going to leave all of Bob's shit?" Don asked, derisively giving the shredded tent a slight kick. One more loose end. He'd have to figure out a different story.

Samuel scratched his chin, considering. "It's a shame to leave it here – could be ransacked by animals or thieves. We'd be leaving behind some top quality items. The sleeping bag alone probably set the guy back a few hundred bucks."

"Well, I'm not carrying any of it. My stuff weighs a ton already," Don said.

"Probably the best bet would be to leave it here. It'll be a good marker for when the authorities come. It might be wise to leave things undisturbed."

"Authorities? What do you mean, authorities?"

"Well, someone will have to come and check out these disappearances. The police will be notified, and of course there will be a search party, although I don't know how much good that will be." Samuel looked around him. "The Stein is one hell of a big area, over a thousand square kilometres. By leaving the tent here, it'll allow them to focus on this immediate area." Samuel looked at the tent again. "Jesus, but that's a mess. Wonder what ripped it like that? Something with claws. You think we'd have heard something."

Shit, shit, shit! Don was going to have to get rid of all their belongings, too. Oh, Christ, this was growing more complicated by the fucking second. What was he supposed to do – drag all this stuff out singlehandedly? He was going to need help, maybe get Ben and Arne in here. They shouldn't have made him come alone. They should have to get their hands dirty, too. This was as much their job as it was his. If they'd been here in the first place, this wouldn't be happening to him. It was all their fault.

Don focused his thinking. The tent. He couldn't leave the tent. They had to take it with them. "Samuel? I think we should take Bob's belongings with us."

Samuel sighed. He was getting tired of this stupid little man. "I told you, we're leaving it *here* for the authorities."

The air crackled with tension. Don's shoulders began to straighten and he felt bolder, more in control. "I said: TAKE IT!"

Samuel jerked back as if he'd been slapped. His brown eyes blazed for a moment, then grew dull. He slumped forward slightly and his head dipped subserviently towards his chest. He moved towards the tent. When he spoke his voice was a whisper. "Yes, Mastah."

"What's that?" Don demanded. "I didn't hear you!"

"Yes, Mastah!"

Don struck Samuel solidly across his face with his open hand. "That's better. You'll carry this all yourself, got that, boy?"

"Yes, Mastah."

"And not a word about this when the bitch comes back." Don grinned cruelly. "That is, *if* the bitch comes back."

**

"See this?" Dean asked Jesse, bending to the faintly smouldering fire. "The coals are still hot. They probably left here half an hour ago." Probably right after she saw him at the creek, Dean added to himself. Probably left the creek and ran back here to tell the rest of the group that a crazy man covered in animal blood and berry juice stopped by to exchange pleasantries while she bathed. Probably got the hell out of here as quickly as they could... not that Dean blamed them. Hell, he would've been here sooner except he wanted to clean up a little before coming to make apologies.

Who would think that blueberries would stain so badly? He'd scrubbed and scrubbed, but still he couldn't quite remove the faint purple sheen from his chest. Served him right – act like a lunatic and get marked like a lunatic. Thank God he didn't have to return to the office for another week or so. Wouldn't that be great? Show up at a trial with a purple face? Impress the hell out of the judge.

The girl was gone. Dean felt both relieved and dismayed. He would have liked a chance to redeem himself, fully clothed and fairly clean.

"What happened here, Uncle Dean?" Jesse asked.

"Looks like they left in a hurry. They should have put the fire out... oh!" A sudden gust of wind whipped through the campsite, swirling around them, throwing dirt and smoke into their faces. It was a heavy feeling, making it hard to breath, and it carried a bad smell... the foul odor of decay. The wind swirled purposefully for a few seconds then stopped as abruptly as it started.

Dean brushed the dirt from his eyes and a strong sense of foreboding washed over him.

Something was wrong. Very wrong.

He knelt and fingered a tuft of fur at his feet. Only it looked more like... human hair? The ends were bloodied. "Jess, come look at this," Dean said. "Jess?"

No answer. He swung around to look at the boy, surprised to see Jesse standing still, his face pale and eyes blank.

Just like before.

What the hell was going on?

Dean leapt to his feet and ran to the boy, shaking him. He didn't like this, didn't like it one bit. "Jesse, snap out of it, damn it, snap out of it." The boy didn't respond and Dean went to pick him up, and then he heard it. The thump-thump-thump sound from yesterday. Crashing and banging, coming from all sides, coming from – no that was impossible – inside of Jesse, and Dean became afraid.

Last time, he slapped the boy, an action so abhorrent that Dean loathed repeating it, but since it had worked before and the thumping was growing louder, he tried it again.

There was no reaction. Jesse's eyes remained blank and his mouth smiled a little, the tiniest bit, and he was very still except for a slight sway to the sound: *thump, thump, thump...* as if he was at some ghoulish disco.

"Come on, Sport, we have to get you out of here." His words were tense, panicky. Last time they remained still and the thing passed them by, searching and seeking, ultimately turning away when it detected no motion. But this time they were in the open and the thing honed in on them. Dean could feel it, feel the earth vibrate with every thump.

"Snap out of it, Jess! We've got to go... got to..." But the boy stood blankly, swaying and smiling, *thump-thump-thump*, so Dean elected to carry him, to pick him up and run. Jesse, who weighed maybe seventy pounds, suddenly felt like he weighed five hundred.

**

"There it is!" screamed Don Blume. "I hear it, I hear it! It's back. It got Benta and Bob and now it wants us!"

Jackie froze. She heard it too. *Thump-thump-thump.*

It arrived suddenly, just like last time, and it sounded not too far off. "It's in the direction we came from."

"The campsite?" Sam suggested.

Jackie nodded and listened, forcing herself to remain calm. There wasn't must else she could do.

∗∗

Dean tried again. He put his arms around Jesse's waist, braced his feet and strained with all his might. No use. The boy wasn't budging.

Thump-thump-thump. It was growing louder.

Dean looked around wildly. The campsite offered little protection. The semi-hot remains of the fire, a tuft of hair and some scattered coffee grains.

Thump-thump-thump.

Jesse was smiling widely. Dean shuddered. What was it that transfixed the boy so? Was he in shock?

Thump-thump-thump.

Dean patted his thigh – good old Smith and Wesson, his Saturday night special. Didn't make these like they used to. He hadn't used this thing in a long, long time. He hoped he wouldn't have to.

Thump-thump-thump.

He hoped it would stand up to whatever it was crashing through the brush, thumping and bumping, descending upon them.

∗∗

"Why won't it stop?" Don cried, kneeling to the ground and curling into a fetal position. "Somebody make it stop! Please, oh, please. MOTHER! MAKE IT STOP!"

Jackie looked away from Don and spoke abruptly. "I saw a man, earlier. At the creek, when I was taking a bath. He was covered in blood and had funny markings on him. He was with a little boy. Maybe this has something to do with them. Some kind of ritual thing."

"A man?" Samuel asked, and Don Blume stopped moaning. "What kind of man?"

"I don't know, a regular type of man, I guess."

"No, I mean, what race was he? Native Indian?"

"No, at least, I don't think so. He had shaggy blond hair and was tall. Really tall, maybe six-three or six-four. The boy, though, he could have been Native. He was dark skinned... but I couldn't tell for sure. I only saw the boy for a moment."

"And they were covered in markings? What kind of markings?"

Jackie shrugged. "I don't know, slashes and that kind of thing. It looked pretty random."

"Blood?" This was from Don Blume, still lying in the fetal position, but listening attentively. "I heard you say blood."

"I think it was blood. The man said something about hunting and the boy was holding up some kind of skin or something. It was brown and fairly small, maybe a rabbit. I really didn't look closely. Why do you ask, Sam? Is it important?"

"I don't know. Possibly. It might account for that noise... maybe even the others' disappearances. Maybe we're dealing with some kind of madman."

"My God," Jackie whispered, her face growing pale. She listened to the thumping sound in the distance, trying to determine if it was growing louder or closer or more intense. "My God."

**

There was no escaping now. The thumping was all around them and the wind had mysteriously picked up, swirling and beating against them. They stood, unprotected, in the middle of the small clearing that had recently served as campsite. Dean's hands clasped Jesse's waist and he gripped the boy tighter –

Thumpthumpthumpthumpthumpthump

– listening to the noise surrounding them. He buried his face in the boy's shiny, dark hair, feeling the warmth of Jesse's skin, smelling the sweet, little boy scent. He kissed Jesse's head and whispered, "I love you, Jess. I love you."

"No," Jesse moaned. "Go away."

And then it stopped.

The forest was still. Neither thump nor breeze marred the perfect calm. No birds sang, no squirrels chirped. The only sound was Dean's softly spoken words, "I love you." Repeated again and again.

Jesse looked up and smiled. His eyes had cleared and he returned Dean's embrace, and Dean was surprised to find the child almost weightless as he reached to be lifted into Dean's arms. "I love you, too, Uncle Dean."

They stood that way for a long time.

CHAPTER SIX

The old Indian hadn't returned but things at Empire Forest Products Head Office, Survey Division, started to go wrong immediately after his second visit.

Little things. Annoying things. The kind of things that could slowly drive a man insane.

Computers failed, documents were missing, phone lines went dead at inopportune moments (even though B.C. Tel couldn't locate the problem). The air conditioning failed on the hottest day of the year and stayed broken despite the repairman's best efforts. Pencils broke and pens ran dry. Desks became wobbly and coffee spilled over important documents, three times in one day. Even the donuts were rancid.

There was no replacement yet for Timbee. Applicants lined up for the job but by the time they reached the interview office they turned away, sometimes so quickly they left their belongings behind. That left a void which Arne Johansson and Ben Hoight had to fill, a position neither relished, although if asked why, each would have a difficult time explaining. Neither tried to think about it very much and tensions began to rise. The little disasters, none so important on its own, combined together to cause both trouble and unexpected conflict. Arne and Ben, best friends for fifteen years, fishing partners and poker buddies with nary a harsh word spoken toward the other, began to do the unthinkable. They began to squabble. To bicker over inconsequential things – like who should open the mail, or who had to fill out the tally forms. The arguments grew until they became of a more personal nature, and soon they began questioning which wife was prettier or the better cook and whose son was the superior athlete. It grew and grew until Ben told Arne his wife had an ass the size of

Alberta and was more stupid than a jersey cow standing in its own shit. Arne did the only thing possible in a situation like this: he popped Ben a good one right in the kisser. Soon the two men, well past their prime with stomachs bigger than their bank accounts, were rolling around, sweating and punching and blurting every bad name they could think of.

It was precisely this moment that Reginald K. Bloodsworth, the founder and president of Empire Forest Products, happened to wander into the room. "What the bloody hell is going on here?" Reginald thundered, and feeling rather dazed, the two men stopped fighting to look up at their imposing boss.

It soon became apparent that neither man was going to answer. Actually, neither could, even if it meant saving their own lives. Ben tried to speak but nothing came out, not even the faintest of squeaks. Arne just sat with his mouth closed and his head hung in shame. He knew he'd blown it... only three more months and he would be up for a promotion. He could kiss that goodbye.

"Since neither of you two imbeciles has the decency to answer me, I'll expect a full report in a half hour. Get off the floor and clean this wretched pig sty – and report to me in thirty minutes. Well? What are you waiting for? Get to it!"

Arne and Ben silently watched Bloodsworth stalk from the room and then they looked at each other. Still neither spoke. Ben put his hand out to Arne which Arne gratefully accepted and the two men struggled up. "What *is* going on here?" Ben asked.

"I don't know. Some pretty scary shit."

"Maybe... maybe that old Indian wasn't such a flake after all. Maybe we should have paid attention."

"Do you think?"

Ben shook his head. "I don't know. I don't know *what* to think anymore. Come on, let's clean this mess up. We have a lot of explaining to do."

**

Dean was thinking along much the same lines. Something awfully weird was going on around here. The thumping sound was unexplainable. The right side of his brain desperately searched for a creative explanation while the left, analytical side screamed: *'There is none, idiot, get out of here!' 'Pipe down,'* the right side suggested, *'everything has an explanation, we just need to think outside the box.' 'Not this,'* the left side answered. *'Not this.'*

Too many things didn't add up. Jesse's bouts with illness, if he could call it that. It was more like a fugue state. First thing Dean planned to do when he got back to the city was take the boy for a full physical examination. And maybe a psychological one, too. Perhaps he'd sign himself up for one as well – two-for-one discount.

And looming over everything, like a hideous specter, the allegation of sexual abuse. Dean hadn't thought it through, yet. He hadn't wanted to – kept putting it off for examination later. Coward.

But it was difficult – sexual abuse was heinous, especially when a child was involved. A child he knew and loved. Didn't this sort of thing happen to someone else? *Nice cop out,* he chastised himself.

Adding to the mix was Dean's reluctance to return to the Stein. This was his first trip in fourteen years, fourteen *long* years. If you'd asked him last week, or yesterday, or even ten minutes ago, he would have answered that his hesitation to return to the Stein was from a promise made to Eddy. Now he wasn't certain.

Possibly there was another reason – but he wasn't sure if he wanted to find out.

He was afraid to find out. Double coward.

And, last but not least, the woman. The woman with the beautiful voice and pretty face, the woman he'd seen bathing in the creek. This had something to do with her. He didn't know how he knew, the knowledge seeped from his core. This was linked to her. To her and Jesse and him. Somehow, they were in this together.

A whole lot of strange thinking for a man who liked everything neat and tidy. A man who demanded proper explanations. A man who'd eschewed religion because it wasn't logical; a man who strode for complete control over every aspect of his life.

And now, that was out the window. This was parallel thinking. He couldn't explain it and he couldn't understand it. He had to trust it, blindly follow instinct with an open mind. He had to have faith.

They were in danger. Especially the woman – her danger was omnipresent. It felt vital to find her, to save her. His heart pounded with the urgency of it.

**

They made good time, it was faster backtracking. Part of it was due to the terrain, now they were hiking mostly downhill. They were carrying less equipment – with the exception of Samuel, who was laden with Bob Vance's pack, plus his own. Now that they numbered only three, there was less waiting around. A sense of urgency prevailed; no longer were they stopping for scenic outlooks.

Samuel led, Don took the middle and Jackie felt content to lag behind. She felt safer that way. Sure, there was something weird in this forest, but there was something even creepier about the two men ahead. She couldn't put her finger on it – she just felt it.

Don Blume was less tense now that Bob wasn't there to rile him. That's not to say he was relaxed; every muscle in his body screamed for release and Jackie knew he, like herself, would be glad to see the last of the Stein.

Samuel was quiet, unnaturally so. Jackie didn't know the guide well, only what she saw of him in the past few days, but she knew enough to recognize the black man had undergone a subtle change. The first day he had been downright chatty, exuberant and full of life. Now he looked tired. Dull and wasted. As though he had nothing to live for. He walked with a stoop, as if he carried a heavy burden upon his strong, dark shoulders that had nothing to do with the backpacks. There were subtle yet tangible undercurrents flowing between the two men that she didn't understand.

The thumping sound hadn't returned, thank God. Not a peep. She wondered what it could be, but didn't wonder too hard – as if thinking about it could somehow summon it. Superstitious maybe, but there would be plenty of time to ponder that phenomenon once she was back in the city. When she was safe.

Samuel stopped abruptly in a meadow clearing and reached for his water bottle. "It'll be dark in a few hours," he said, taking a long swallow. "We'll continue hiking until dusk, then set camp."

Don pursed his lips but said nothing.

Jackie felt overwhelmingly disappointed. She'd known realistically they wouldn't make it out of the Stein by nightfall, but they had been walking so fast and for so long that part of her still hoped. Desperately hoped. She followed Sam's example and retrieved her own water bottle. "I don't remember seeing this meadow before. Did we pass through here on the way in?"

"Nope, this is a shortcut. This trail is more rugged but it'll shave off a half day of hiking – if we leave at sunrise tomorrow, I reckon we'll reach the parking lot by noon."

"I have to confess, Samuel, I'm a little confused. I thought the jeep was due south but we've spent the past hour walking north-west."

"You're right, of course. See that mountain ahead? Last time we went around it, tomorrow we'll go straight over."

Both Jackie and Don Blume gaped. "But it's so high! The rock face is completely bald – we can't climb that."

"Relax," the guide said, smiling. For a moment he looked his old self. "There's an aboriginal trail, almost like a tunnel. It's faint, but enough wildlife uses it to keep it viable. The trail winds through the mountain pass. As you walk through, there are vistas of lakes and peaks so sublime you'll believe you're in Heaven. An experience of a lifetime."

Jackie said nothing, and Don Blume's eyes narrowed. Samuel looked at both of them and chuckled, shaking his head. "City folk. Always fussing."

**

"Oh oh. Trouble here."

"What is it, Uncle Dean?"

"These tracks – look, now there are only three. What happened to the other four sets?"

"Maybe the group split up?"

"Maybe. I didn't notice any tracks branching off, but it was difficult to tell. Back at their camp there were so many footsteps in every direction it was impossible to tell exactly how many people were there. Same goes for the trail we've been following – footsteps back and forth, back and forth. But here: three of them take a different trail."

"Which three?"

"Good question. See this print here? It's large and deep, so I'd guess it belonged to a tall, heavyset man. The other one is smaller, but still large enough to indicate a man's foot. And this one here? That must be the woman's... looks like a perfect size seven to me."

"Oh, I see. The imprint of the number seven, on the sole of her shoe."

Dean laughed. "You're on to me. Thought I was dazzling you with my superlative tracking skills."

"Which way should we go?"

Dean answered without hesitation. "This way." There was a subtle pull in that direction – as if the trail was guiding him.

Why had the group split? Did it indicate trouble? Surely, they must have heard the thumping that permeated the forest yesterday. Had it scared them into scattering?

"Have you been here before, Uncle Dean?"

"Nope, this is one trail your Dad and I never explored. Let's see if we can find it on the map." Dean pulled a weathered, dog-eared copy of the Stein Hiking Guide. He flipped through the pages, mumbling. "I figure we should be right about here. This is where the trail branches. That way goes to the parking lot and this way goes..." His eyes followed the dotted line up the map. "Oh, Christ! They're heading to Devils Lake."

**

Sam said they were hiking along Victoria Ridge. This narrow band balanced somewhat precariously above a creek, affording magnificent views of the sheer slopes of canyon walls. Jackie stopped abruptly and pushed a sweaty hank of hair from her eyes. Hiking was too mild a word – they were climbing.

"Easy, now," Samuel said, his eyes crinkling in the waning light. "Another few minutes and we'll make camp at Meadow Lake. It's real pretty – you'll like it."

Jackie hunched her shoulders to adjust the weight of her backpack and grimaced wryly. "That's what you said about this place."

"Did I lie?"

"I don't know – too tired to appreciate the scenery. Ask me again when we get to the campsite – I'm going to unload this pack from Hell, soak my feet for two or three hours and sleep like a baby. Then, maybe I'll be able to appreciate some of this natural splendor."

Samuel chuckled, noticed Don's frown, and dropped the grin. They pressed on. The trail became more exposed as they continued to climb and the denser Douglas fir gave way to sparser pines. They noticed the wind here, whipping abruptly about their faces, and for a moment the trio froze, listening grimly for the accompanying *thump thump thump*. It never came and Samuel told them to relax, that it was always windy along this ridge.

Then they were there, at a little lake as pretty as a postcard. Meadow Lake was aptly named and Jackie was delighted as she dangled her feet in the cool water, sharing company with some meadow voles until a long-tailed weasel scared them off with his approach.

She left the setting of the camp to the men. They didn't want or even seem to need her help, and she was glad to spend time alone. Oh, Samuel was pleasant enough, although sometimes his eyes became frighteningly vacant, almost as if he was suffering a stroke, mainly when he was in contact with Don Blume. And Don? He had been mercifully silent most of the day, looking away whenever Jackie glanced his way and generally avoiding eye contact. Once, when he'd stopped to retie his bootlace and Jackie, lost in thought, had overtaken him instead of waiting for him to finish, heard him mumbling: *"S'all her fault. Fucking bitch. Just wait until I tell Mother. Fucking bitch."* She stared at him, startled, and was horrified to see the hatred in his eyes. Then it was gone.

At that moment Jackie resolved to go it alone, then realized she had no idea where they were. If they'd been on the trail they'd taken earlier, she might have a chance, but this was unfamiliar territory. This trail was difficult to follow, with lots of low-lying bush and no markers. Sometimes the trail was so indistinguishable Jackie wondered how Samuel could follow it. But still the guide forged doggedly ahead.

Samuel promised the hiking would be easier tomorrow and Jackie had to take his word for it. It did seem as though they were headed in the correct direction again, her compass pointed true south. She liked Samuel but didn't know him well enough to trust him. And, considering recent events, the strange noises and missing people, Jackie didn't trust anyone.

Anything could happen to her out here.

Like it happened to Jerry?

A sickly fear rose in her chest. If she did disappear, no one, save for this little group would know her whereabouts. She hadn't told her parents about this venture into the Stein. She knew it would upset them. They weren't young anymore, and with Dad's illness and her Mother's inability to cope, combined with the heavy grief over their only son's disappearance, they lived life precariously. If something happened to Jackie, their only remaining offspring, it would truly send them over the edge.

Stupid! She told herself, even though she knew her reasons were perfectly altruistic. But why hadn't she told her friends? Or coworkers – even though it was summer, she kept in touch regularly with several. *Because, Jackie old girl, you were afraid to. You spent four long years building good relationships with the other teachers and you didn't want to blow it.* Sure, she was emotional after her brother's disappearance, but who wouldn't be? Jerry was, after all, her friend as well as her brother. Maybe she let work slide a little, most people understood, and she made certain the kids never picked up on it. The Principal, Teddy, had been wonderful. But the hurt wasn't going away, and by June, people were starting to get fed up. No one said anything. No one looked at her askance, nor hinted subtly she should be getting on with her life. But Jackie knew they were thinking it. She was thinking it, too. Maybe it was time to put things in perspective, time to lay Jerry to rest.

But she couldn't. She had to know. She had to really know that he was gone, find irrefutable evidence before she could start living again. Start laughing again.

Did that mean she was crazy? If she was a different kind of woman, someone more open with her feelings, like her friend Jayleen, psychotherapy might help. Lord knows it helps Jayleen. But Jackie wasn't Jayleen, and she knew that babbling to some stranger about childhood injustices wouldn't solve her problem. Finding the truth about Jerry would. And, fearing no one would understand, Jackie elected to keep secret her whereabouts. Now she regretted it.

It may have been the worst mistake of her life.

**

Devils Lake. Even now the name sent chills racing down Dean's spine. *How could he have forgotten Devils Lake?*

The memories rushed back in a sudden swoosh, emotions so long buried Dean was surprised they weren't dead. *Dead?* Poor choice of words. Those memories were as alive as Devils Lake.

They were having a boys' weekend, just after Dean met Emily Ann but long before Lyn got pregnant with Jesse. Just Eddy and Dean and an overweight, ginger-haired kid named J.J. Fleishenheimer. J.J. was acne prone and desperately out of shape, not to mention out of style and sync with the other kids in town. But he had an honest face and a friendly manner, and the thickest Bronx accent Eddy ever heard. This fascinated Eddy, who'd never travelled farther than Kamloops, and certainly never met anyone who'd been all the way to New York City, let alone lived there. So they befriended the Irish-looking boy with the Jewish name and invited him to camp in the Stein. It was Eddy's idea really, and as usual, Dean went along with it. Eddy's ideas usually turned out great.

Usually.

Eddy thought he'd teach them some Native ways. (The parallel that Dean was now teaching the same skills to Eddy's son struck him ironic in the extreme.) The whole idea was a grandiose show-off scheme on Eddy's part, but J.J. seemed game, and Dean was too. They'd hunted and fished and played silly animal games, and then they'd stumbled onto an unmarked trail to Devils Lake.

This part of the Stein was unknown to them, which was strange since Eddy knew the valley so well. They were seventeen, almost legal adults in the eyes of the law, but still children in more aspects than not, hell-bent on foolish pride and cocksure as only young males can be. They competed at everything – who could hold his breath underwater longest; who could skip a stone farthest; who could shimmy up a tree quickest. The games never ended.

When they came across the unmarked trail, Eddy suggested they follow it. It was steep and narrow but the climb was well worth it. They felt like they were on top of the world. They felt like Gods. Then everything changed.

Oh, God. How could he have forgotten Devils Lake?

CHAPTER SEVEN

On the day Ben Hoight's wife left him, (a lovely, gentle woman to whom he'd been wed twelve years and sired two children) he contemplated suicide. It was the worst day of his life. Or so he thought.

Why did Margaret leave? Because she was scared. Pure and simple: scared. Of *what* she was unwilling (or unable) to expound. To give the poor woman credit, she tried. She really, really tried. But the words never came. Only a heavy shaking and tears. Plenty of tears. Then she bundled up Arnold (age eight, named after his father's best friend and co-worker) and Ben Jr., age five-and-three quarters. Arnold told Ben Jr. it was stupid to add the three quarters but Ben Jr. did it anyway. He always said it proudly, like a badge of honor, which made all the grownups laugh and made Arnold even madder. Then he'd call Ben Jr. a whole lot worse than stupid, always when Mom or Dad was out of earshot, of course. Sometimes he even said the "F" word, but Ben Jr. really didn't mind. He basically tuned his brother out, realizing that Arnold was bigger but Ben Jr. was smarter. Arnold knew this too, and that's what made him really mad. He wasn't above giving his brother a good thumping every time he thought he could get away with it, but he seldom did – Arnold was the kind of boy destined to get caught at everything he tried, there would be no free rides in life for Arnold – which made him even more pissed off. Although the cycle seemed endless, Ben Jr. realized that Arnold would not be bigger forever and thus was content to bide his time. However, when he was really annoyed or was feeling frustrated with the injustice of having a moronic giant for a brother, Ben Jr. would calmly mention that *he* was named after their father, and Arnold wasn't. That usually made Arnold hit the roof and thump Ben Jr. real good, but Ben Jr. decided it was worth it.

So Margaret threw some clothes in a suitcase, grabbed the Visa Card from the freezer, (plus the Sony PlayStation with all twenty-seven games thanks to Arnold's complete refusal to leave home without it) and took the family van to God-knows-where. She wasn't saying and Ben Sr. certainly had no clue. It couldn't have been to her mother's. That sorry woman had been dead and buried for a good ten years.

What Margaret had managed to convey was that she still loved him but was desperately afraid to stay with him any longer. It seemed his dear wife was having recurring nightmares which started (if Ben had his calculations right) about the same time Jerry Hackett and Wendall Scott disappeared. Ghoulish dreams about bizarre animals and burning bones and lots of blood. Night after night she dreamt that Ben killed her, and now her dreams showed him killing the boys. It had gotten so bad that Margaret started taking sleeping pills but that didn't help – the nightmares kept coming. She couldn't sleep, she couldn't think straight. The only thing she could manage to do was eat, and she gained twenty pounds. Hadn't Ben noticed?

Ben couldn't say he really had. Sure, she'd been grumpy lately, but he chalked it up to woman stuff, you know, the PMS thing, or whatever the hell they were calling it now. He never noticed the sleeping pills. And the weight gain? Well, Margaret wasn't exactly a slim woman and an extra twenty pounds wouldn't show. Maybe if he'd seen her naked lately... Ben tried to remember the last time they'd made love and he realized he couldn't. It had been a long, long time and Ben hadn't even noticed.

Now she was gone. For God knows how long. There was no food in the fridge (Margaret had apparently been on an eating binge just before her departure) and Ben hadn't the slightest clue how to operate the oven. Or the microwave, other than reheating coffee. Or the washer and dryer. The washer alone had more bells and whistles than a jetliner. No way could he operate the washer and dryer. Shit.

Worse yet, his ass was in a sling at work. Old man Bloodsworth really laid into him after he caught Ben and Arne fighting. Arne was still mad because Ben said all those things about Arne's wife (it didn't help to apologize because both men knew they were really true). No replacement for Timbee and no word from Don Blume, although that was to be expected. No one foresaw that man's arrival for another three days at least.

To cap it off, his newspaper was missing the sports section, the liquor store was out of his favorite brand of beer, and Ben had a nasty suspicion he was developing a boil on his butt. Right on the fleshy section, the part where you sit.

So suicide crossed his mind, and he considered it with detachment, weighing the pros and cons, even going so far as to decide the various methods. (Gunshot in the mouth was his personal favorite: quick, easy and painless if done right. Death would be instantaneous, a real masculine way to die. A little messy, but then, what did he care? He wouldn't be around to clean it up.) Then he got over it. He ordered in pizza, choosing the house special: loaded with onions, mushrooms, salami and a particularly greasy brand of pepperoni which Ben loved but Margaret wouldn't let him eat – said it made him fart.

And fart he would. All over her side of the bed. That would teach the silly bitch a lesson.

Damn the house was quiet. He wished the kids were here, fighting a little so he could yell good-naturedly at them. He wished Margaret was here so he *could* make love to her – all of a sudden he was desperately horny.

**

It was the wrong side of midnight and Jackie was dreaming. She *knew* she was dreaming, *knew* she was asleep, but still she couldn't wake up. After awhile, she gave up struggling and nestled deeper into her sleeping bag to enjoy the sensation.

Her brother was alive, sitting hunched down at the end of her tent, talking to her. She couldn't see his face very well. Although the moon outside was round and bright, inside the tent it was dark. Her brother's face was shrouded, and Jackie guessed if she moved a little to the left she would have a better view. Problem was she couldn't. Not only could she not waken, she couldn't move. She was experiencing that common inertia experienced in a dreamlike state: her body felt leaden and impossibly heavy, as if her flesh was filled with quicksand.

Jerry was massaging her foot through the sleeping bag. He was stroking just right, the way she liked it. Not so hard that it hurt, but hard enough not to tickle. She smiled with sleepy pleasure. Jerry had been rubbing her feet like this since she was five.

Strange how real it felt for a dream.

Now Jerry was talking, although Jackie couldn't make out his words. He was babbling nonsensically. His words had rhythm and Jackie thought he might be speaking some strange kind of language, although certainly not one she could identify. Funny sounds, all mixed up like kaleidoscope pieces.

She sensed he was frustrated, that whatever he was trying to tell her was important, perhaps urgent. But the inertia that held her body also threatened her mind, and she couldn't concentrate. She felt heavy, drunken.

Jackie's mind wandered and she remembered the time she and Jerry were playing in the woods at her grandfather's house. She was hiding and Jerry was seeking, and Jackie was very good at this game. She was a quiet child and knew how to remain perfectly still, especially when the hiding spot was as good as this one. She lay motionless in the dark cave, feeling the damp warmth of the earthen floor, waiting for Jerry to find her.

But he never did. Presently she fell asleep and when she woke it was dark and she couldn't find her way back to grandfather's house. There were all sorts of sounds in the woods, night sounds she wasn't used to, and she became afraid. There was a search party, which of course she knew nothing about, and when one of the rescuers passed by the cave, Jackie remained hidden. She was frightened by the unfamiliar person and heeded her mother's advice: never talk to strangers. This one knew her name and called to her but still she hid, fearing it might be a trick and fearing her mother's wrath.

It was Jerry who found her, seven hours after she initially hid, and he took her hand and led her back home. She felt safe with Jerry. He seemed so much older that day and Jackie knew then she could always count on Jerry to save her.

The stroking on her foot gave way to sharp pain and Jackie gasped, refocusing her attention on her brother. He was fading now, and although the moonlight had illuminated his form only minutes ago, she could barely see him now. His long fingers grasped her foot and she tried to pull away, but failed. The pain intensified and Jackie awakened, felt the sleep strip away layer by layer. The lethargy lost its grip as she regained consciousness. She was able to sit and she blinked her eyes, looking at her brother. He was very faint now, a gossamer image evaporating like smoke. She leaned closer and for the first time saw his face.

Jackie gasped. It would be fairer to say she saw what was left of his face.

This was crazy. Nothing more than a sleep induced hallucinogen. *But it seemed so real.* Too real. She shook her head to clear the image but the monstrosity that used to be her brother remained. He began to speak and his head shook slightly; long, pallid strips of loose flesh hung from his face, exposing the grey bone beneath. Jackie felt the scream rise in her throat but the figure shook its head and brought a decayed finger to what used to be lips, was now an open jawbone with charred stumps of teeth.

She tried to look away but couldn't – her face was frozen, gaping at her brother. *No, not her brother,* Jackie thought wildly. Her brother had nothing in common with this... this... creature.

Jerry began to speak. She sensed the difficulty he was having, the tremendous effort it took to move the damaged throat. What used to be his Adam's apple was now a well-cooked remnant of punctured bone moving up and down in a desperate effort to function. The whispered words rasped softly and Jackie strained to catch them. Her eyes widened as their meaning became clear. With a voice far removed from that of a living creature, her brother spoke the words: *GET OUT!*

**

Don Blume regarded Samuel sourly. The black man was singing gaily, his deep voice chanting some sort of primitive verse. Something was happening to Sam and Don didn't like it. He wasn't sure exactly what change the guide was going through, but it made Don uneasy. Like he was losing control. Samuel was growing stronger, while Don was growing weaker. Don's brain was muddled and his thoughts were becoming increasingly unclear. Flashes of brilliance still came to him, but not as often, and not as profound. Sometimes Don thought he was losing control.

There were so many loose ends to think of. Like the fire pit. What if someone found it? It might cast suspicion on his avalanche story. A thousand questions screamed in his mind, casting doubt on his plans. What if someone found the missing bodies? What would he say then? And when exactly should he kill Jackie and Samuel? And why hadn't he put out that fire? It burned like a beacon, smouldering away next to bits of Bob Vance's scalp. Those coals could burn for hours, maybe days, sending up a smoke signal for anyone interested enough to take a closer look. Everything was unravelling. *Oh, why hadn't he thought to put out that fucking fire!* It was all so bloody messy, so untidy.

Think, Don. *Think, think, think!*

His head throbbed with the effort as he willed his brain to conjure a viable solution. THINK! What would Mother do? (A flash of pain at the thought of that dear woman) and then it came to him. Brilliant! Don could say a grizzly attacked them, killing Bob. That would explain the bits of scalp. Maybe even the others. Yes, that was it – he would change his story. The damn bear stole into camp, attacked the group in a frenzy and hauled Bob out, then killed the others. And their bodies? Why, it ate them. Seemed plausible, nice and tidy. No loose ends. *Mother would be proud.*

His brain was growing fuzzy again and Don forced himself to think some more before it completely clouded over. The Bob Vance problem was solved, but what about Samuel and the bitch? He had to do something, soon, while he still could. Samuel was growing stronger and Don was growing weaker, and pretty soon Don wouldn't have control over the black man. *Think,* Don, *think.*

"She's coming!" Don said to Sam, his voice thick with apprehension. "She's coming to get us. Now!"

"What?" Samuel asked, his sing-song halting.

"Stop her, Sam! Stop her before she kills us!"

"You mean, Miz Jackie?" The black man's voice was doubtful, his gentle brown eyes full of confusion. "Why, Miz Jackie never'd harm a fly."

"You're wrong! You're a fool, letting silly sentiment cloud your vision. She's plotting, I tell you, plotting right now. *This very moment!* I'll bet she's thinking of ways to cut off our heads. Cut off our heads and slice out our hearts. Then she'll eat them raw."

"Noooo."

Don noticed the black man's hesitation and he gratefully pounced on it. "I'm right, I'm always right. It's a plot. She's in cahoots with Bob, and remember what you did to him, Sam? Do you remember how you took care of Bob, how you squeezed the life from him?" Don yelled triumphantly, feeling the power wash over him like a man of God. He had his strength back! He was right and Samuel was wrong. They were all wrong. He had to show them the way, to lead them so they could be as pure as he.

"Mastah Bob was a bad man. He was gonna hurt you. He was gonna hurt Miz Jackie."

"That's right, boy. He was gonna kill us. He was bad. He was infected. And now she is, too. She'll be coming for me. *Coming for you.* Right now she's plotting, waiting there, pretending to be good. But she's evil. We must stop her before she kills us."

"Yes, Mastah."

"Can you do that, Sam?"

"Yes, Mastah."

"Can you stop her? Can you stop her now? Can you stop her like you stopped Bob?"

"Yes, Mastah."

"Then do it, boy! Kill her now before she comes for us. Don't be fooled by her softness, by her beauty. She's evil, she must be eliminated."

"Yes, Mastah." Samuel slowly moved his large bulk toward the tent door, his eyes dull and blank. "Yes, Mastah. I kill her now."

**

Dean stiffened. They were close: he could sense it. Instinctively, the same way he slept and breathed, without effort. Jesse began to lag and Dean couldn't blame him. It was late now, darkness had fallen hours ago, but they had to keep going. "C'mon," he admonished the child, "just a little farther, Sport. Not much longer." Jesse protested with a murmur and Dean urged him again, then turned his attention to the trail ahead. Not much farther. Perhaps a kilometre. Maybe less. If they picked up the pace they could go the distance in twenty minutes. Fifteen if they ran.

A lone wolf cried in the night, far away and his eerie howl echoed through the forest, sending chills down Dean's spine.

His sense of urgency increased. Ten-fold. A hundred-fold.

Now the short distance seemed insurmountable, as far away as the moon. He reached for Jesse's hand and began to run.

**

Jackie emerged from her tent, sprinting. She had the foresight to grab her jacket but nothing else. Her brother's warning still pounded in her ears and she stopped questioning. Questions could come later, reaction to reality (dare she call it reality?) must come now.

She dodged into the forest cover, as quickly and quietly as possible, and when she was sure she was safely hidden, she stopped briefly to assess the situation. *What was she running from?*

A sudden movement caught her eye and she squinted in the dark, trying to decipher it.

Samuel.

Going to her tent.

Jackie relaxed. Samuel was coming to help.

**

Kill, thought Samuel. Kill the bitch. Rip her face off. Squeeze the life from her throat.

Stop her from hurting the Mastah.

**

Faster... faster. Dean ran, the sweat stinging his eyes. The boy protested, dragging behind his uncle like an anchor. Dean tugged harder but the boy lost his footing and they both fell. The child began to whimper and Dean read the fear in his eyes, felt the fear in his heart. Not much time. He had to hurry. He sensed it was almost too late.

"Wait here," Dean implored. "Wait here, Jesse, for a few minutes, and don't move, no matter what. Understand?"

Jesse remained quiet, his breath coming in short puffs, curling into the night like cigarette smoke. Dean pressed his face to the boy's and repeated again, urgently: "Understand?"

Jesse nodded. Dean repeated the instructions: *Stay here! Don't move! No matter what! I'll be back shortly!* When he was certain Jesse comprehended completely, he slipped off his backpack and began to run.

**

The relief Jackie felt as she saw Samuel was palpable. He was looking for her, she could tell. It was hard to see him in the dark but there was enough moonlight to identify his form, to see he was headed for her tent. She began to move quietly, walking slowly from her hiding spot, walking towards him in the clearing.

**

The danger intensified again and now Dean knew it was almost too late. He urged his legs to go faster, heard the pounding. The pounding of his footsteps, the pounding of his heart.

**

Samuel reached the tent. He had stopped thinking clearly and was operating on something akin to autopilot. Don Blume's objective ran clearly in his mind. *Kill the bitch. Kill the bitch. Kill, kill, KILL!* Like a neon sign flashing in the darkness, these words illuminated his way, setting the stage for his actions. Any hesitation was gone. Remorse, compassion and human decency ebbed from his soul until it was empty. Now he was empty too, a finely-tuned killing machine, fully charged, all pistons firing. He bent his large frame and looked inside.

**

Jackie was getting closer to Sam. He was still a hundred feet away, his back toward her. She had reached the edge of the clearing now, the heavy tree cover behind her. She could see Samuel entering her tent. She started to cry out to him....

**

Faster, faster. Dean's heart pumping until he felt it would explode. *Thump, thump, THUMP!*

**

The tent was empty. The bitch was gone. Samuel bellowed in rage. He began to straighten, turning suddenly, staring into the forest in a direction not far from Jackie.

He bellowed again, letting loose his pain and frustration. He pounded on his chest: thump, thump, THUMP!

**

Jackie froze with the first bellow. She knew it was coming from Samuel and it didn't make sense. Nothing made sense. He turned and she witnessed madness in his eyes, the hatred and the fury. She saw him beat his chest and heard the thumping.

Samuel bellowed again and Jackie knew true fear. Samuel's expression was chilling and the pounding on his chest was primitive, bizarre. But all of that dimmed in comparison to the realization of the thumping.

The Noisy Thing was back.

CHAPTER EIGHT

Ben Jr. closed his eyes tightly and tried for the hundredth time to go to sleep. But he couldn't. He kept remembering the horrible events of that afternoon, kept thinking about how it was his fault. Every time he closed his eyes, the afternoon unfolded before him, like watching an endless YouTube loop.

....Ben Jr. was bored. He was at the Three Oaks playground watching his brother Arnold do back flips off the climbing bars. Arnold repeated his exhibition again and again, never varying the routine. First he would climb to the top bar, hook his feet under and let his body fall backward so he was upside down, hands hanging loosely below his head. Then he'd purse his lips together; blow his brother a 'raspberry' with an accompanied remark, something like: *Chicken shit, Baby stink-breath, 'fraidy-cat*, or something with the 'F' word. Ben Jr. watched his brother, hanging there with his tongue sticking out and his shirt free, exposing the beginnings of a fleshy belly. *He* wasn't going up there to hang upside down. It was dangerous. It was stupid. It was boring.

But there wasn't much else to do, especially if you're five-and-three-quarters, in an unfamiliar park near your Auntie's house. Even if you were mature for your age.

So Ben Jr. sat, watching his brother and contemplating life. He liked his Aunt Bettie and her three cats (whose names he still wasn't sure about) and her tidy house, but he missed his dad and his friends back home. Arnold was a lousy brother and an even lousier playmate. "Baby-baby-doo-doo, diaper-full-of-poo-poo," called Arnold, contorting his face into a disgusting grimace. He completed his back flip with a flourish and began to re-climb the bars, right to the top, probably for the three-hundredth time this morning. Ben Jr. sighed.

"Your brother should be careful. He might get seriously hurt," a raspy voice said, and Ben Jr. looked around in surprise. He hadn't seen the old man arrive.

"Yeah," he agreed. The old guy was different looking, real old with long grey hair and wrinkled brown skin. He was dressed like some guy on TV, only better looking. More authentic and very wise. He had pale blue eyes, bluer than anything Ben Jr. had ever seen, kind of like a robin's egg or the sky on a spring day. When he smiled it reached all the way to those blue eyes and it made Ben Jr. feel warm and happy inside. "Are you an Indian?"

The old man nodded. "I was."

Arnold hurled another insult, back flipped and began to climb the bars again. Ben watched silently then turned his attention back to the Indian. "My brother can be a jerk sometimes."

The old man nodded but didn't say anything.

"He's eight," Ben added, feeling compelled to explain his brother's behavior.

The Indian nodded again. He began to speak slowly, his voice quiet and rhythmical. "You do not want to be here, do you?"

Ben Jr. shook his head. "No. I want to go home."

"It is not right to be kept from your home. A person's home is all he has, and it is frustrating when forced from where you belong, especially when you have no choice."

Ben nodded emphatically. The Indian hit the nail right on the head, Ben should be home. He didn't belong here; he belonged in his own house, with his own bedroom and friends. Back with his Dad. All the injustices welt up in his five-year-old throat, unable to be verbalized. A tear slid from his eyes. He was tired of being harassed by his brother, tired of being shuttled back and forth with no choice and no say. He was tired of being treated like a baby.

Ben turned to speak but the Indian had vanished, gone as quickly as he'd appeared. He blinked his tears away, stood and squared his shoulders and walked to the climbing bars. "Arnold, I want to go home."

Arnold was hanging upside down, arms loose, ready to back flip. "Stick a sock in it, Shit-head."

"You stick a sock in it," Ben Jr. yelled, and before he could think twice, he reached forward and punched his brother in the stomach as hard as he could.

Arnold made a strange *ooophing* sound and uncurled his toes. He fell in a heap at Ben's feet, and Ben remembered the old Indian's words: *Your brother should be careful. He might get seriously hurt.*

**

The thumping was everywhere. Jackie ran through the darkened forest, feeling the branches scratch her face, feeling her clothing tear, feeling Samuel's hot breath. He was closing in, almost had her within his grasp but she wrenched free and the thumping sound intensified. It hurt her ears but she couldn't cover them, couldn't think, could only run.

She was lost now. She'd left the trail ages ago and was trampling through bush, everything a blur in the darkness. She would never find her way out. She heard Sam bellowing behind her and she dodged to the left, ducking to avoid a low branch and silently prayed she would at least have the opportunity to find her way out – if Samuel caught her that wouldn't be necessary. She'd be dead.

She heard a 'thwack' and realized Samuel must have bumped his head on a low branch. *Good.* She gained a few moments. She feinted to the right in a desperate attempt to lose him and kept running, trying to be silent. She knew her breath was coming in savage gulps and endeavored to steady it. The thumping sound was everywhere and she didn't know what direction to turn to avoid it, so she kept straight ahead, keeping her thoughts on Samuel, on the immediate danger.

Jackie couldn't hear him anymore. Maybe the branch knocked him out? Maybe it killed him. Maybe he was lying with blood gushing from his head...should she get help for him? No, no what was she thinking... the man was trying to kill her! *And where was Don Blume?* What part had he in this? Where was she going? Should she stop to assess the situation? No, she should keep running.

She strained to hear noise behind her, any indication Samuel was still in pursuit, any clue he was gaining on her, but it was difficult to hear past her own labored breathing and the thump-thump-thumping noise permeating the forest.

She kept running.

She turned to avoid a tree and then turned again, and now she had no idea which direction she was going. It was too dark. She couldn't see the moon. She couldn't think! She had to stop, had to decide. She could hide, or climb a tree, or play dead... God no, that's what one did with bears, not lunatics. She had to do something...

She ran straight into Samuel, crouched low, waiting for her. "Kill," moaned Sam savagely. "Kill the bitch!"

"No," she screamed. "No!"

But it was too late. Already his large black hands were closing over her throat, already she could feel the airway constricting as the pressure increased. She couldn't breathe, couldn't think. Her struggles were growing weaker and the thumping sound started to dim.

**

Dean was too late.

He knew he was too late – yet still his feet continued to propel him. The thumping sound grew proportionately as he ran forward. It was impossibly loud; hypnotic. *Thump-thump-thumpthumpthump.* Dean had an insane urge to stop and sway to the primitive beat and he fought the lethargy flooding his body. In his peripheral vision he saw movement...dancers? Strange animalistic forms. A surreal vision writhing in tandem.

He was too late. The girl lay ahead, less than a hundred feet, but her body was still and lifeless. *Dear God, like Em's.* He was too late... again.

An enormous black man stood above her, his hands around her throat, squeezing, squeezing.

He was too late. He had failed. The girl was dead.

The violence was overwhelming. Rife. Palpable. The macabre dancers were feeding off it, the thumping increased its tempo. Movement was everywhere.

Except the girl. She lay still.

"Nooo!" Dean cried, the words an agonized moan.

The black man looked up. Eyes wide, he stared like an animal caught in headlights. He looked at Dean vacantly then glanced at his own hands, at the woman. He seemed surprised, confused. Before Dean could shout another warning, the black man bolted into the forest.

The thumping ceased abruptly.

The beast-dancers disappeared.

The woman lay unnaturally still, her neck tilted to one side.

Dean knelt and cradled her head. Her throat was red, dark bruises already starting to form. He felt for a pulse. "Please," he whispered, "don't die."

Her eyes flickered for a moment and Dean expelled a breath he hadn't known he was holding. She moaned and swung her hands to her throat, coughing. She looked at Dean for a moment then closed her eyes, and with Dean holding her head, she turned her face to one side and began to vomit.

**

"Feeling better?" Dean asked softly and Jackie nodded.

The truth was, she felt awful but it easier to nod than speak. She still hadn't caught her breath.

Dean studied her critically. "I doubt it... you look like hell."

"Thanks," she mumbled, throat raw. "I'll try to primp up next time some psycho strangles me."

He smiled slightly. "You still have a sense of humor, guess that counts for something. What did that guy have against you, anyway? No, don't try to answer... there's no time. I have a feeling your rather large friend may be back as soon as he recovers his wits. Can you move?"

Jackie nodded and struggled to get up. Holding onto Dean for support, she stood and managed a few shaky steps. "Yep, ready for a marathon." Her voice was rough and hoarse.

"Good." He looked around, scanning the forest. What he wouldn't give for night vision goggles. "Are you able to walk?"

"Yeah."

"Excellent." She was leaning heavily on him but her pace was respectable.

After a little while, she rubbed her neck. Her throat was raw and parched, and her words were a whisper. "I'd trade my soul for a sip of water."

"Keep this up, and I'll get you all the water you desire." He kept his voice low, continually scanning the forest for signs of movement.

"Promise?" she croaked.

Was that a flicker of movement to the left? No, just his imagination. "You bet... if you walk faster, I'll up the ante and make it champagne."

"Champagne?"

"Yeah, and not the cheap stuff either. Top of the line. Hell, if we get outta here in one piece, I'll throw in the best steak dinner you ever had."

"What are we talking here, Dom Perignon or Cristal?"

"Bottle of each, of course."

"Ah." She swallowed convulsively. They'd made it a few hundred metres. Her mind kept returning to Samuel, to her throat, and she spoke barely above a whisper, trying to keep her mind occupied. "Porterhouse or filet mignon?"

"Porterhouse, everyone knows that."

"Yes, what was I thinking?" They were trotting now, putting distance between them and Samuel. Her throat unconstructed and she breathed more freely. "You're the guy from the creek."

"The very same. Keep going, we're almost there."

"Where are we going?"

"To meet a little friend of mine."

"That is the *worst* pickup line ever."

It took him a moment, then he let out a quiet bark of laughter. "I have way worse lines than that. Hey, you're limping; did you hurt your ankle?"

"No... It's okay. Just a little sore... everywhere." She had her arm over his shoulder and he was bracing her; he was a lifeline. She couldn't see where they were going, just followed along blindly, allowing him to lead...

a complete stranger. "By your friend, I assume you mean the kid at the stream this morning?"

"So you were paying attention. I thought you were too busy screaming to take in details."

"Well, it's not every day two fellows covered in blood and war paint interrupts my bath."

"And it's not every night someone tries to kill you?"

"Yeah, I lead a pretty exciting life." She coughed in an attempt to introduce moisture into her throat, but the action made her wince. "Jesus, it's dark out here. Do you really have any idea where you're headed?"

"Yes, I do, although at this point I'd settle for as far away from *your* friend as possible."

"Why do you assume he's my friend?"

"Isn't he? He was in your group."

"How did you know that?"

"We were tracking you."

She stopped abruptly and eyed him warily. "Well, that's creepy."

"Sounds bad but the explanation is reasonable, if not completely silly." He raked his hand through his hair and looked around, half-expecting someone or something to come crashing through the woods. His adrenaline was pumping. "I can tell you now or I can fill you in when we're safe – your choice."

The sound of a branch breaking crackled in the distance and Jackie started moving again. "I'll choose door number two. It'll give us something to discuss over the steak and champagne."

"Well, you can never underestimate the power of good dinner conversation. Turn here. Watch your step, its rocky."

She climbed down the embankment, holding his strong, warm hand for guidance. They jogged along in silence, their footsteps making little noise on the forest floor. After enough time and distance passed, Jackie felt her heart rate steady. For the first time, she began to take in their surroundings. "Hey, notice something strange?" Jackie asked.

"Everything's strange tonight. What in particular did you have in mind?"

"It's quiet here... too quiet. And dark. Earlier there was moonlight and now..." She shuddered. "And now there's no wind. I know you can't always feel it down here but usually you can hear it in the trees."

Dean was silent. "You're right. It is too quiet. I don't like it... something's wrong. Can you go any faster? We're almost there."

"Sure." They were running now, Dean in front, holding Jackie's hand tightly as he led her through the trees. *She was right, things were way too quiet.* The silence was a bad sign, an omen. A forest was supposed to be filled with sounds. It was a bustling ecosystem, home to thousands of noise creating animals and insects. The stillness was unnatural.

Every time it was this silent, the Noisy Thing appeared soon after.

Yet, it had just stopped, not fifteen minutes earlier. Could it start again so soon?

He thought of Jesse, alone. They were close now, just a few more minutes and they would reach the spot where he left the child. "Hold on, Sport," he said under his breath. "Hold on."

Not much further.

They were almost there.

"Mister?" Jackie said softly, and it took Dean a moment to realize she was addressing him. "Do you hear that?"

"What?" He frowned. His concentration was broken.

"That noise... can you hear it?"

They had reached the spot now. His backpack was lying on the trail and Jesse was nowhere to be seen.

"Jesse!" Dean called, quietly at first, then louder. He let go of Jackie's hand and began to search wildly. "Jesse!"

There was no sign of struggle. No broken branches, no heavy footprints. Nothing was disturbed, their backpacks untouched. Jesse was gone.

In the distance, like a beat of wild thunder, the thumping noise had returned. Jesse was gone and the Noisy Thing was back.

PART TWO

...ascent to Hell

CHAPTER ONE

Reginald K. Bloodsworth sat behind his massive cherry-wood desk and contemplated the two men before him. Imbeciles, he decided. Two loathsome, idiotic, lazy imbeciles with pathetic excuses and even more pathetic lives. What was this bloody *crap* they were spouting? He cleared his throat, and Arne and Ben shut up.

"Let me get this straight," Bloodsworth said, stroking his heavy jowls. "An Indian –"

"Old Indian," Ben interjected, and then closed his mouth quickly as Bloodsworth fixed him with a withering glare.

"An *old* Indian shows up in your office and voices some rather vague threats. Ominous threats about logging the Stein, saying we'd better cease and desist at once. You neglect to take him seriously and he tells you Don Blume is as good as dead. You still don't listen and he begins to shadow you. Your personal life goes awry. Ben's pleasant little wife decides to leave him, and you two gentlemen, the best of friends, find yourselves engaged in physical blows... am I getting this right so far? Yes? Good. To finish off, in your words Arnold, not mine, this old Indian gent magically appears at a playground and pushes Ben's oldest son off the play equipment and the child breaks his arm."

"Well, no Sir," Ben began nervously. "He didn't exactly push my son. Arnold fell on his own accord, but I think the Indian had something to do with it."

"Ah. I see. I see. Anything else?"

"No Sir, that about sums the situation up."

"I see." Bloodsworth remained quiet for a moment, still stroking his jowls. He was a large man, well over three hundred pounds and he formed an intimidating figure to his employees. His bearing was regal; his back ramrod straight. Although he had lived for almost four decades in Canada, Bloodsworth spoke with a strong British accent. He was a monarchist and adored the queen, and secretly thought most Canadians were little more than savages. These two imbeciles were more savage than most.

"I see," he continued, his voice rising to thunderous proportions although he hadn't moved a muscle. "What do you propose we do about this bloody situation?"

Arne looked at Ben. Ben looked at Arne. Neither man spoke.

"Well?" said Bloodsworth.

"Uh, we don't know, Sir. That is, at this particular time we have no recommendations."

Reginald K. Bloodsworth rolled his eyes to the heavens and prayed for providence. Why did he continue to live in this colonial backwater? Why was he forced to deal with such pure stupidity? Because, he reminded himself, allowing his blood pressure to resume normal standards, it was idiots like these which made him the wealthy man he was today. The *exceptionally* wealthy man he was today. And for that he had to occasionally put up with nonsense like this. Sometimes his position was little better than nanny to a bunch of squalling brats.

"To begin with," Bloodsworth said, "this is the most ridiculous bunch of bloody nonsense I have ever heard. I'm of half a mind to fire you both. Your performances have been tawdry and unacceptable. Production is lagging and this silly business must stop."

Reginald paused. He enjoyed his pause, enjoyed watching the two men squirm, and decided to milk this one for all its worth. A small measure of comfort, perhaps, but he owed it to himself to get what little pleasure he could from life. The pause stretched to thirty seconds when Reginald K. Bloodsworth deigned to speak again. "Fortunately for you, your story has been somewhat corroborated by an employee from the second floor, in public relations I believe. He has seen this Indian gent as well, and since he has been an impeccable employee *(unlike you two, his gaze seemed to say)*, I must believe him.

"As for this other business, the personal problems, I find that harder to stomach. Still, my public relations man has reported some odd developments in his own life as well. A coincidence? I think so. This bloody voodoo business is rubbish and the rumors must stop. Do you hear me?"

Both men nodded. Then Arne spoke tentatively. "Sir, the Wendall Scott – Jerry Hackett business... do you think it could be related?"

"We will not speak of that again," Reginald said, his voice exploding throughout the luxurious office. "That was... unfortunate, but totally unrelated. Do you understand me?"

"Yes, Sir. Perfectly, Sir. But –"

"There will be no 'buts' and no further questions. I have made my decision. Since you two seem so concerned about this affair, I am dispatching you into the Stein. Locate Blume and see how he is progressing with his tour. Find out if he has allayed the suspicions of the Hart woman. Warn him of the possibility of a lunatic roaming around, for that is what your old Indian gent is, a radical lunatic who is making idle threats to halt our logging production. He is not the first cuckoo out there and I am bloody well certain he will not be the last. Do you have all that, or do your tiny little brains need me to put it in ink and Xerox it for you? No? Splendid.

"When you have finished this assignment you may report to me, and perhaps, just perhaps mind you, if your performance is satisfactory, you might still have jobs upon your return. Understand? Yes? Bloody good. Now get the hell out of my office."

**

Dean combed the forest, searching. He was looking for an indication which way the boy went. Footprints, crushed twigs, anything. He was frantic but quietly so. The danger that was Samuel still lurked, waiting for them to err, to show themselves. Jackie sensed Dean's urgency and followed him silently, straining to see the lost child in the darkest hours of night.

Dean agonized over the missing boy. The first panicky sensations gave way to a sinking, sick feeling that ravished his gut and made his heart pound erratically.

The most gruesome scenarios poked his imagination. Jesse: laying broken and torn, alone in the dark. Jesse: attacked by some beast. Jesse: terrified and crying for Dean in the night... crying and crying, only Dean never came.

The nightmare continued and the minutes ticked by, adding up. No, it worse than a nightmare – from a nightmare one woke up.

The visions continued until he lost focus and felt ill, before he forced himself to stop and regain control. Surrendering to his emotions would help no one. He needed to remain calm and level-headed, for Jesse's sake. For his own. For the woman walking two steps behind him.

Taking deep breaths, he began to evaluate the situation. Jesse was well versed in wilderness survival. Dean had taken him camping since before the child could walk, and his Native family took him into the forest often. He was a brave boy. He might be nervous alone in the woods but he could handle it.

Jesse also knew first aid, and as long as he didn't sustain serious injury, he would be able to cope. If he was injured... No. Dean forced himself to focus on the positive. There was no reason to believe Jesse was injured. He likely wandered off, perhaps frightened by the noise and action. Dean cursed softly. He had been very clear in telling the boy to stay put – Jesse wouldn't have moved without good reason.

One thing was becoming certain – Jesse was not in the vicinity Dean left him. They had searched in the immediate area thoroughly. Which left three alternatives: he was hiding, he'd left the area voluntarily, or he was taken out. But which direction?

Devils Lake.

The name came unbidden, so powerfully, as if whispered in his ear.

It was ludicrous – but Dean had the uneasy premonition it was true. It was more than a hunch. The more he pondered, the more certain he became. The feeling became stronger and stronger. He would find Jesse at Devils Lake.

Why?

It was the direction of the Noisy Thing, for one thing. Also the route this woman's group was headed when the black man suddenly went berserk and started attacking her. Where was the rest of her group? He had counted seven to start, now only three – where were the others? And what business did they have to be in this dangerous, out of bounds area? This trail wasn't listed on current maps. Had they been drawn to it? Jesse certainly was: Dean thought of the look in Jesse's eyes yesterday when Dean called it by name. The boy clamored for more information and Dean hadn't known what to tell him, kept the description textbook and dry. Could the strange events in the Stein be connected somehow to Devils Lake?

He began to hesitatingly traverse the trail to Devils Lake, ready to reverse direction at the first clue he was on the wrong path. Jackie followed behind silently. Five minutes along, he saw a footprint on the path, clearly illuminated by the small flashlight which he kept pointed low. He knelt and placed his hand over it. "Jesse," he whispered softly. A few minutes after that, he found Jesse's Ninja toy, arms twisted into an arrow, pointing the way.

Jesse was leaving him clues. Dean was on the right path. And all things pointed to Devils Lake.

Dean bowed his head. *Devils Lake.* That heinous, mysterious place the Ancients avoided. Even the landscape wasn't to be trusted: difficult terrain formed by a rock slide so catastrophic that it carried debris for several kilometres. As a boy Dean had no ambition to trek this foreboding, dismal place, even before the incident with J.J. Fleishenheimer.

He had to go to Devils Lake. There was no other way.

**

The long night stretched to dawn and the first pink-grey streaks appeared in the eastern portion of the sky. Finally, Dean halted and cocked his head to one side, examining Jackie critically. "We need to talk."

She nodded and sat wearily on a mossy stump. They were in a clearing and she could tell it would be a sunny day. Everything was damp but the morning sun would dry things out and the steam would rise from the forest in great, smoky tendrils.

She was exhausted. They had searched through the night. Her throat hurt, inside and out. Her feet ached and she was so tired she could curl up and sleep, right here on this stump. The adrenaline rush that accompanied the first, harried scramble through the brush had evaporated and now her fatigue hung heavily in every atom of her body. She pushed the straggles of hair from her eyes and willed her energy to return. And she remained quiet, waiting for Dean to speak.

"I must find Jesse. That is my first priority."

Jackie nodded. "Of course. I'll help."

He frowned. "It's not necessary. I can give you a map showing the way out, but I can't take you. Too much time would be lost."

"No, I'll stay with you. This involves me too; I need to find out what happened to my brother."

"It's dangerous."

Jackie managed a shaky laugh. "And walking out of this forest alone isn't? You think that lunatic isn't lurking out there, waiting for me? Besides, I feel a responsibility for the child. If you hadn't left Jesse to find me then he wouldn't be gone."

"It couldn't be helped. You were in immediate danger.... there was no other way. He couldn't keep up and there wasn't time. As it was... another minute or two...."

"I know. And believe me, I thank you. If you hadn't come...." She looked away.

Dean knelt and took her face carefully in his hands, stroking her neck softly with his thumbs. He felt her flinch and backed off. "Those bruises are really something. You are literally black and blue."

"Not really my favorite colors. At least, not today."

"Can't say they suit you. Lucky he didn't crush your windpipe."

"It felt like he did, at first."

"If you are staying with me, we need to get a few things straight. Strange things are happening here. I've never seen anything like it... too many bizarre incidents to be a coincidence. I haven't the faintest idea of what's going on, but I think things might be related – shh, let me finish. I know it seems odd, and totally illogical, but I think what's happening to you may be connected to me. Crazy, eh?"

"Well, yes, but I guess no crazier than everything else."

"Yes, that's it. Everything is crazy, nothing seems normal anymore. It's like regular thinking can no longer apply, do you see what I mean? We need a parallel type of thinking."

"I'm confused. I'm not sure exactly what you're saying."

"I know. Sorry... I'm not sure myself. Let me think on it a bit and when I figure it out I'll let you know. But for now, tell me why you're here and what relationship you have with the man who tried to kill you. Be completely honest, don't leave anything out, no matter how trivial it might seem."

"Why?"

"I have a feeling it might be important."

"Do you have these feelings a lot? What are you, clairvoyant or something?"

"Nope, not an intuitive bone in my body. At least, until I came here. Until now I was a regular, straight-laced lawyer, strictly business, very dull."

The image of him at the stream came to mind, bare-chested and smeared with berry juice. "Somehow I doubt that. Where do you want me to begin?"

"For starters, what's your name?"

Jackie laughed, the absurdity welling up in her bruised throat. "We've been tramping through this god-awful forest for an entire night and we haven't exchanged names? Now I know I'm going crazy!"

He held out his hand. "Well, crazy lady, I'm Dean Stockton, pleased to meet you."

"Jacyln Hackett Hart. Hackett's my maiden name, Hart is my married name. Jackie to my friends."

"You're married?"

"Was. A mistake at nineteen. To my high school sweetheart. Lasted three years and ended in a happy divorce. We're still friends. We get together for coffee and movies a couple of times a year and exchange gag Christmas gifts. We're great buddies but lousy partners. Thank goodness we realized it and had the sense to get out."

"Okay, Jaclyn Hackett Hart, Jackie to your friends, what are you doing here, in the middle of the Stein Valley with a madman chasing you?"

"That part is harder. I came to find my brother. He's been missing since spring, April eleventh to be exact. He's a forestry technician who went missing with his partner, Wendall Scott. Apparently vanished from thin air. They haven't found any bodies."

Dean frowned. "There are lots of ravines and cliffs around here, lots of avalanche potential, especially in the spring."

"That's what their employer, Empire Forest Products, said. The thing is, Empire changed their story. First there were rumors they were murdered, that there were photos of their remains. After a few days, Empire announced they were simply missing. But the search was called off. Why would they do that? Why would they call off a search party so quickly? The men were equipped for inclement weather, they could have survived indefinitely.

"The Empire representatives were helpful... at first. Then suddenly, everyone clammed up. No one would talk to me, everyone was evasive. I tried going in person, but everyone I originally spoke with disappeared, ostensibly transferred to other departments. That doesn't make sense: even if transferred, they should still be reachable, right? Their replacements didn't know anything about it. How can two men go missing and their coworkers know *nothing* about it? It was like hitting a brick wall." Jackie's voice became bitter. "As if my brother never existed."

"So you came to find out yourself?"

"Yes. I'm an elementary school teacher so I have the summer off. I know it's a long shot, but it seemed the only thing left to do. I have six weeks to find something... anything. Some clue, do you understand? I'd love to find proof that my brother is alive, but realistically, I know that's unlikely. I'll settle for answers so I can lay him to rest."

"Have you found anything?"

"No. Nothing. Only...only...."

"Go ahead, tell me."

"Okay, this is going to sound weird but you asked for it. I feel, with certainty, my brother is dead."

"How?"

"I saw him. His image, his spirit I guess. Look, I know that sounds flaky. At first I didn't believe it – couldn't believe it, thought it was a figment of my imagination. But he came to me again, last night, and warned me. He told me to wake up, to run. That was just before Samuel came to kill me. My brother knew and he was warning me. He saved my life."

Dean looked at the sky, considering. Parallel thinking. As good a time as any to apply it.

"There's more. He wasn't... whole. His face...." She stopped, cringing at the memory. "His face was gone on one side, flesh hanging in strips. And it was charred as if he'd been burnt. I knew then he was dead."

Dean studied her, eyes narrowing slightly, and Jackie spoke: "You don't believe me."

"Yes, I do. I believe that's what you saw, or what you think you saw. I just don't know what it means. Can you tell me more?"

"What else?"

"Anything. The group you were with. Tell me about them."

"I don't really know them. It was a tour group, arranged through a website that specializes in adventure tours in this area. You know, white-water rafting, back country ATV rides, that sort of thing. I thought of coming here alone, but when I saw there was a guided camping tour, it seemed perfect. Three days in, three days out, plus one in the middle to relax. Seven days in all. This would have been our fourth day."

"Did anything unusual happen?"

"Oh boy, where do I start? The first night, a woman named Benta Sturm disappeared. She was German, a professional photographer. She was on assignment to take photos of the pictographs, you know the ones?" Dean nodded and she continued. "We were sharing a tent – she got a few shots the first day but decided to sneak off and take night images. She said something about moonlight. She was nice, very intense. I really liked her. She never came back so Samuel, that's the guide who... well, tried to –" She put her hands around her throat and stuck her tongue out, "you know... uh... strangle me. Up until that point, he was a pretty decent guy. Anyway, Sam spent the next day trying to find her, by the time he got back, it was almost nightfall so we decided to stay the night and hike out in the morning, to arrange for the search party."

"Did he find anything?"

"A piece of metal. Just before Samuel returned, we heard the thumping sound for the first time. Don Blume went berserk."

"I know. I was there."

She stared at him incredulously. "You were there? You saw us?"

He grinned sheepishly. "I was your 'bear' in the woods. Jesse and I were tracking you. That's why I'm here – supposed to be giving Jesse an authentic aboriginal experience, teach him his roots and all."

"So Don *did* hear something. Huh. I thought he was making it up."

"He did seem rather high strung. So, that's when I first saw you, well, not all of you... just your legs."

He also saw her bathing naked. She could tell by the glance he gave her that he was remembering, too. Awkward. Jackie decided to address it. "You made up for that the next time you saw me... assuming the creek *was* the next time?"

"It was, and I didn't peek."

"Not at all?"

"Just a little. But I stopped looking the moment I realized what I was, uh, looking at."

"Really?" Her voice was doubtful.

"Almost the very same moment. Right up until you started screaming like... well, like some guy covered in tribal war paint was watching you bathe. You've a good set of lungs."

"Kind of feel like using them again."

"Sorry, go on."

"We decided to abort the trip and go for help. I didn't think we were hiking in the right direction but Samuel assured me we were, that he was taking a short cut, and no one else seemed concerned so I went with it. What choice did I have? It was either stick with the group or find my own way out. Sam was acting a little off – nothing major, just not himself." She frowned. "Actually, I can't say that. I don't know him. Maybe that was his usual behavior."

"So, night two, instead of leaving the Stein, you find yourself in deeper."

"Exactly. The next morning, before I went to wash up in the stream, we noticed Bob Vance was gone. Nothing amiss, except his tent flap was ripped to shreds. And maybe something else... we found some bloodied hair... well, maybe a piece of scalp to be exact. Who knows, by then, things had gotten very weird, the men were fighting."

"Fighting?"

"Arguing. It was very strange, the guys kept getting, um, more primitive and childish as time went on."

"All of them?"

"No. The Asians seemed unaffected, but of course I can't be sure. They didn't speak English."

"And you? Did you feel any different?"

"No. Just scared."

"So then what happened?"

"After Bob disappeared, the Asian guys left. Can't say I blame them, I was tempted myself."

"Is it possible they had anything to do with the strange occurrences?"

Jackie frowned. "I don't think so... but I guess it's possible. Anything's possible. This whole place has gone crazy."

"Okay. So, up to this point, some of your group was acting oddly, aggressively, right? And some weren't. Fifty-fifty. For some reason, certain people seemed to be affected and others weren't. So what's the common denominator?"

"Everyone affected was male."

"Yes, but not all the males. What about the German woman?"

"Can't say, I only had the one day with her. At that point, everyone seemed relatively normal." Jackie sighed. "It doesn't make sense."

"You seem unaffected, I feel okay, but Jesse... he's acting oddly. If we can figure out why some are exhibiting personality changes while others aren't, we might be closer to discovering what's happening. Can you tell me more?"

"No, that's about it. We were leaving the valley when Samuel attacked me."

"You weren't leaving. This trail doesn't lead out, it goes to Devils Lake."

"Devils Lake? What's that?"

A muscle twitched in his jaw. "The heart of the Stein. Your guide was leading you to the very center."

The idea stunned her. "Then... it was premeditated," she whispered. "Samuel had every intention of killing me, all along. I can't believe it, he seemed so nice. I *knew* we were going the wrong way, I knew it! When I questioned him, he became agitated." Her voice trailed weakly. "My God, I feel sick."

"Here, take a deep breath. That's it, keep it steady. You've had a hell of a shock, you have every right to feel sick."

Dean sat beside her. "Jesse started acting strangely almost as soon as we arrived in the Stein. I thought he was sick, had the flu or something, but he kept telling me he was okay. My gut told me to take him home but he said...." Dean looked at the ground, this was difficult. He still hadn't worked out Jesse's allegations of sexual abuse. "He said his Aunt's boyfriend was... doing things to him."

"Oh... I understand."

"But I don't. Children don't lie about that sort of thing. I know Penny Littlefoot. She was like a second mom to me when I was Jesse's age. I was over there all the time, visiting Eddy. And I've met her boyfriend Harry. There was nothing, you understand, *nothing* to indicate Harry is capable of that sort of thing."

"People can fool you."

"Apparently so." Dean's voice became low. "If only I had known, but I had no idea. Nothing."

"You can't know everything."

"No, I guess not. But damn it, I should have known." He shook his head, as if to clear the mental cobwebs. "After Jesse told me, I didn't know what to do. I was waiting, I guess. Waiting for answers, waiting to figure out what to do. If I'd left earlier Jesse would still be with me."

"And I'd be dead."

"Of course, forgive me. Maybe I should crawl out of this well of self pity and do something constructive."

Jackie inclined her head. "Now you're talking. What about the thumping sound?"

"The Noisy Thing? Haven't a clue. You?"

"Nope. Never heard anything like it, but I'm a city slicker. Closest thing was Eminem Night at The Bucket of Blood." She saw his look of incomprehension. "It's a night club."

"Rapper fan, are you?"

"Oh, yeah, me and Snoop Dog, we're tight."

He smiled. "Good to know."

"Especially when it's a charity event."

"Ah."

"Hey, don't give me that look. We raised twelve hundred dollars for kids in Africa. It's to help build a school." She looked around. "Although my classroom could technically qualify as zoo at times, this wilderness stuff is new to me. I thought maybe the noise was an animal."

Dean shook his head. "Animals can make loud and odd sounds – but *nothing* like that. I have no idea what it is, but I'm guessing it must be tied to this. The Noisy Thing is the key to this mess."

"The key?"

"Well, the key, or the end result. Either way, I don't think it's good."

"So, what now?"

"That's the million dollar question. I think some answers may lie at Devils Lake, and although I hate like hell to go there, I don't think there's any other way."

"Devils Lake." Jackie shivered. "Why does that name give me the creeps?"

"For good reason. Can you move again? Yes? Good." Dean stood and held out a hand, pulling Jackie to her feet. "Legend has it that Devils Lake is home to powerful spirits. Come on, I will tell you on the way."

"All right," Jackie said, not sure she wanted to hear this. She looked surreptitiously over her shoulder, half expecting Samuel to crash through the trees. She had a feeling that evil waited at Devils Lake.

∗∗

"Goddamn!" complained Arne Johansson as they left the office. "Who the fuck does he think he is? God?"

"He *is* God," Ben Hoight mumbled. "Or he might as well be."

"Yeah," Arne agreed. That old fucker was as close to God as they would ever see. Shit.

"I don't want to go into the Stein," Ben said tentatively.

"Me neither."

"You don't think... you don't think whatever killed our guys is still out there, do you?"

"Nah. And it wasn't a thing, it was an accident. Just like the boss says."

"Yeah," Ben agreed, but the conviction wasn't in his voice. "I hate the forest. All those mosquitoes and bugs and wild animals. Gives me the fuckin' creeps."

Arne was silent. "Me too," he said, finally. Ben was his best friend, the closest pal he'd ever had, but he still wouldn't admit the truth. He was so goddamned scared of going into the Stein Valley he was about to shit his pants. It was *his* signature that graced the men's work orders, *his* signature that fudged the thin line between truth and fiction, *his* John Hancock that okayed falsified documents. The old fucker Bloodsworth knew it, too. Had known about it since day one, encouraged it. Not in so many words but Arne knew which side his bread was buttered on.

And now it came down to this. Bloodsworth was punishing him, sending him into that devil's den. Arne wasn't quite sure what really happened to Hackett and Scott those many months ago, but he'd heard rumors. And so had Ben.

They had good reason to be scared.

Very, very good reason.

His mind raced furiously, looking for a way out. He could quit. He was fifty-one, not too far from retirement. He could quit and hide for the rest of his days in harmonious seclusion.

But it was too late for that.

This thing had grown too big, too fast. Poor old Ben had no idea. His good buddy had no clue what they were really up against and Arne wasn't sure he understood it himself.

They turned a corner, and from the slant of his left eye, Arne saw the old Indian, just for a moment before the old man turned away. The Indian smiled slightly, not much but enough for Arne to catch it.

That scared him more than anything.

Ben was still complaining, jabbering about getting supplies and how he didn't have proper equipment. Ben hadn't noticed the Indian but that didn't surprise Arne. Ben wasn't meant to see him. The Indian was for Arne's eyes only... this time.

The Indian could seek him anywhere. Hunt him and torment him like an animal.

There was no place to hide.

**

As the sun rose higher in the sky, Jackie fought the urge to keep her eyes open. The increasing warmth added to her fatigue. She struggled to keep moving, struggled to keep her eyes on the trail. One foot in front of the other, again and again, until the monotony threatened to overtake her. Think of something, she thought desperately, so she focused her attention on the man in front. Very tall. Blonde hair that hadn't seen the inside of a barbershop for a while – not quite to his shoulders. Never a fan of long hair on men but she had to admit the shaggy style suited him. Wide shoulders. Strong, muscular legs.

Look how he kept turning back, every so often, checking if she was all right. Not necessary, she thought, but nice all the same. She was tired, of course, but otherwise fine. The soreness in her ankle had dissipated and no pain lingered to remind her of last night's ordeal.

Her neck and throat were another story. The bruised flesh still ached and throbbed. It would take longer to mend. But she was lucky; she didn't have to walk with her neck. The situation could be worse. She could be dead.

Dean looked back, again, his eyes flickering over her quickly before returning to the trail ahead. He offered no conversation and Jackie was thankful. Silence was easier than idle chat.

He was a remarkably attractive man, in a rugged, outdoorsy sort of way. Seemed intelligent and witty and obviously brave. Last night left no doubt of that. But what else did she know about him?

Nothing.

He'd asked a lot of questions but hadn't shared much.

Here she was, hiking through unfamiliar territory, searching for a child she didn't know, following a man she knew nothing about.

Except that he saved her life. Don't forget that. No matter what else happened, she was still better off with him than without. Samuel was lurking out there, somewhere. The Noisy Thing was there too, and the only other person she knew here was Don Blume, one unbalanced individual at the best of times.

A sudden, horrible thought: What if Samuel killed Don Blume? What if Samuel was responsible for Benta's disappearance? And Bob Vance's?

The idea made her panic, made the world swirl uncontrollably for an instant so she almost lost balance, and Dean was there instantly, holding her elbow, steadying her.

GET OUT! Her brain screamed, *RUN NOW!* She forced her mind to compose and fought the urge. Impulsive actions were rarely useful and often acerbated the problem. She'd learned that the hard way.

Like her marriage. After that fiasco ended, Jackie promised she'd never do an impulsive thing again. So far she had lived up to that. She had a great job, working with people she respected and kids she adored. She had a nice little townhouse in an emerging neighborhood, bought when Vancouver real estate was on a downturn, which made it marginally affordable. By doubling payments and living a Spartan lifestyle, she'd made a dent in the mortgage. She had several close friends, dated regularly but without real interest. She had a cat, the perfect companion. Fed it twice a day, stroked it on occasion and stuck out extra food when she was away for the night. Why let things get complicated?

Too late, Jackie baby. Things got complicated the minute your brother disappeared. And things were growing more complicated by the second. She didn't even know where she was. Somewhere in the Stein, heading to place called Devils Lake.

The name sounded ominous.

The man in front of her stopped and offered his hand to help her over a log which had fallen across the path. A man who obviously had his own set of problems; a man she knew nothing about. For all she knew, this man could be responsible for Benta and Bob Vance's disappearances.

His hand remained outstretched. Things were complicated. Her brother was dead – she'd seen his corpse as clearly as if it were in front of her. Someone tried to kill her last night, tried to choke the very life from her. Something bizarre was happening in this forest. Everything was topsy-turvy. Her nice, orderly life was quickly unravelling and she hadn't a clue what to do about it.

The hand beckoned. Strong and masculine. His smile reached his eyes and he took a step towards her, reaching for her.

Jackie thought hard. What had he said earlier? Ah, yes, parallel thinking. His words, but what did they mean? Maybe something like throw caution to the wind and follow your gut. Take a chance.

She swallowed twice, her bruised throat dry.

She looked into his eyes and took his hand.

For better or worse, her decision was made.

**

Dean looked at Jackie as she took his hand. Poor little thing, she was scared. He could see that clearly and he didn't blame her. She'd been through a hell of an ordeal, and if he suspected right, it might get worse.

His brain was racing furiously. All thoughts were on Jesse. He had to find him; it was his fault the child was missing. What had he been thinking about leaving a nine-year-old alone in a dark forest? He must be crazy.

Well, crazy would explain everything else. Maybe that was it. Maybe he had gone insane and he was dreaming this.

But crazy didn't cut it. Crazy meant he wasn't responsible for his actions and that was the coward's way out. He had known exactly what he was doing last night when he left Jesse alone. A calculated risk that went sour. Everything was his fault.

He turned to check on the woman again and smiled. His eyes showed none of his inner turmoil, a cheap courtroom trick. Never let them suspect you're floundering. Never let them see you're scared. His smile turned to admiration. Boy, but she was a trooper. Kept up with his long strides without complaint. This wasn't even her fight.

Then again, maybe it was. Things were so screwed up he couldn't tell for sure.

It was an unwinnable dilemma: if he hadn't left Jesse then this lovely young woman would be dead. That would have been his fault, in a way, if he'd been able to stop it and hadn't tried.

He was responsible for both of them.

He couldn't have been in both places at once.

He'd helped the person with the most urgent need.

He'd done the right thing.

Dean breathed a little easier. Now he would find Jesse – *had* to find Jesse, and the three of them would get the hell out of this damnable forest and never set foot in it again.

Almost in response to his thoughts, a thump-thump-thumping sound began in the distance, the beat carried in the wind along the tree tops. It was more than that, Dean realized. He didn't just hear it, he *felt* it. The ground vibrated with it. Hypnotic, rhythmic.

"Do you hear it?" Jackie asked, her voice a whisper.

"Yes," he said. It was coming from the direction of Devils Lake. He felt a cold shiver run down his spine. He squeezed Jackie's hand.

They were on the right track.

**

Jackie couldn't be certain but she thought it was early afternoon when Dean finally stopped. The sun was high and the day had grown warm enough for the mosquitoes to disappear.

They had been hiking steadily forever. She couldn't remember ever being this tired.

"Hungry?" Dean asked.

"I could eat a horse."

He chuckled. "Jerky and dried fruit will have to suffice."

"Sounds heavenly."

"Are you always this easy to please?"

"Only when I'm starving. I was starting to eye those ferns over there, they're edible right?"

"Sure, fiddleheads."

"Yum. Here, let me open that package – my nails are longer."

They munched in silence for a few minutes. "I'm afraid I don't have much left in the way of food. Jesse and I had planned to hunt and trap our meals."

"Is that why you were covered in blood at the stream?"

"Sort of." He frowned. "Jess was acting strangely then. He seemed to get a kick out of the kill, too much so now that I think about it. It's not like him. Usually he's a passive, loving sort of child. Last year we came across a wounded bird and Jesse tried to nurse it back to health. Poor kid did his darndest. We called the SPCA and they told us what to do, and Jesse did everything right. The bird died anyway. They usually do, you know. They die of fright; their tiny hearts just give out. Jesse was crushed. Cried for hours, then insisted we give it a decent burial." Dean allowed himself a small smile. "Problem was, it was winter and cold as hell. The ground was frozen solid and we couldn't get the shovel in. We had to settle for burying it above ground. Jesse found the nest and laid the bird in it, then covered the whole thing with rocks. He made a cross and everything. When we came inside he was nearly blue. He never said another word about it; he is very mature that way. Damn grave is still there."

"Why are you here? I mean, why did you come to the Stein?"

Dean was silent for a moment. "Jesse's like my own kid. I love him more than anything. After his parents died, I wanted to keep him with me, to raise him as my own son. The elders of his tribe convinced me otherwise. You see, Jesse is Native, and that is special: a wonderful thing. We tend to trivialize it in our society. White men have traditionally disdained aboriginals and show little regard for Native culture and heritage. The white man has done his very best to annihilate the Indian ways. It is a terrible shame, really, because their culture is so rich and strong.

"Jesse has a right to that culture. I couldn't deny him that, anymore than I could deny the color of his eyes. What could I offer him that his own tribe couldn't?"

"Love?" she asked.

"He has plenty of love there. Jesse is a child of the entire tribe. Natives are like that. Theirs is a global family, not individualistic like ours. They take care of their own.

"The elders pointed out that Jesse would be raised by nannies if he lived with me, and they were right. I work long hours. My schedule is erratic, sometimes I work past midnight. Often, if fact," he admitted, sheepishly pushing his hair from his eyes. "That kind of existence is no life for a child."

"So you spend time with him in the summer?"

"Summer, Christmas, Easter, long weekends. We do guy stuff. Fishing, boating, that kind of thing. But I also try to show him the other side of life. We go to galleries and museums. I took him to the ballet last year, and boy, he hated it. Bored silly. I have to admit I was too. Maybe he was a little young. I'll try again in a few years. But this time I'll make sure he knows the story beforehand."

Jackie smiled at him. "You seem like a nice man, Dean Stockton."

"Tell that to my coworkers. They call me shameful things behind my back."

"Why is that?"

"Oh, I don't know." He swept a tendril of spider web from a branch and it hung off his hand in silken threads. "I guess I throw myself into my work when Jesse's not around. It's been suggested that I'm a hard ass."

"Ah. So, is there a Mrs. Hard-Ass lurking around?"

A facial muscle twitched. "Not anymore. I'm... I'm widowed. Nine years, now."

"Sorry... that's rough."

"Yeah, it was. Seems we both have emptiness in our lives...you've lost a brother and I've lost a wife."

"Yes, I suppose we do."

He studied her for a moment, then turned away, rubbing his hands together to rid them of the sticky web. "Well, let's carry on. If we don't get moving, I might lose another person – Jesse is very precious to me. Think your legs can stand more hiking?"

"Sure," she lied. Fire shot through her thighs and she rubbed the muscles briskly to get the circulation going.

"Good," said Dean, "because from here on in the trail starts to climb. Now we really have to work."

"Oh. Great."

"If we make good time, we might just be able to make Devils Lake by dusk."

Jackie said nothing. Devils Lake was ominous sounding at best and she didn't relish the thought of arriving there after dark.

**

"Do you hear it, do you hear it?" Don Blume chanted as Samuel approached. Don's body was swaying back and forth to the beat. *"It's back, It's back, It's back and It loves me. Do you hear it?"*

"I hear it," Samuel said.

Don swirled, hips moving to and fro like a belly dancer. Perspiration ran down his face in rivulets. He had stripped his shirt and was standing naked from the waist up, chest gleaming with a sweaty shine.

"Did you kill the bitch, kill the bitch, kill the bitch?" he sang, swaying back and forth. He raised his hands high above his head, an act of piety.

Warring emotions erupted across Samuel's face. "No. I lost her."

"Nooo," cried Don, falling to his knees. *"You've failed me, failed me, failed me."*

The struggle grew within Samuel and he fought to remain impassive, but Don's chanting, and the thump-thump-thumping of the forest reached out to him and stroked him, caressed him, smothered him.

Minutes passed. *"Failed me, failed me, failed me,"* Don continued, his voice low.

Samuel broke down. His proud shoulders stooped and he knelt before Don with eyes averted. "I's sorry Mastah. Old Samuel's sorry, Mastah."

"You are bad, Samuel. You are evil. You have let her get away. She must be destroyed."

Samuel looked at Don, slack jawed and clearly beaten, but with love and devotion clearly in his eyes. "I get her, Mastah. Old Samuel get her, this time fo' sure."

Don Blume began to cry. "You promise, Samuel? *You promise, promise, promise?*"

"I promise, Mastah. This time I kill her fo' sure."

**

"You know what you are Ben? A pig."

"What the hell are you talking about, Arne?"

"I'm talkin' 'bout you. It's what you are. A real fuckin' animal. Look at the way you eat. You're a slob. No wonder your wife left you."

"Take that back!"

"No. You have mayonnaise on your lip. Can't you keep your goddamned sandwich in your mouth, for Christ's sake? You disgust me."

Ben grew red and flustered. "Why are you saying this, Arne? What are you trying to do, hurt my feelings?"

"No, I'm just pointing out a few facts of life. You eat like a pig, you dress like shit, and that phoney way you comb your hair has been bugging me for years. Why do you comb it over the top like that? D'you think those few scraggly hairs are hiding the fact you're going bald?"

"Arne! You are my best friend in the whole world and you are really starting to scare me. What's gotten into you?"

Arne stared at him, his face ugly. His eyes had narrowed to little slits in a way Ben had never seen before, and his lip turned up at the corner, in a kind of snarl. *Primitive-like.* In fact, Arne looked like he wanted to rip Ben's face off.

"Arne?" Ben said more softly. "Are you okay, pal?"

Then Arne's face began to do a funny thing. The redness abated and the furrows filled out. He began to look like Arne again. "Arne?" Ben said again.

"Yeah?" Arne asked, looking confused.

"What the hell just happened?"

"I dunno."

"Geez. We've been in this goddamned forest for only four hours and you're already starting to get weird on me."

"Sorry."

"Well, Jesus H Christ. Don't do it again."

"Okay. Hey, got any of that sandwich left?"

"Nah. I dropped it on the ground when you started yelling at me."

"Oh. Sorry."

"S'okay. We're both under a lot of pressure. Say, do you have the maps or do I?"

"You do. They're in your pack."

"Grab one for me then, will you Arne? I want to see where we are."

"Okay." Arne rummaged through Ben's pack and handed over the maps.

Ben studied the diagram and conferred with his GPS, which he shook a few times. It just didn't seem to be working right, but he wasn't sure. It was a complicated device, not easy like his TomTom in the car. "I guess we're about *here*. Say, have you been in the Stein before?"

"Yeah," Arne nodded. "Couple of years back, when I was still doing field work."

"Which way do you think the group went?"

"Well, usually they head along this trail." His finger traced a dotted line on the map. "There's a campsite here, see? Since we came from a different starting point, we'll intersect here. We'll probably meet them on the way."

"Unless they went somewhere else."

"Why would they do that?" Arne asked.

"Don't know. Just a thought. Look at this place, Devils Lake. Ever been there?"

"No." Arne shivered. "Why do you ask?"

"No reason. Just kind of jumped out at me. Say, Arne?"

"Yeah?"

"Think there's any truth to what the old Indian said about Don being dead?"

"Nah. The old guy's just crackers, that's all."

"Yeah," Ben said. "That's what I thought, too."

**

The clouds seemed to come from nowhere, rising eerily in the clear blue sky around 3:00 p.m. The first dribble of rain hit at 3:15 and by 3:20 the dribble had turned into a deluge. When it became apparent the rain would be heavy, Dean set up the pup tent and they ducked inside. "No use going on," he said.

"Why not?"

"We'd be drenched in two minutes, and I have it on good authority there's no laundromat around the corner."

"You're kidding. The tour guide never told me that."

"Yeah, but the tour guide tried to kill you."

She threw him a baleful look and he apologized. "I'm sorry. That was in bad taste."

"Maybe, but it's true. So what do we do now?"

"Wait. It probably won't last long."

"And if it does?"

"Then we stay put for the night. I guess we could both use a rest... we've been running on pure adrenaline."

"I thought you wanted to reach Devils Lake by nightfall."

"I do, but its unwise trekking in this rainfall. The mountains are a dangerous place, especially in inclement weather. Anything can happen, and we wouldn't be much use to Jesse injured. It's better to wait it out."

The rain beat against the tent. "Does this kind of weather happen often?"

Dean shrugged. "Who knows? I've seen it before. The mountains tend to create their own weather. Have you noticed how mountain peaks are often shrouded in cloud? Natural phenomenon. It's a different world up here... hey, you're shivering. Let me get you something dry to wear."

"My stuff is back with Sam and Don Blume. They're probably rooting through it right now. I hope it's raining as hard on them as it is on us... oh."

"What?"

"I just thought about Jesse. Poor kid, he must be scared stiff."

Dean frowned and was silent for a moment, considering. "As long as he's uninjured, he'll manage. He's a bright kid and an experienced woodsman. Jesse's lived near the Stein all his life and he probably knows it as well as I. He'll find shelter, even if it's just against a tree trunk. He knows how to build a lean-to, I taught him myself." Dean paused. "This holiday was supposed to be a ritual for him, following ancient traditions. The Natives sent a young boy into the wilderness to survive on his own, it was a rite of passage. If he came back he was a man. If he didn't..." Dean hesitated. He didn't want to think about that.

"That's barbaric."

Dean shrugged. "Life's hard, especially back then. Can you imagine what it must have been like to live that kind of life? Always at the mercy of the elements? I suppose that's why aboriginals feel so connected to the land – instead of fighting it, they learned to embrace it."

Jackie listened to the rain pelting on the thin nylon tent. It was vicious yet oddly tranquil. As though she and Dean were the only two people in the world, safe and cosy.

He gave her a flannel shirt, miles too big, and obligingly turned his back as she stripped off her wet shirt. The tails came to her knees, encompassing her like a warm blanket. As she settled, he in turn removed his own wet shirt, leaving his chest bare. "Only one spare," he said.

"Ah." She averted her eyes, wondering where to look. There wasn't much option in a tent this size. His chest was muscled, tanned, and with just a sprinkling of fine, fair hair. "Well, uh, thank you."

"Here, you can use Jesse's sleeping bag. He won't mind."

"Thanks." She unzipped it and slipped inside. "It's a bit short but feels heavenly. I'm so tired I could sleep anywhere."

Dean yawned. Now that he was immobile, fatigue washed over him. "Let's grab a power nap while it's raining, and we'll get going again when it lets up."

"Okay... and Dean?" she said, closing her eyes.

"Yes?"

"Thank you."

"For what?"

"For everything... the food, the dry shirt, the sleeping bag..." Her speech was broken by a big yawn. "Thanks for saving my life."

He would have responded but he could tell by her breathing she was already asleep.

**

"Jesus Christ, how the *hell* do you put up this tent?"

"I dunno," said Ben. "I've never camped before. Doesn't it come with instructions?"

Arne fixed Ben with an exasperated glare, rain running off his face in wide rivulets. "Does it look like I'm holding instructions?"

"No."

"That's because there are no instructions. Now help me figure this out, it shouldn't be too difficult... oh, shit. Our supplies are getting soaked. Do you think you could move them under that tree? Maybe they'll stay drier."

Ben looked at the sky. "I doubt it. There isn't a dry spot in this whole godforsaken hellhole. Boy, she's coming down. I don't think I've ever seen it rain this hard."

"Me neither."

"Kind of creepy, eh?"

"Yeah. Everything here is creepy. I wish that fuckin' Bloodsworth was standing here getting his ass soaked instead of us."

"Yeah. Arne? I think this pole is supposed to go through the middle, like this. See?"

"That's good," Arne said admiringly. "Then this other pole must go here. Now she's standing."

Both men stepped back to look at their handiwork. The dome shaped tent was lilting badly to one side, the top saggy and uneven.

"It doesn't look quite right," Ben said.

"Who cares? It's standing, let's go inside."

They climbed through the small entrance and stripped their saturated clothing. Ben sat shivering. *Jesus Christ,* he thought, *this was supposed to be summer. How come it was so goddamned cold?* "Arne?"

"Yeah?"

"We left our supplies outside."

"Oh shit!" Arne climbed back out, dashed bare-assed to their supplies and dragged the stuff inside. "Well," he said, his voice heavy with disgust, "at least one thing is certain: things can't get much worse."

**

Don Blume and Samuel Hudson sat in the torrential rain, oblivious to the deluge. Each man was absorbed with his own thoughts.

Don sat, stupefied. He felt confused, unsure where he was.

Unsure who he was.

He remembered his name, his mother, and recollected faintly why he was here, but it was meaningless.

The rhythm coursed through his body and he allowed himself to sway with it.

He was cold. He knew he was cold, realized he must be cold, but couldn't feel it. Oh, his fingers and toes were numb and his skin ached, but the cold didn't go to his center. There he was warm. Warm and content and filled with purpose.

Only he wasn't exactly sure what that purpose was.

He could ask Samuel but it was too much effort. Talking had become difficult, words wanted to come as grunts now. Everything was more basic. He felt a desire to eat, to sleep, and at some point, he felt a diminished urge to seek warmth.

But, like speaking, this too had grown more difficult. He couldn't actually remember how to go about it.

Don lifted his heavy head, squinting through the hammering rain to see Samuel. The black man was sitting there, his shirt off, ebony skin bare to the elements. He was smiling. How could that be?

Don frowned and made this mouth into an 'O'. "Ooh-oooh!" he grunted. That didn't work.

He tried widening the 'O' and moved his tongue. "Sssaaammmm"

The black man continued to ignore him. Either he wouldn't, nor couldn't, hear him. Or maybe, like Don, he couldn't respond.

**

Samuel's thoughts were very different from Blume's. He felt inner warmth, contentment, peace. For the first time in his life Samuel was truly happy.

He felt the cold but chose to ignore it. It was better since he'd removed his shirt. After the rain started, his back began to sting unbearably, the cloth abrasive and binding. Samuel stripped it off, tearing the fabric, hearing the buttons pop all at once. He dropped the offending garment onto the ground.

Something strange was happening, but Samuel didn't think it was strange at all. At some deeper level he understood it, accepted it. To his conscious self he simply watched, taking it all in.

His dark skin, always smooth and hairless, had begun to develop welts. A series of fine, raised scars crisscrossed his chest, his upper arms, along his shoulders and all the way down his back. There was no pain. It was as if they were old injuries, healed over time.

This made Samuel feel angry. But like the welts, the anger was old. The anger was deeply rooted and tacit.

He felt powerful. Incredibly strong and potent, almost regal.

His back was straight, his welted shoulders muscular and proud. After all, he was African-American.

No, he was African.

Samuel had found his roots.

**

The old Indian stood at the gateway to the majestic valley that was called the Stein. He saw the rain and welcomed it. He was at one with the elements. Large droplets fell on his upturned face, caressing weathered skin.

He thought about his native soil. He thought about the rain. He thought about the people in his valley.

And he smiled.

CHAPTER TWO

Dean listened as the rain slowed to a din, splatting lightly on the tent walls. He had slept soundly but awoke with a start, unsure why. The blackness inside the tent was suffocating. He guessed it was past midnight, perhaps later. He could check his watch but hesitated to wake Jackie. Sometime during her sleep, she had shimmied against him, her body seeking warmth. Her head lay resting softly upon his arm, her back towards his belly, spoon style.

It was strangely intimate to be this close to a virtual stranger, yet she lay so trusting, so vulnerable.

It also felt nice.

Too nice to dislodge her, even though his heart urged him to leap up and resume searching for Jesse. His head disagreed. It was folly tramping through the woods in the dead of night, especially on a trail as perilous as this. There was no moon, obscured again by heavy cloud cover – it was as black as India Ink. The rain would hamper their progress. Track marks, if there even were any still visible after the deluge, would be impossible to find in the dark. It wouldn't be safe... loose soil, raging creeks, even a washout might be expected. One slip could send them careening off the trail into a canyon.

Still, he hesitated. Every minute not searching for Jesse was a minute lost. Jesse's trail grew colder every second. Was he making the right choices? Dean sighed.

He focused his attention on other matters, like the faint, flowery scent of Jackie's hair. His chin rested on her head and her dark hair fanned up to tickle his nostrils. He could feel her warm breath on the back of his hand, deep and rhythmical.

When had he last had sex? Too long, apparently.

The sleeping bag between them did little to camouflage her buttocks as they pressed against him, her curves fitting so naturally against his own. She felt good. She felt right. The vision of her at the creek came to him unbidden; the brief glimpse of her soapy breasts and the water running in rivulets over her belly. His groin twitched appreciatively and he gritted his teeth, willing himself to think of something else.

What was the story behind the guy who tried to kill her? Samuel Hudson, she'd called him. He suspected he knew the outfit Hudson worked for: Fraser Valley Adventures. They'd been around for years now, a reputable business which specialized in river rafting, heli-skiing, fishing, big-game hunting, even dog sledding if you had enough money and were willing to go north. Tour guiding was their bread and butter, both in the Stein and the surrounding areas.

Could they be involved with Jackie's brother's disappearance?

Not likely. What could they possibly gain? Adverse publicity would negatively impact business, and they'd had enough of that with the spate of recent rafting accidents. They'd lost two experienced guides and six rafters (two Canadian, three American and one Aussie) in the past eighteen months, in two separate accidents. Both on the Fraser River, which bordered the eastern ridge of the Stein.

And what about the avalanche last winter that buried alive two heli-skiers and paralysed a third? That was in the news for weeks, especially since one of the skiers had been an Olympic hopeful with a promising commercial career.

No, Fraser Valley Adventures could ill afford any more negative publicity.

Perhaps her brother had seen something and Fraser Valley Adventures was trying to cover it up? And now Jackie was sticking her nose into matters where it didn't belong.

Why do these absurd ideas always come in the middle of the night?

But the idea did bear further exploration. If not Fraser Valley Adventures, then possibly someone else. But who?

And why would anyone want to harm Jackie? To shut her up?

It also didn't explain the thumping noise, nor the missing members of Jackie's group... unless that was staged to frighten her?

It certainly didn't explain Jesse's bizarre behavior.

Jackie moved restlessly in her sleep and nestled closer. She made tiny snoring sounds, like a purring kitten. She was sleeping deeply and that was good. If she was staying with him, she needed to keep pace. She required rest, especially considering what lay ahead.

What other theories could he consider? Dean let his mind wander for a moment, but no ideas surfaced. The slate was as clear as a blackboard, he'd hit a wall. There must be something else that made sense, something which linked the whole mess together. Could it be possible they were all here by chance? By accident?

Parallel thinking, Dean reminded himself. Throw away everything you know to be true and examine the rest. Start with immediate threats: Find Jesse. Escape (or defeat) Samuel. Avoid (or confront) the Noisy Thing. Explore the idea of two more missing people, the German and the American. And the Asians, he reminded himself. Don't forget the Asians – just because they left voluntarily didn't rule out mishap. So where did that leave him? Four people, five including Jesse, presumed missing. What a mess.

And not a solid shred of evidence. Only a gut feeling and a whole lot of wishful thinking. There was nothing substantial, only supposition. All the evidence, all the facts were purely circumstantial.

What to do now?

Keep going. Pray to find something useful. Check out Devils Lake.

And what if Jesse wasn't there?

Had he made a terrible error in judgement not going to the authorities immediately, mobilizing a search party and combing the area? No, that would have taken too long. More than a full day's hike out, another half-day to get everything organized. Far too long to leave a young boy in the forest.

It occurred to Dean that Jesse was having his authentic ritual after all. Alone in the woods with no food, no protection. Could Jesse have wandered off on purpose? He'd been pretty set on keeping everything as realistic as possible.

Jackie stirred again, this time turning to face him. "Shhh," she mumbled, her voice heavy with sleep. Her eyelids were moving rapidly; she was dreaming. "Shhh. It's okay. Everything will be fine." She reached up to cup his head with soft fingers, and gently stroking, she drew his head towards her chest.

He allowed it, knowing he shouldn't, surrendering to the softness of her breasts, with only the thin flannel lining of her shirt acting as a barrier. He felt soothed like a baby. For the first time since his wife's death, since all he knew in the world turned upside down and crazy, Dean closed his eyes and drifted into an effortless, dreamless sleep.

**

As the first shards of dawn overtook the little tent, Jackie glanced down at the sleeping man and studied him. His face, so serious yesterday, looked peaceful in repose. The tiny, furrowed lines above his brow were smooth, making him appear younger, more vulnerable.

How old was he? Early thirties, perhaps. What was he like? Certainly an outdoorsman, as evidenced by the weathering of his skin, the crinkles around his eyes, even in repose. What was he like in real life? What captivated his interest? Did he enjoy his job? Was he good at it? What were his passions?

And the private man? The fellow who came home after a long day's work and put on his slippers? What kind of man was he then, when the world wasn't looking?

He woke all at once. There was no lingering between states, she saw that immediately. One moment he was deep asleep; the next fully alert. His dark lashes flickered once, then she felt his gaze as it rested on her.

"You've been watching me."

"Yes," she agreed.

He was silent for a moment, studying her, and she remained calm under his bold stare. "You talk in your sleep," he said.

"So I've been told."

An irrational stab of jealousy. Where had that come from? "By whom?" he questioned, narrowing his eyes slightly.

"Oh, just about everybody – my brother, my school girlfriends, my ex. Apparently I used to let him know what I *really* thought of him."

"Hmm. That sounds... bad?"

"Well," she answered dryly, "it sure didn't help the marriage. Especially near the end." Her cheeks were rosy, a little flushed, and all of a sudden she felt self-conscious. "What? Why are you looking at me like that?"

"It's just... uh... you're beautiful."

Jackie snorted. "Yeah, right! I'm disgusting... my hair feels like it's been picked at by crows and my teeth are... ugh," she ran her tongue over them, "wearing little angora sweaters. Gross."

He raised a hand and smoothed her hair. "No, I mean really beautiful. None of that phoney crap. Now, lying here, you look... exquisite." His hand lingered, then moved slowly downward to stroke her cheek, to feel the smoothness of her skin. It was so fine, so perfectly unblemished that it made the dark bruises around her throat all the more ugly.

"Do these still hurt?" he whispered.

"Yes."

His fingers traced the bruising, ever so lightly, barely touching it. She caught her breath and gazed back at him. The moment stretched.

"We should get up," she whispered, finally.

"Yes." But still his fingers kept moving, softly. There was something about her features, so intriguing... so beguiling that he wanted to keep looking, to keep touching. It wasn't that she was pretty, although she was. He'd known plenty of attractive females and none had affected him since.... since Em. And Emily Ann had been so lovely herself, so bubbly and cute.

But Emily Ann had been a girl. A sweet, exuberant girl filled with unrealized promise.

Jaclyn Hart was a woman. Loyal and independent enough to trek the Stein, searching for a lost brother. Stubborn enough to keep looking for answers. Fearless enough to trust a complete stranger.

She excited him, enticed him with clear blue eyes that studied him evenly, as though she was seeing his soul. He could lose himself in her, he thought.

That was... terrifying.

She bent downwards and met his lips with her own, making the first move, tentatively. They shared one single soft kiss that seemed to last for eternity. When they broke apart, it was him, and he turned away, his head swirling in confusion. When he spoke, his voice was crackling, gruff. "We'd better get going. I'll put on some coffee."

"Okay. I'll put on some clothes. Uh, wait, that didn't come out right."

But he was already hightailing it from the tent, scrambling as if he was on fire.

**

"It's a beautiful morning," Jackie said, mostly to break the silence, and it was. Little evidence of last night's storm remained, only the ground cover glistening damply in the morning sunbeams. Tendrils of steam wafted everywhere: from ferns, mosses, stumps and trees – the entire forest was ridding itself of excess moisture. It was ethereal.

Dean glanced at the clear, blue sky. "Should be a decent day."

"Amazing, isn't it? It's like the forest has been cleansed." She looked at her grubby hands. "Wish I could say the same."

He tossed her a damp cloth, heated with water from the tiny Primus stove. "This'll help. What do you take in your coffee? I have powdered milk and brown sugar."

"Brown sugar sounds good. Go on, add another spoonful... don't be stingy."

His mouth quirked. "Are you always this bossy?"

"Just until I get my caffeine, and then I'm delightful."

He passed her a collapsible mug and she took note – this guy took his camping seriously. Their hands touched briefly at the exchange and she felt a jolt of electricity. Dean turned abruptly away, keeping his back to her.

Both the hot cloth and coffee were pure heaven. Again, the silence stretched. He was not a chatty man in the morning, was he? "Dean.... about what happened in the tent..."

"Forget it, it was nothing." His tone did not invite further discussion. He busied himself around the makeshift campsite, keeping his back to her. Deliberately.

Jackie sipped her coffee. So that's how it was going to be. She should feel flustered or embarrassed or something. Instead she felt... safe. Sure, two could play this game. If one wanted to play games. She didn't. "Objection overruled, councillor. That *was* most definitely something. I won't speak for you, but coming from my end, it was... definitely the high point of my week."

His shoulders stilled.

"Of course," she added, "it's been a shitty week. But all in all, it was a pretty good kiss."

At that, he turned and stared at her. She could see the warring emotions on his face. "Don't kid yourself," he said gruffly. "It was a *great* kiss." And he smiled. This time, it reached his eyes and she saw joy. Plus fear... uncertainty. His face was a kaleidoscope of emotions. "Finish up; we need to get going as soon as possible."

"Of course." She looked at the trail – it didn't look so bad in the daylight.

He began packing the supplies, dismantling the tent. Within ten minutes, everything was ready to go. "Did you have enough to eat?" he asked.

"Plenty. Thank you. I couldn't stuff in another dried prune if I tried."

He swatted a mosquito. Last night's water was bringing them out in droves. Without asking he passed her the Deep Woods Off. "Better use this or there will nothing left of you." He studied the blip of blood left behind. "Well, at least someone got a good breakfast. I know that wasn't exactly Eggs Benedict, but the dried fruit and nuts will give you energy – you're going to need it. Keep a handful in your pocket to munch on as we hike."

"Hey, I'm not complaining. Nuts and dried prunes are very... uh, satisfying."

"You're kind of a lousy liar, aren't you?"

She smiled. "Guess so. To be honest, dried prunes are... yuck. The coffee, however, was amazing."

His mouth twitched, and she thought she saw a hint of a dimple under his stubble. "Jesse doesn't like them much either. Tell you what, when we get out of this, I'll cook you a four star breakfast – how does that sound?"

"Hmm, I seem to recall an earlier promise of steak and champagne. Now breakfast, what am I getting myself into?"

"Are you chickening out?"

"Depends – are you a decent cook?"

"I know my way around a few pasta dishes. Hardly any of them involve prunes."

"That's a relief."

Without asking, he retrieved the bug repellant and turned Jackie around, lifting her hair from her nape, and gave it a little spray. "That should do it. Ready to go?"

"Yes." She picked up the backpack. It weighed a ton.

"I'll carry that." He swung it over his shoulder like it was nothing.

"Let me take something."

"Are you sure?"

"Of course, Dean. I'm able-bodied."

"That you are." His gaze raked over her and suddenly she did feel like blushing. "Okay, if you carry Jesse's backpack it would be a huge help." He positioned the smaller carrier and adjusted the straps so they rested comfortably on her shoulders. The small sleeping bag hung tightly off one side. The whole thing was compact, light. She frowned. "I can carry more than this."

"No, that's enough. I wasn't kidding when I said the trail gets rough from here on in. Oh, Jackie? When we get there, to Devils Lake, stick close, all right?"

"Why?"

"Safer that way. I have no idea what we'll find."

"Sounds ominous."

"Likely nothing will happen, but..."

"But?"

"Well, there're some things about Devils Lake you should know. Mostly folklore, but the aboriginals believe its pretty powerful stuff. You see, legend has it that Devils Lake is a source for dominant, evil spirits."

"Do you believe that?"

"In evil spirits? Hmm, no, but I've seen things in the courtroom make me wonder. But regardless of what I think, the local Natives certainly believe, and that deserves respect. So profound is their superstition that even today they avoid this area. If they must pass through, they blacken their faces to avoid being seen."

"By who?"

"By the devil who lives in the lake."

"You're having me on."

"I kid you not."

"C'mon. That sounds rather farfetched."

She looked at him like she was waiting for the punch line and his mouth quirked. "Many of our myths have

Native origins. Sasquatch, for example, was reported by tribes throughout the Pacific Northwest. This area, in fact, is considered a hotspot for sightings."

She couldn't help but look over her shoulder, scanning the woods. "Big Foot? That's a little spooky."

"And don't forget Ogopogo. He was described by First Nations people over two hundred years ago. They called him the *Lake Demon*."

"Jeez, the devil who lives in the lake. C'mon, really?"

Now he laughed outright. "I swear. You can Google it."

"Are you suggesting Devils Lake has its own little Loch Ness Monster? And, if so, do you think there's a link?"

"It's just a myth," Dean said, leading the way through a thicket of branches. Once again Jackie had no idea where the trail was and how he was following it. "But then again, perhaps myths are based in truth. Are you a religious person, Jackie?"

"No, not really. I mean, I believe in something, but not in an organized, church-going way."

"Would you say you're spiritual?"

"I suppose."

"Most people are, whether they realize it or not. Throughout the ages, people have felt the need to believe in something they have no proof of. God or a Divine Being. It's the same worldwide, regardless of culture or religion. Easterners call him Buddha, we say Jesus Christ, the Arabs pray to Allah. Some cultures have Polytheism but it still amounts to the same thing: humans have a innate need to believe in a Supreme Being, even though there is no practical proof."

"Yes, I guess that's true."

"What one culture defines as God, the next calls heathen. We continually disregard others' beliefs, even though they mirror ours."

"What are you getting at?"

"Native mythology bears the same consideration and respect as other religions. Remember, we're talking about Ancients here, people with limited language and a need to explain common events. If a rain storm happened, or a bad hunting season, they might think that a certain God was angry. It's really no different from the Ancient Egyptians and Greeks. They had gods for everything but some historians believe during that period of history there were many unnatural disasters, like earthquakes and floods. The current doctrine is that these events were caused by a comet coming so close to earth's orbit that it was visible to the naked eye. Surviving literature and artwork supports that theory, and the Ancients, in a great effort to understand these cataclysmic events, decided the Gods were displeased."

"So, you're suggesting we use religion to explain things we don't understand?"

"Sure, and I believe it's where many myths start. Here, watch out for this branch. Can you squeeze by? Good." After she'd passed, he slipped in front of her again, taking the lead. "We still do it, you know. When something happens beyond our control, we say 'It was God's will'. Or, 'It was meant to be'."

"Yeah, but how does this pertain to Devils Lake?"

"My point is that to us Native Mythology sounds simplistic and far-fetched but is it much different from our own? Although the stories seem implausible, the Ancients creating them were using their limited knowledge and language to explain some very real events."

"Are you suggesting we heed the pictographs' warning of evil spirits?"

"Not exactly, just that we can't overlook or dismiss something because it doesn't mesh with our own belief system. That's what Jesse's father taught me. Keep an open mind."

"All right, I'll try. But if we see any two-headed snakes, I'm outta here. Seriously."

Dean chuckled. "I hate to be the bearer of bad news but two headed-snakes are not a myth, they exist. An aberration of nature."

"Really?" She looked alarmed. "Well, that's more disgusting than dried prunes. This just keeps getting better and better." She took a deep breath. "Tell me more about Devils Lake."

"Are you sure you're up for it? You look a little pale."

"Yeah, why not? Let's keep the bad news rolling."

"Well, Natives believe there is a devil in the lake. Some tell of an old woman with flowing hair who floats around the lake on a log, chanting. Some say goat herds have been turned to stone. Reports of young girls dying while swimming abound, and of an animal, half-dog and half-bull, that attempts to swim the lake but disappears halfway across."

"Yikes. Do you believe it?"

"I believe the Natives believe it. Eddy did, and.... well, I've never told anyone this before, but something happened to a friend of mine at Devils Lake."

The silence stretched between them, which allowed Jackie to catch her breath. The hiking was harder now, the incline steep. When it became apparent he wasn't going to elaborate, Jackie pressed. "Can you tell me about it? It might be relevant to what's happening now."

Dean exhaled noisily. "That's what I'm afraid of. The summer I was seventeen, Jesse's father and I spent a few days camping in the Stein with a red-haired kid named J.J. Fleishenheimer. We came across this trail to Devils Lake. Eddy didn't want any part of it, but J.J. started teasing him, calling him chicken. I was intrigued – I'd never seen Eddy shy away from anything before. I'm ashamed to admit I joined in the goading, until finally Eddy relented and agreed to take us."

"But he was still reluctant?" Jackie guessed.

"Very, but when you're seventeen and your best friend is calling you a coward, you really have no choice. Eddy said he'd take us in for a quick look, but only if we promised to leave immediately."

"So you promised."

"Of course, since it was the only way we'd get to see it. The trail was unmarked but Eddy knew the way in. Behind his back we were already scheming to convince him to stay the night once we arrived at Devils Lake. At this point the challenge was too tempting. We were seventeen and felt we had to prove our manhood by showing how brave we were. That we were also stupid and foolhardy never entered our minds, or if it did, we pushed the thought away. If Eddy said something was dangerous, we should have listened. Eddy didn't say things lightly, and he was never wrong.

"It was late by the time we got near. Eddy suggested turning back but we refused, so he shrugged and continued on. Eddy was in the lead, J.J. in the middle, and I was pulling up the rear. We were really close when one of my boot laces snapped. I shouted for the guys to go ahead, that I'd catch up. It took me six or seven minutes to locate a spare lace in my pack and thread it up. Usually Eddy would have waited – he was a real stickler for staying together – but I think at that point he was so pissed off he didn't care."

Shivers ran down Jackie's spine. "What happened next?"

"I heard an awful scream, and I dropped my pack and raced down the final descent. When I reached the lake, I couldn't believe what I saw. The lake itself was incredibly beautiful. The color was different from the other lakes around here which are either black or greenish. This was pure turquoise and the late afternoon sun made it sparkle like a million diamonds.

"Near the bottom of the trail lay J.J. – in a crumpled heap like a broken rag doll. Something startled him so badly that he lost his footing and tumbled down the trail, falling over a moderate sized rocky embankment. His back was broken, and he was babbling away, but it was nonsensical. Eddy stood tight lipped, glaring at me."

"That's a horrible story! What scared him? What did J.J. see?"

"I'll never know for sure. I thought I heard J.J. say something about ghosts and evil spirits, something about heinous creatures half-animal, half something else. But he wasn't speaking clearly. Thank God we had the good sense not to move him or he'd never have walked again. Eddy volunteered to stay with him while I went for help. I ran all the way but it still took over thirty-six hours before the rescue helicopter came for him. Eddy and J.J. had to spend the next two nights at Devils Lake.

"J.J.'s back mended, but he was never the same. Before the accident, he was witty and smart-mouthed. Afterwards, he seemed... well, catatonic. Like the life had been sucked from him. His family took him back to New York about six months later. Decided the great outdoors wasn't so great after all. Can't say I blame them."

"What about Eddy? Surely he saw what happened that day?"

"I'm certain he saw something, but he refused to talk about it. I badgered him for ages and his response was to look me squarely in the eye and say we shouldn't have gone to Devils Lake. That we didn't belong there. And then he made me promise to never go back again."

"To Devils Lake?"

"No, to the Stein. Whatever Eddy saw during the thirty-six hours he spent at Devils Lake with J.J. was enough to convince him never to set foot in the Stein again."

"Did you go back?"

"Not until now. We still went hiking and camping, just in other places. So, not only did I break my promise never to return to the Stein, but I'm going back to Devils Lake."

The shivers running down Jackie's spine intensified. "Why did you come back?"

Dean shook his head. "I've been asking that myself. On the surface, it was to take Jesse into his ancestral home. Yes, we could have gone elsewhere, but there is no other place like the Stein. I mean, look at it," he spread his arms wide, "it's gorgeous. Where else can you access old growth forest of this magnitude close to Vancouver? Yes, there are provincial parks and other forests, but nothing like this. It's so unspoiled." He was silent for a moment, then added, "But truthfully, I think I was meant to come back – it was calling me. My best childhood memories are from the Stein, Eddy and I combed these woods like it was our own personal playground. We'd spend days, even weeks at a time here. There's a purpose for me here." He cleared his throat. "I feel as though something is drawing me to Devils Lake."

"That's the way I feel too," Jackie whispered. "Like we're being pulled magnetically."

"Exactly."

"Are you afraid?"

"I'd be lying if I said I wasn't. Mostly, I'm afraid of what we'll find. Hold up – look at this."

Jackie glanced at the piece of torn purple cloth, so filthy the original color barely showed through. "What is it?"

"A piece of Jesse's t-shirt. Maybe he snagged it, or maybe he left it for me to find. And here..." His voice grew silent.

"Dean? What is it?"

"Here, near the edges. See this dark stain? It's probably just dirt but it could be blood."

"Oh, no!"

Dean's face was grim. "We're on the right track but Jesse's in trouble. I think we can safely assume he didn't leave the area voluntarily. Whoever, or whatever has Jesse, forced him."

"He can't be that far ahead. We've been making good time and he's just a child."

"Yeah." His face was grim. "I keep telling myself the same thing. Come on." He tucked the cloth into his jacket pocket. "We'd better hurry."

**

Ben studied the map. "Which way, Arne?"

"Uh, let's see." Arne took control of the map and circled his finger. "This is the tour route. The group should be right about here, and if we go this way, we should intersect them."

"But that's not right – that trail leads us further in, and look at the elevation, it's a sucker's climb."

Arne turned the map around, looked at it from all angles. Usually he had excellent mapping skills but this looked like gibberish. He consulted the GPS but it wasn't any help. The problem was, there were very few named places, save for a few lakes. It wasn't like you could punch in "hotels" and get a direct heading. He was embarrassed to let on just how confused he was. Ben might be his best friend but Arne was his superior in seniority.

One of the lakes popped out at him, it seemed to rise off the map. "Here," he jabbed. "This is the way."

"Devils Lake?"

"I have a feeling we should go north. I can't explain it, just a strong feeling."

"Boss doesn't like strong feelings, Arne. He likes it when we follow orders. Plus, it's over a thousand square kilometres here, wouldn't do to get lost."

"Are you questioning me, you little pissant?" Arne's lips stretched wide, showing his teeth. The smile was one Ben had never seen before and it gave him the creeps. It was reminiscent of a jack o'lantern, and not the friendly kind, either. It was ghoulish. "What the boss doesn't know won't hurt him. Besides, I'm tired of taking orders from that asshole."

Ben remained silent.

"Well, aren't you, too?"

"Yeah, I guess so. I've been taking orders from Bloodsworth longer than I've been taking them from my wife."

That elicited a chuckle from Arne, and Ben felt himself relax. His friend was back to normal.

"What about this idea? We can follow the trail here, see? It starts off to the center but deviates up here to the north. We can decide which direction to go where it forks."

"But what if the group comes back the first way? Then we'll miss them."

"So what? I could use a little R & R. Neither of us has taken a vacation in years.... I say we make the best of a lousy situation. Look at this place; it's beautiful now the rain has finally stopped. I could stay here for a few days with no pressures."

"No boss breathin' fire down our necks."

"No wives to nag us."

Ben let that one slide. He missed Margaret. "We could sleep until noon."

"Yeah. Maybe do a little fishing."

"Except we don't have any fishing gear."

"You're such a goddamned pessimist, Ben. When did you get to be such an old lady?"

"Ah, stick it up your butt, Johannson," Ben said, starting to laugh.

Arne smiled. "That's my Benny. Now we're cooking."

"So, it's settled then?"

"Yep. We'll go north."

An ominous thumping noise sounded, far in the distance. Both men strained to hear it, unable to discern the direction it came from.

"Jesus! What the hell is that?"

"Dunno," said Arne. "Sounds like blasting."

"Yeah, except it's rhythmical."

"And too close together."

"Like someone's blasting a boom box with too much bass."

"Never heard anything like it," Arne said.

Ben had to agree. It was strange sounding, almost otherworldly. Definitely creepy. "Could be an echo," he said finally, grasping at straws. "Don't you think, Arne? Arne?"

Arne declined to answer and Ben turned away from the thumping noise to face his friend, but what he saw made his blood chill. Arne stood, mouth split again in that hideous smile, and he rocked back and forth, back and forth. His eyes were glazed, as if in a trance.

"Arne?" whispered Ben, horrified. Involuntarily, he took a few steps backwards but found himself on a precipice, further retreat was blocked. "Arne, cut it out, you're scaring me. Arne! Stop it! Jesus, Arne! Can't you smell the smoke? The smoke! I think the forest is on fire!"

**

Don Blume, busily engaged with his hands around Samuel's throat, paid no attention to the Noisy Thing. He did hear it, on some primal level, but he ignored it, concentrating on the task at hand: namely, to force Samuel into submission.

The black man refused to be forced.

Don tried to think where he went wrong. Yesterday he had complete control over the black man and now, barely able to speak, the situation reversed.

Where had his strength gone? His hands felt limp. He was barely able to exert any pressure on Sam's neck, and the little he could was dismissed by Samuel. Not dismissed – totally ignored.

Last night had been spent entirely in the storm. He had fallen asleep, finally, in the wee hours before dawn, exhausted and drained, curled into a tight ball on the cold, wet ground. Sleep seemed to help; when he woke his strength had returned, marginally. He was able to speak again and his powers of reasoning were somewhat restored.

He valiantly tried to remember his name but was unable to. He did remember his objective, to kill something, but he was unsure of what. Then he saw Samuel, sitting still on a stump, regally staring into the forest.

It came to Don that Samuel was his slave, but Samuel didn't seem to understand this. Don tried calling the man *'boy'*, tried browbeating him into service yet

Samuel ignored him. Don searched his limited resources but came up empty. Samuel had to do his bidding, he had to.

Don grew frustrated and decided to kill the black man, but his weak hands were ineffectual weapons against the other's brawny neck. Don was infuriated but that emotion took up too much energy, and finally, as the thumping noise increased its tempo, he fell back, exhausted. He wanted to cry but couldn't remember how.

Samuel Hudson stood suddenly, glancing at Don as if he was an annoying insect. His large head was cocked to one side as he scanned the forest before turning his attention back to what used to be Don Blume.

"I go now," he stated.

"Go?" Don asked, relived he could speak again. It seemed to help when he hadn't tried for a while. "Go where?"

"There. It calls for me."

"But... but what about me?"

"You stay here. It doesn't need you."

Don felt true fear. "No! I can't stay. Let me come with you, please. Puh-lease!" He grasped the black man's calves. "I beg you." His head was beginning to hurt. His tongue was starting to thicken and the words were becoming more difficult to formulate. His strength ebbed.

"If you desire," Samuel's voice had changed, grown deeper and melodic. It had the singsong quality of the islands, a true tribal tone. "Do not expect aid from me."

"Thank you," Don said, struggling to his feet. "Thhhank-ooohh."

Samuel turned away, his bearing strong, head held high. His shirt, discarded during last night's rainstorm, remained off and his skin, marred with the crisscrossing of scars, gleamed darkly in the morning sun. He started to walk, his stride strong and sure. He neglected to follow the trail; he had his own course: true north, to Devils Lake.

**

"I hear it," Dean said in response to Jackie's questioning look. "Our noisy friend is back."

"It's hard to tell which direction it's coming from."

"Yes, especially when it's so far away. Seems to reverberate off the mountains."

"Do you have any idea what it might be?"

"No. You?"

She shook her head. "It's sinister sounding, even this far away. Up close, its –"

"Diabolical."

"Yes."

"It appears to be mobile, whatever it is. Able to move vast distances fairly quickly."

"Maybe there's more than one."

Dean looked at her. "I hadn't thought of that. It would explain a few things, though. Listen, even though it's far away, the forest creatures are silent."

"They sense danger, too."

They walked quietly, both listening as the faint *thump-thump-thumping* echoed through the trees.

"Dean? What happens if we run into it?"

His mouth tightened. "I don't know. Let's cross that bridge when we come to it."

Suddenly, it was louder, as if it was all around them. Dean stopped and grabbed Jackie, holding her close, but the thumping stopped moments after it began.

Then there was silence.

"That was weird. It's like... it's listening to us," she said, after a few moments. "Like... it knows we're here."

"Yes, it does feel that way."

"What does that mean?"

"Maybe that we're getting close. Can you carry on?"

She nodded. Dean led the way, climbing up a boulder as the trail took a sudden upward surge. He held out his hand and helped Jackie up the steep incline.

The path twisted in a hairpin curve, and now they were walking in the direction they'd come. "I don't remember this," Dean said, frowning.

"It was a long time ago, maybe you've forgotten, or maybe the trail was altered."

"Maybe." His tone was doubtful. "I find it hard to –"

"Dean? What is it?"

"Turn away! Now, Jackie, don't look!"

But it was too late. Jackie had already seen the bloody corpse, hanging execution style by its neck, swaying slightly in the breeze.

"No," she whispered, unable to take her eyes off the grotesque form. "That – that used to be Bob Vance."

CHAPTER THREE

They cut down the body and buried it as best they could, with branches and rocks. Jackie kept her eyes on the torso, refusing to look at the corpse's face. That first glance would stay with her forever, especially as the body swung around and she saw the clump of hair missing from the back of the head. They'd been correct earlier; that *was* a piece of scalp found at the campsite. She'd fought the urge to vomit.

Dean turned to Jackie. "You don't have to continue on, you know. You can change your mind."

She looked at the rudimentary grave. "I'll take my chances with you."

"It's dangerous. This," he said, pointing at the noose, still swaying in the tree, "proves it."

"I understand. But I feel safer with you than alone. Please don't try to change my mind."

Dean sighed. "I should, but God help me, I want you by my side, too. Selfish, maybe."

"No, practical."

"Is that the tone you use on your school kids?"

"Yes," she said, smiling a little. Part of her was amazed she could still smile after the gruesome task they'd just performed, part of her thought she'd never smile again. "How could you tell?"

"Because you sound like a schoolmarm. Stern and serious." Dean looked at the grave. "I'm still not sure we did the right thing burying him. The authorities might see it as tampering with evidence."

"We couldn't just leave him, Dean. It's not... decent. You said yourself he'd be prey to animals."

"I know, but he was past caring."

"Bob Vance deserved a proper burial."

"You're right, and realistically, by the time the authorities arrived there wouldn't be much left of him. There are a lot of scavengers in these woods – buzzards, coyotes, wolves, bears. We've been so focused on human threats that we'd best not forget that. Okay, let's get moving. I don't feel like spending more time here than we have to."

"Wait. We should say a few words. Prayer or something."

"I thought you weren't religious."

"No, but as you reminded me, I am spiritual. Come on, it's the proper thing to do."

"All right. Make it quick, though. Do you want to do the honors or shall I?"

"I will. I knew him." She cleared her throat. "Dear God, please accept Bob Vance into your Kingdom. I didn't know him well, but he seemed like a decent man. He had great plans for this valley, to develop it and make it a place for many to enjoy. While I didn't personally agree with his plans, I knew he was firm in his convictions. His death was tragic. Please don't let it be meaningless. Amen."

"Amen."

"Okay, let's go."

They walked along in silence. The trail was too thin to walk abreast, so Dean led, and Jackie kept pace, keeping only a foot or so space between them. Dean was the first to speak.

"What did you mean about Bob Vance having great plans for this valley?"

"He was a realtor, from California. He wanted to develop a tourist resort."

"That would have been impossible. This is parkland. The government would never allow it."

She snorted. "Yeah, right. But ask yourself: for how long? Read the newspapers: there's consistently a push towards privatization and commercialization. I read recently that allowing leases and private partnerships in provincial parks is being considered. Not just the Stein, mind you, but any provincial park. I'm talking commercial development like restaurants and concession stands within park boundaries, not to mention accommodations. Coming soon to a park near you: all the comforts of the city."

"Hmm. I wonder." Then he shook his head. "I spent a lot of time in this valley as a child, it's the same now as it was then, pristine... untouched, old-growth forest. It's been this way for thousands of years and some hotshot wants to change it."

"Tragic, isn't it? It's not like there aren't a million other spots to put a resort. Why is everyone so keen on destroying our few remaining rainforests?"

"Greed. There's a great deal of money to be made, for a select few. Then it's gone, ruined. At the rate we're going, old growth forest will be a thing of the past. The forest industry argues that second and subsequent growth forests are just as good. It's not true. When forests are leveled, more than just trees are affected – the entire eco-system is destroyed. Animals, fungi, vegetation... things we haven't yet discovered are lost forever. Have you ever seen a clear-cut forest?"

Jackie shook her head. "Only on TV."

"It doesn't do it justice. A clear-cut forest is a mass graveyard. It's devastating – so ugly it'll make you weep."

"But public awareness is growing, more and more people are protesting. They can't continue forever."

"We don't have forever. The next few decades are critical, a turning point. Unfortunately, stumpage fees are up. The price of timber is rising, everyday. This timber will go to Asia, Europe, the United States... anywhere people are building. Forestry companies, both local and abroad, were hurt so badly during the recession they'll do anything to dig themselves out. Lumber brings revenue for the province, which in turn fills government coffers. The public bears pressure on the government to increase funding for social programs... where do you think that money comes from?"

"It's an ominous cycle."

"Indeed. Previous generations left us with a terrible environmental mess and we're not doing enough to change it. Future generations will be left with nothing."

"Dean," Jackie said suddenly, tugging on his backpack. "Do you hear that?"

He stopped walking. "No."

"The birds. They're singing again."

His face broke into a smile. "Yes."

"I think it's a good sign. Where there are birds, there's life."

"Yes," he agreed. But silently, Dean thought: *It could also be a trap.*

They broke for food as the sun rose overhead, stopping by a pretty little lake. Earlier predictions of warmth proved true, and they both had removed jackets hours ago. The meal was a granola type mix, with dried apples, washed down with pure, cold stream water. The trail had become ridiculously steep; there were parts akin to mountain climbing. It was more treacherous that Dean recalled. Jackie was grateful for the break, but Dean continued to pace.

"What is it?" she asked, finally.

"Nothing." But he was frowning.

"Dean, something is definitely bothering you. And I'm guessing it's not the fact that we're eating rabbit food instead of getting our burger fix at the drive thru. Now, spill the beans or I'm going to hog the rest of these chewy, tasteless hunks of brown crud. What are these, anyway?"

"Dates." He sat down, raking a hand through tousled hair. "Something is wrong here. This trail... it shouldn't be this steep."

"Maybe you're remembering it wrong. Last time you were, what... seventeen? That's a long time ago, maybe it just seems steeper."

"No, but thanks for the old-age crack. Just for that, I'm eating the rest of the dates."

"Be my guest. Seriously." She passed him the bag. "Next time we go traipsing through the woods, running from homicidal maniacs and searching for lost children, I will pack the food. Could we have taken a wrong turn? Maybe this is the wrong trail."

"I've been asking myself that for the past two hours, ever since we buried Bob. I've gone over it in my head a hundred times, triple checked the map. This has to be it."

"Are you sure?"

"Yes. See this?" He pushed a crumpled map in front of her, pointing vigorously at a splotch of blue. "This is where we are. This lake is called Earlobe Lake, I remember it quite well. Eddy and I went swimming here, but J.J. refused to. The map shows Earlobe Lake right where it should be, and I've confirmed it with the GPS. I was half hoping we wouldn't come across it. Then it would prove we'd taken the wrong trail."

A sense of foreboding stole through Jackie. "I don't understand."

"Don't you see? The topography is all wrong."

She looked closely at the map. "No, I'm not sure I do."

"We've been travelling at about five, six thousand feet, give or take. See the forest green color? Now, back here, where it turns brown, is where we found Bob."

"Yes, so?"

"According to this, we should have been climbing in altitude, which we have, but not to this degree. We should have gained only a few thousand feet, putting us at six or seven thousand. That is significant since the average mountain peak here is nine thousand feet, give or take. We should have been hiking steadily up, but not climbing like we did. My guess is that we're past eight thousand feet. That doesn't make sense at all."

'No, you're right. It doesn't. According to this map, if we were at eight thousand feet, we'd see ice-fields."

"Exactly. We would also feel cooler."

"The air is warmer."

"Much warmer."

There was silence as they contemplated that. Then Dean spoke again: "This map shows Earlobe Lake at the summit. The trail levels out, which is how I remember it. It should all be downhill to Devils Lake, but look."

She followed his outstretched finger.

"It's straight up."'

"There must be some mistake," Jackie agreed. "Maybe we're over here, on Siwhe Mountain."

"No, impossible. We would have crossed this creek, which would have been difficult." Dean cleared his throat. "There's more. Look at this." He held out his hand, showing a compass. Jackie looked closely and she could see the needle spewing madly.

"It's gone haywire."

"Something is interfering with the magnetic field. It started just after we found Bob and has been growing steadily worse."

"Maybe that proves we're on the wrong trail. How can you be sure what direction we're going?"

"The sun," Dean said, rubbing his eyes in frustration. "I've been tracking the sun, and we're headed due North."

"Of course," she said absently. "I know about the sun, I teach it to my students, but, oh…. There must be some explanation."

"That's why I haven't said anything. I thought perhaps the trail was rerouted, but Earlobe Lake proves that theory wrong."

"What does it mean?"

"No idea, I guess we just keep going ahead and find out."

"How much longer until Devils Lake?"

"Can't say for sure. Yesterday, even this morning I could have calculated it exactly, but everything has changed. We should have been here hours ago. It's taking us twice as long to get where we should, probably because of this altitude gain. Judging from the looks of the trail ahead, it's going to get worse."

"Will we get there before dark?"

"I hope so. We'll hike until dusk, if you can keep going."

Jackie nodded.

"If we don't make it tonight, we'll at least be within striking distance of Devils Lake, and hopefully we'll find it early tomorrow morning."

"But Jesse would be out here, alone, one more night."

"Yes." Dean's voice was hard. "I don't know what we're up against, but it would be a grave mistake to underestimate the situation. We don't want to end up like Bob. We can't help Jesse if we're dead."

Jackie flinched. "That's harsh."

"I know. Okay, we'll keep going, but be careful of your footing. If you get tired, let me know, and we'll take a break. Don't worry about speaking up, fatigue is as real an enemy as anything else out here. One mistake and you could end up with a broken leg, or worse."

"Got it."

"Look, Jesse's a smart kid, and brave. If he's still alive, he can last one more night."

"If he's alive. You mean –"

"I don't mean anything. We'll find him, today or tomorrow… one way or the other."

With that, Dean began to lead the way and they lapsed into silence as they resumed climbing the steep trail ahead.

**

Samuel moved fluidly through the forest, his bare muscles rippling. He was unhesitating in his direction: true north. When a boulder or stump blocked his way he simply climbed over it. The only time he deviated was to avoid trees or other immovable objects, then he adjusted his direction immediately upon passing. Don Blume was hard pressed to follow: many times he fell behind, only to find a sudden adrenaline rush which allowed him to keep up with Samuel. For reasons unfathomable to Don, it was imperative he remain with Samuel.

On they went. The trail began to rise and Samuel kept up the grueling pace. Only once did he stop. He had come across a small brook and he hesitated slightly, looking down at the clear, burbling water. Samuel frowned. The water was important. He studied it for a full minute before he knelt and cupped his hands, drinking deeply.

Don caught up with him, panting. He looked frightfully deranged: his thin hair stuck up wildly, his eyes glazed. He was sweating profusely from exertion, and when he came to the brook he fell into it madly, taking wide gulps of the precious liquid.

Samuel watched him with curious detachment, then began to jog north again.

"Wait," cried Don. "Rest! Neeeed resssst."

Samuel ignored him, continuing forward. Don picked himself up and staggering erratically behind, followed.

**

Ben Hoight was scared shitless. He watched as his friend – transformed into something evil – turn normal again. The burning scent dissipated at the same time Arne twirled to Ben, frowning. "What is it, buddy? You look like you've seen a ghost."

"Get away from me," Ben shrieked, sidestepping him. With the precipice to his rear, there was nowhere else to go.

"Ben? What the hell is wrong with you?"

"Me? Me? What the hell is wrong with *me*? You're the one who's gone fuckin' looney tunes."

"Benny?"

"Stay away! Don't come any closer or I'll...." Ben looked around wildly, grabbing a pointy stick. "Or I'll poke your eyes out."

"Benny, what's gotten into you? It's me, Arne. Now put that stick down and let's talk about this rationally."

"Rationally?" Ben's voice was on the verge of hysteria. "How can you talk about rationality when you keep turning into... into... shit, something so fucking weird I don't even know what it is."

That stopped Arne. "What do you mean?"

"Just now. You went all creepy, just like before."

"I don't understand."

"Well, neither do I."

"Look, Ben. I don't know what you think you saw, but as you can see, I'm all right now. Aren't I? Now, please put down the stick before you hurt someone with it."

Ben slowly released his hold on the stick. Maybe he had imagined it. Arne looked as normal as can be. Ben felt a little foolish. Maybe it was that new blood pressure medicine his doctor had given him. Maybe he was reacting with it or something. He'd have to ask Margaret if there were side effects. She's done a short stint as nurse's aide when she was a teenager and she might know.

"Sorry, Arne," he said.

"S'okay, buddy. We're both under a lot of stress."

"Yeah."

"Let's go... we've got a lot ground to cover."

"Okay. Arne? What do you think that thumping sound was?"

Arne frowned. "What thumping noise?"

"You know, a minute ago, just before... well, you know."

"I didn't hear anything."

"Sure you did. We thought it might be blasting. Don't you remember?"

Arne shook his head and Ben sighed. Maybe he'd been imagining that, too.

"Where are you going?" Jackie asked.

"To find us dinner."

"Oh."

Dean turned to look at her. "Is something wrong?"

She studied the idyllic setting before her. They had reached the meadow a half hour earlier and pitched the tent. The beauty of it astonished her. How could anything so perfect looking feel so wrong?

She shook her head.

"Tell me," Dean prompted.

"It's... it's just that I feel nervous being alone. It's almost dark."

"I won't be long."

"Okay." Her voice sounded unconvinced, scared even to her own ears.

Dean searched her eyes and was disturbed by the trouble they reflected. "We have to eat, Jackie. We haven't had anything since lunch and that was only a handful of granola and dried fruit."

"I know," she said deprecatingly, rubbing her stomach. "I recall that. Ugh. Go ahead, go."

"What's really troubling you?"

Jackie sighed. "Nothing. Everything. This whole thing is crazy... I'm feeling so frightened. I *hate* feeling this way – so dependant. I'm starting to feel afraid of my own shadow. Every time I turn around I see Bob Vance's mutilated body hanging in the woods. I see Samuel lurking behind every tree..."

"Do you want to turn back?"

"No, of course not."

Dean began unbuttoning his shirt. "Do you know how to use a gun?"

"What?!"

"A pistol. Are you familiar with one?"

"Yes... sort of. I used to go down to the Rod and Gun club with my dad and brother when I was a kid."

"Good." He reached under his shirt. "Take this. Careful now, it's loaded. The safety clip is here, and you loosen it like this. You have five shots, plenty enough to hit your target. Got it?"

"Yes. I guess so."

"Good. And Jackie? If in doubt, use it."

Later, when he came back with a rabbit under one arm, he asked if she wanted to keep the gun. "No," she said, returning it handle first. "You take it."

"Are you sure?"

"Positive. Just because I know how to use it doesn't mean I'm comfortable with it. It's better off with you.... but thanks for the offer."

"Ever skin a rabbit?"

"God, no."

"Watch closely. This is how it's done."

"Do I have to?"

Dean smiled. "No, you don't have to do anything you don't want to."

"Does that include eat it?"

He laughed, holding up the hare. "You say that now, but just wait 'til it's cooked. You'll be begging me for some. Roast rabbit is delicious."

She wrinkled her nose and stood up. "Do you mind if I wash up a little? I noticed a little brook over there."

"Were you wandering about?"

"A little. I was searching for berries." She held up the coffee cup shyly, the only thing she could think of collecting them in. "I think these are edible."

"Well, they're no dried prunes, but they'll do." He paused for a moment, carefully selecting his words. "I don't think it's a good idea."

"Why? I'll yell if anything's amiss."

"I saw footprints."

She sat abruptly. "Footprints? What kind of footprints?"

"Human. Part human, anyway. They were indistinct."

Jackie shuddered. "What does that mean?"

"Probably nothing. Just poor imprints, that's all. There were two sets. One of them was barefoot. And the other... I recognized the sole prints. From before, when I was tracking your party."

"What are you saying?" she whispered.

"Could be coincidence – somebody has the same sneakers, same size. But I think Hudson and Blume are in the area."

"No! How can that be?"

"I don't know. They weren't tracking us, at least directly. Their footprints came from a different direction. Apparently they weren't following any trail, just trekking straight through the bush. They probably don't know we're here. Yet."

"Let's get out of here!"

"No, it's safer here. My bet is they still think we're ahead, not behind. Of course, there's another possibility: they might not be tracking us at all."

"What do you mean?"

"They could be going to Devils Lake. On their own accord. Remember, that's where Hudson was leading you when he tried to kill you."

"But why? What's drawing them to Devils Lake? Could they be after Jesse?"

"I hope we find that answer when we get there. Whatever is happening at Devils Lake must be luring them as well. Our answers lay there."

"And our danger."

"Yes. And our danger."

**

At night, she called out to him, and Dean took her into his arms. Again they had coiled together, instinctively, even though Dean remained awake. They had agreed to sleep in shifts: two hours on, two hours off. It seemed safer that way. A good night's rest no longer seemed tantamount when so much danger lurked.

"Shhh," he murmured, stroking her hair. She had been dreaming, awful tormenting dreams about her brother and Bob Vance, and even Benta Sturm. They danced a macabre dance, their bodies hideous and decaying. They beckoned her, came closer and closer, holding out long bony fingers where the flesh hung in great, rotted globs.

More horrible than the putrefied vision was the urge she felt to join them. To dance with them. To move to the beat of the strange, hypnotic music. To be one of them.

"No!" she cried.

Dean shook her gently and she turned on him, fingers outstretched like claws. "No!"

"Shhh," he said again, holding her. "It's all right, just a nightmare. Open your eyes, sweetheart. It's me, Dean."

She woke, chest heaving. The dream faded but not the memory. "Oh, boy, that was truly horrible. The Quentin Tarantino of nightmares."

He held her against his chest, stroking and murmuring soothing words until he felt her breathing relax. Still he continued, until her breathing quickened again, and he looked at her with alarm.

"Make love to me," she whispered.

"No, it wouldn't be right. It's the dream talking. You don't know what you're saying."

She raised herself on one elbow and looked him squarely in the eye. "I know exactly what I'm saying. I need you to make love to me. Now. Please, don't make me beg."

"Are you sure this isn't just sleep-talking?"

"Absolutely sure." She reached downwards and found him, already aroused, and she stroked him wantonly. "See? Would I do this if I was sleeping? Now, are you going to fuck me or not?"

"Ahhh......." His breath caught, it had become difficult to talk, to think. "You'll regret it in the morning."

"No, I won't." She spoke softly, her fingers deftly moving in circles. His cock twitched and stiffened further. "Please," she whispered. "Who knows what tomorrow will bring? At least we can control tonight. I want you, Dean Stockton. I want you *inside* me, I *need* you inside me." Her mouth sought his, hungrily kissing his unshaven chin, searching upwards for his lips. "I need you."

Her words were his undoing. He rolled over so he was above her and his hand slipped down to caress her shoulders, to cup her breast. "You smell like the forest," he whispered. "Like pine trees and ferns... and, oh... like Heaven."

"So do you," she murmured. "Like Christmas." She guided him into her, unsheathed. It was wanton and reckless, irresponsible.

"Jesus," he groaned. "I should be using a condom."

"S'okay," she panted, pulling him closer, deeper. "I'm on the pill."

"Ahh," he groaned. His lips explored her jawline, her earlobes, her throat, before finally moving upwards and claiming her mouth. "I love a woman who plans ahead."

He was deep now, striking to her very core, filling her completely until she thought she'd lost her mind. She groaned and her eyes rolled back, and she grabbed his head, her fingers entangling in his long, tousled hair. "Mmm. Yes, don't stop. Ahhh...." She felt she should explain, she was on the pill not because she was rampant sexually but because... because... ah, who cared. Words and explanations no longer mattered. Were no longer technically possible. She pulled him closer, moaning, and lost all rational thought.

They made love to the beat of the music, to the heat of the night. And when it was over, and they lay spent, Dean reached for her and they made love again.

CHAPTER FOUR

Don Blume awoke slowly, coiled rigidly on the cold, hard ground. He couldn't remember getting there, didn't recall lying down to sleep the night before. In fact, all his recollections were dim.

He felt odd; different from before, but since he couldn't recall what *'before'* was like, he wasn't certain. His pants (he thought they were pants) were tight, and when he tried to stand up straight to remove them, he found it difficult.

Sometime during the long night his body had changed. Now, instead of standing tall, he was more comfortable hunching slightly, his arms trailing in front. His spine had become rounded, almost bulbous. Course hair covered his body – his bare back, his long arms, his face. Only his palms remained unchanged.

But his fingers! Elongated, with fingernails shaped into claws. He studied them with wonderment.

Then quickly lost interest. His newly changed body already seemed normal.

But the pants – they constricted. They hurt.

Don clawed at the offending garment, trying savagely to unfasten the odd round thing at the waistband. He howled his frustration, his rage, barely noticing the change to his vocal chords as he finally ripped the fabric off his hairy, stocky legs.

"Uh-uh-uh," he said.

He had lost the ability to speak.

"Come. We go," Samuel Hudson said, appearing regally. Sam pointed to the mountain before them.

"Uh-uh." Don sniffed the air. Something excited him – the wind, the faint scent of the female in the breeze. He remembered something dimly; some forgotten promise and he struggled to capture the image. For a fleeting moment he did: the female. She did this to him. All females were bad. All females were Mother.

Mother? What was that?

"Uh-uh." He shook his head. The female excited him. He would rut with her. Then he would kill her. Hunt, rut, kill.

Or maybe he would kill first, then rut.

"Uh-uh." He sniffed the air again. She was close. Samuel would lead him to her. She would be his.

Don tried to smile, but he had forgotten how.

"Some holiday this is," Ben muttered.

"What was that?" Arne asked. "Did you say something?"

"No." But he was *thinking* plenty. Something peculiar was happening to Arne, and even though he appeared normal, Ben knew the truth. Arne was different.

For one thing, he seemed driven. He insisted upon hiking the forest through the night. It wasn't easy, crashing through this bush. They weren't following a trail, yet Arne seemed to know precisely which way to go.

Early in the morning, while it was still dark, the terrain began to steepen and now they were climbing straight up. This was ridiculous. Where was the fishing? The lazing around and sleeping until noon that Arne promised him only yesterday? Arne had become a harder task master than Reginald K. Bloodsworth.

"Come on, buddy, keep up," Arne called from ahead.

Ben growled. *Stupid fucking cocksucker.* Where did he get off thinking he was the boss? Okay, technically he was, but since when did he start acting like it?

Since they'd entered this blasted forest.

Since they'd heard that freaky noise, that thump-thump-thumping sound.

Since that crazy old Indian appeared in the office a week ago.

Well, what was he going to do about it? No one said he had to follow orders from a crazed lunatic, even if that lunatic was his best friend. He could refuse to go any further. Just dig in his heels and tell Arne to go to hell. He could even take off – Arne was so goddamned far ahead, he probably wouldn't even notice. He could innocently claim to Bloodsworth they became separated – who would be the wiser?

Arne appeared before him, suddenly, startling the crap out of Ben. He'd been completely deaf to his approach. Arne's voice was stern: "Come on, Benny. We don't have all day. We have a rendezvous to make and we wouldn't want to miss it. Would we?"

"No," Ben answered meekly. He quickened his pace.

But inside he was wondering: *what rendezvous?* What the hell was Arne talking about?

**

They stood at the foot hills, staring at the mountain peak before them. It was the first time they'd clearly seen the apex, before it had been obscured by the surrounding forest and cloud cover. Dean reached for Jackie's hand. "This is all wrong," he whispered. "It doesn't even look like a mountain – look at how flat it is."

"Like it was sheared off."

"Reminds me of a volcano."

"Yes, like that crater on Maui."

"Haleakala," said Dean, nodding.

"How on earth are we going to get up there? We'll need a helicopter."

"No, I think we can make it. It looks steep but see over there?" he said, pointing. "That gorge winds its way up – like a natural trail. We'll try following that."

Jackie groaned. "How long will that take us?"

"Two, maybe three hours."

"My calves are aching already."

He grinned. "Are you sure that's all that's aching? Considering last night?"

"Umm..." Her face colored and she found herself studying the ground, her sneakers, the pretty little wildflowers lacing the forest floor. Anywhere but up. Last night had been.... explosive. Wild. Nothing prepared her for the total abandonment, all-consuming bliss. "Maybe a few other, uh, *muscles* I haven't used for a while."

"I like it when you blush. I must say naughty things to you every morning."

"Promise?"

He nuzzled her neck. "Are you always this bold, Ms. Hart?"

"When in Rome...."

"Mmm. Too bad I don't have any Italian blood in me."

"What! You're not Italian? Well, that's it, call the whole thing off."

"I can still manage a pretty respectable lingus alfresco."

"I believe you mean linguini alfredo."

"Nope." His tongue traced a light path down her neck, heading for her collar bone, circling the tender hollow above, until she elicited a slight moan, which prompted him to move lower. "I could show you... now."

She pushed him away, laughing. "I believe you, but truly, if we start that now, there is nooo way I'm making it up that final ascent. I will be a puddle of uselessness."

"A puddle, eh?" He sighed, considering. "You're right. Rain check?" His hands grazed lightly over her breasts. So taken by the travels of his tongue, she hasn't felt them slip under her shirt, her bra.

"Dean…"

"I know, I know. Let's get moving."

As he led the way, she remarked, "Speaking of moving, has anyone ever told you that your ass is spectacular?"

"Not since last night."

"Just making sure."

He turned and smiled, pointing to his groin. His erection was visible through his denims. "I'd love to continue exchanging banter…. but… you win, obviously. This is making it difficult to concentrate, let alone hike. Anymore and I'm likely to toss you down and take you right here."

She smirked. "Later?"

"It's a promise."

"Deal. By my account, you owe me a steak dinner, bubbly, breakfast *and* a sexcapade. That's quite a tally you're running, Mr. Stockton."

"No worries. I *always* pay my debts."

**

Three hours later they stood on the precipice, staring into the center of the crater. Neither spoke. They looked down with awe and dismay.

"What is it?" Jackie whispered, finally. Unconsciously her hand entwined with Dean's, but the warmth she felt did little to allay her dread.

"I'm not sure…. it looks different from anything I've ever seen."

"Like its own world."

"Or the center of our world."

His words shocked her. That's exactly what it looked like: the center of the world. Trees at the top of the crater gave way to deeply sloping sides. The landscape was barren, rocky… dry. It was as if the earth thrust forth from the core of the crater and pushed billions of tons of soil and rock outward, creating a mountain of worthless rubble, devoid of life.

But the nucleus of the crater was a different story. It was difficult to see from this distance, but it appeared the terrain altered radically. Instead of the surrounding wasteland, here the crater gave way to a platform of sorts. The colors, even from this far away, were explosive. Brilliant hues of reds and greens oscillated like the heavy air of an oasis. Blues intermingled with purples, and colors never seen before vibrated, gushing with an intense urgency from the vortex.

The chanting started low, then began to rise. It was the thumping sound a thousand times stronger, until it filled the crater and the valley beyond. It radiated with painful intensity, and instinctively, Jackie placed her hands over her ears to stop the pain.

"They know we're here," Dean shouted, and although she couldn't hear him, she knew what he was saying. It was in his expression, the same terror that echoed hers.

Then he grew excited and began to point.

Jackie followed his outstretched finger, squinting to make out the dancing figure below. Halfway between the crater's inner rim and the thriving center stood a body, piteously small.

Dean was yelling, shouting frantically. "What?" she called, and he repeated it, but she still couldn't hear.

She looked straight at him, concentrating on his mouth, watching the words as they formed.

"Jesse! That's Jesse!"

Then it stopped. Suddenly. Inexplicitly.

"That's Jesse. Wait here," he repeated. "I'll get him."

"No! I'm coming with you."

"No... stay here. It's too dangerous. I need you as backup. If something happens to me, I want you to run. Get the hell out of here and send help. This thing... I don't know what it is, but it wants us. We have a better chance of succeeding if we split up."

"Dean..."

"Please, Jackie. I need you stay here. If I have to worry about you, I won't be able to concentrate on getting Jesse."

"But..."

He kissed her quickly, hard. "There's no time. Look – he's moving. I have to hurry if I'm going to catch him before he gets to the center."

"What... happens then?"

He raked a hand through his blonde hair. "I don't know. God help me, but if Jesse reaches the center of that thing, I don't know what will happen." He passed her the gun. "Take this." Before she could object, he'd already turned and begun his descent, half-running, half-sliding.

**

The thumping seemed to spur Samuel on. "Uh-uh," Don grunted, clamoring after him. The black man was moving too fast; this steep hill was hard to climb. Don's shoes, like his pants, were long gone. His feet had grown, elongated like his hands, until they resembled hoofs, and the soles had become tough as leather. It seemed this atrocity should make climbing easier, but it didn't. He had trouble keeping upwards, and finally relented, letting his long arms rest on the ground.

That made a difference and he allowed his weight to shift, so his forearms were taking much of the load. Now it was easier. "Uh-uh-uh!"

Then he saw her. The female. Standing at the top of the hill, silhouetted against the brilliant sky.

And he smelled her. The womanly odor that made his loins burn. This Mother-thing, with her streaming juices beckoning him, taunting him.

Her back was towards him, three-hundred metres away, now two. She was watching something else, paying no attention to the din behind her, and Don concentrated on making his movements quieter. He was a hunter now. Stealthy like a cat. Vicious like a wolf. Ruthless like a man. His bare hoofs made no sound on the soil and he approached her quickly, her Mother-scent overwhelming him until his rage and frustration grew.

**

"Jesus, Arne? What the hell is this?" Ben looked at the jutting mountain before him. "I think we made a wrong turn."

They heard the thumping noise, starting small and growing louder. Arne smiled appreciatively.

"No. This is it."

"What? Are you fucking crazy?"

Arne turned to face him and Ben could see that yes, Arne was indeed crazy. "Jesus Christ, Arne."

Then his buddy approached him and Ben's face blanched white with fear. "Jesus, Arne... what are you doing? Arne? Put that stick down... Arne! No! Don't hit me.... ahhh!"

Ben stumbled backwards, tripping over a root. He fell hard, his hands too busy protecting his face from the raining blows to break his fall. "Stop," he cried, trying to scramble away. The stick keep striking, hitting his chest, his ear, now the back of his head. "Jesus... Arne... You're going to kill me!"

**

Jackie watched Dean make his descent, taking her eyes off him for a moment to scan the valley around her. Had she heard something?

No, just the wind rustling the trees around her. The few trees left on this craggy mountain of rock.

Just the breeze. The cool breeze which felt so good compared to this awful heat.

Nothing else. Not even the song of a bird or the buzz of an insect. Just her, alone with her imagination, standing at the edge of the world.

She patted the gun tucked into her waistband. That, at least, was real. Never a gun aficionado before, she was starting to appreciate their appeal.

She watched as Dean disappeared behind a boulder and breathed again when he reappeared. She wanted to shout out, to tell him to be careful but she knew her voice wouldn't carry. He was closing the gap to Jesse, the child seemed more interested on swaying than anything else, but still the expanse between them was vast. Jesse moved slowly yet steadily forward, and it was only a matter of time until the child reached the seething vortex. *Why was he doing it*? She wondered. *What drew him there?* The chasm between them seemed insurmountable.

"Please," she whispered. "Please."

She heard it again. A rustle. A definite rustle.

The breeze again?

No, the wind had died down. Completely.

She scanned the hillside. Nothing.

She patted the gun again, praying for Dean to hurry.

She thought of her brother, his ghostly apparition grotesquely disfigured. Had this... this seething pit of noise, vibration and color done that to him? She wondered if she'd ever feel safe again.

**

Oh, the glorious scent! He was close now, no more than twenty-metres, hiding behind a scrub of bush. The sun was in her eyes. He saw her looking but she couldn't see him.

If he still had control of his vocals, he would have laughed with glee. As it was he could only grunt softly.

Samuel had disappeared. He knew this should bother him, but it did not. The black man had simply continued walking while Don stopped to stalk his prey. Don supposed he was on the other side of the crater, but even that thought took too much effort so he let it go.

He sniffed the air. It was still; dead. Her scent was fading without the breeze to carry it, but that didn't matter – she was highly visible, even to his weakened eyes.

The prey turned her back to him and he thought about rushing her, catching her off balance. This excited him, so much that he almost gave away his position but he fought for control. She was so close now. Her tender neck was almost in his grasp and his loins burned urgently with the need to take her.

He couldn't wait.

She was his.

He began his attack.

**

The thumping noise began sharply, with no warning. It was different this time, harsher and louder. More urgent. Ben watched with amazement as his best friend's arm halted in midair.

It was all he needed to scramble away from the next deadly blow. He turned over and clamored to his feet in one fluid movement, moving quicker than he had since high school. He didn't spare a backwards glance, too intent on running for his life. He couldn't tell if Arne was in pursuit.... he just kept running through the trees, letting the branches tear at his face, stinging his eyes, not caring... not caring....

The thumping sound was gaining on him. He tried to cover his ears but lost his balance, stumbling slightly before regaining his footing. "No," he screamed, not sure what he was running from anymore. Everything was bad here. Everything was evil.

And it wanted him.

It needed his blood.

He thought about the photographs of Wendall Scott and Jerry Hackett. The mutilated images seared his brain and the truth hit him like a bolt of lightning.

Reginald K. Bloodsworth was wrong.

They were all wrong.

The old Indian wasn't crazy.

He wondered if he'd ever see his wife and kids again.

**

"No!" Jackie screamed, looking down the crater in horror. She couldn't believe her eyes.

Dean had stumbled, lost his footing, and was now tumbling wildly into the crater.

She saw him lash out, trying to latch onto something – anything – to break his fall, but the landscape was too barren.

It was like watching a horror show. She stood, powerless to help, but unable to take her eyes off the debacle.

He was falling quickly now, somersaulting and twisting down the steep hill. She winced as she saw him glance off the side of a boulder, ragdoll style. Then she saw him curl into a ball, keeping his limbs and head tucked in, tumbling.

Jesus. Could anyone survive a fall like that?

She hesitated for a moment, remembering his words: Run! Get help if anything went wrong. She took one last look and made her decision. She began to climb inside the crater.

The Noisy Thing started abruptly and the crater vibrated with the thumping sound.

She swallowed her fear and prayed she was doing the right thing, and began the perilous descent.

**

Don began his final attack, moving as stealthily as his misshapen feet would allow.

He saw his prey move. Watched in disbelief as she disappeared over the edge. Impossible! She hadn't seen him; his animal instinct assured him of that.

He threw back his head and howled his rage, but the sound was lost by the sudden arrival of the Noisy Thing.

He understood it well then. He knew what he must do.

What was left of Don Blume stood up, his wretched body mutilated into a grotesque animal form, swaying to the beat, and he began to follow his prey into the crater.

**

Ben Hoight fell again, closing his eyes for an instant, then opening them in disbelief. He blinked again and again, trying to dispel the haunting illusion in front of him.

He must be losing his mind.

That was the only logical explanation; he had gone mad.

What else could explain the sudden formation of dancers around him, a hideous mixture of man and beast?

They were chanting a strange music, writhing and twisting to the continued beat.

He closed his eyes to shut out the sight, and held his hands over his ears to keep out the infernal thumping noise, but nothing could disguise the scent: the smoky, burning odor of charred flesh.

**

Dean opened his eyes slowly, squinting upwards into the sky. For a moment he couldn't remember where he was.

Then it all came back. With horrifying clarity.

He had fallen. He craned his neck slightly to one side, gauging the distance to the top of the crater. From this angle, it appeared he had plunged a long way. He moved slightly and groaned.

Getting up wasn't going to be easy.

He thought of Jesse and tested an arm, then lifted himself up. Everything was bruised but nothing appeared to be broken.

A miracle.

"It's about time we had some good luck around here," he muttered, quickly scanning to assess the situation. Jackie had disappeared; he should be able to see her silhouette on the rim of the crater but it was as lifeless up there as it was down here – no wait! There she was. But why was she hunched over like that?

He frowned. No time to worry about Jackie. She was smart, she had a gun. She could take care of herself... for the time being.

It was Jesse he must concentrate on now. He saw the child clearly. He was much closer – his fall carried him quicker than hiking could have. He was near enough to call out, but the Noisy Thing was back and it made communication impossible.

He scrambled down the remainder of the hill.

Jesse, still swaying to that diabolical beat, would soon be within reach.

**

Jackie stopped. She saw Dean get up, watched him resume his quest. There was no need for her to go any further.

She watched carefully. He appeared to be limping, but otherwise uninjured. He had closed the distance between himself and Jesse dramatically. "One hell of a way to get down a hill, buddy," she said softly, allowing a small smile.

She took a final look downward, listening to the thumping noise. It was hideous, diabolical. The crater seemed to be seething with it. She shivered and decided to retrace her steps and wait for Dean and the boy at the top of the crater.

She turned, and walked head first into Don Blume.

**

They were writhing all around him, prodding Ben's flesh, and he shrank back in horror. He maintained a fetal position, closing his eyes tightly against the monstrosities before him.

But it didn't help. His eyelids did little to contain the horror; he saw as vividly as if his eyes were open.

There were many. They danced and stomped and flew about him, chanting in a foreign tongue. It made no sense, but still he knew what they wanted. Him.

He lay still, some distant part of his mind still scrambling to hatch a plan, find a method of escape, even though he knew it was hopeless.

He felt ill. He felt like soiling his pants. But he willed his mind to calm, just like the time he was caught cheating on a fourth grade arithmetic exam. He didn't crack then and he wouldn't crack now.

He forced his breathing to remain even and quiet. He thought of Margaret and the kids. He thought about the trip to Hawaii they always said they'd take, yet always put off for one more year. He thought of his sister who he hadn't seen in seven years, his sweet sister who married an awful drunk and ruined her life. He wished he'd had the chance to say goodbye.

He wished he'd had a chance to tell them all how much he loved them.

He forced himself to remain calm as he felt the beast dancers come closer, move in for the kill.

**

Dean was close now. He could see the child clearly... just a hundred metres, then less. "Jesse!" he yelled, but his voice came out weak and cracked. Better not waste energy.

The colors were brighter here. He was, perhaps, halfway to the center of the crater. Still too far to see anything clearly, but Dean sensed the writhing shapes on the platform. The thumping noise boomed loudly, echoing through the hollow, so instead of the thump-thump-thump he had grown accustomed to, a myriad of tiny thumps echoed back and intermingled with the stronger ones.

He felt his eyes shift to the center and quickly looked away. It was difficult; he wanted to look there... longed to look there. Something was drawing him and he fought it, afraid if he succumbed he would be lost for good. He strove to remain focused and to shut out everything but the essential facts.

Jesse was very near now. Dean almost had him. Could reach out and touch him, if only... if only he was a little closer. It was a matter of time, and Dean reached ahead, forcing his feet to move faster, stretching his fingers forward, grasping at Jesse's purple t-shirt, feeling the cotton in his fingers, gaining hold, feeling the fabric rip, feeling the despair and hopelessness as Jesse surged violently toward the center and slipped from Dean's grasp.

And then he was gone.

**

Don Blume had the advantage. He caught the female by surprise. He was uphill; thus his position was superior. She was fighting blindly, staring into the sun.

His ungainly bulk was now his ally and he threw his weight against her, grunting savagely.

He clawed her left shoulder, felt pleasure as her t-shirt tore, felt ecstatic as his scratches drew blood.

The fresh blood, intermingling with her Mother-juices was more than he could bear. He gripped her neck, his elongated fingers squelching her life. He must kill her quickly so he could rut with her.

He squeezed tightly, feeling her tender throat convulse, felt her cough and wheeze, and he grunted his satisfaction.

Her arms flailed madly, then he heard a noise. A loud sound, like an explosion. He grunted again and looked down, surprised to see a thick swath of blood staining his furry legs.

His blood.

How could this be?

Another explosion. Then another. But no more blood.

He stopped for a moment, still holding her throat, willing himself to think.

Then he saw the black thing in her hand, pointing at him, at his chest, and he understood.

A fire stick. A demon tool. That black thing was causing the explosions and making his leg bleed.

He saw her fingers tighten, saw her squeeze the black thing, and he shoved her hand aside. Another explosion followed, but this one went high, high into the sky, and he twisted her hand tightly until she squealed with pain and the black thing fell from her fingers, fell to the ground, and down, down, down the side of the crater.

He tried to grin, but it was impossible. Instead his mouth turned into a leer, showing sharp, pointy teeth.

He opened his mouth and began to move it downwards, towards her tender neck. He would rip the jugular open and taste the fruit of her warm blood, allow the sweet liquid to gush down his throat and into his belly.

**

Dean looked around wildly. Where could Jesse be? Here one second, gone the next. How could that be? Unless...

He wiped the dirt from his eyes and looked again, careful to keep his gaze from the center. There! A sudden ledge... an outcropping below, just big enough to hide a small boy.

It was worth a try.

Dean lunged forward and was rewarded with a flash of purple cotton. Jesse's shirt. He crouched, and there, underneath the outcropping, the small boy lay huddled and dazed. He took the child into his arms, cradling him, whispering.

"It's me, Sport. Uncle Dean. It's gonna be okay, you hear me, Sport? Uncle Dean's here and I love you and everything's going to be okay."

A flicker of recognition flashed in Jesse's eyes. "Uncle Dean?"

"Oh, thank God!" He nuzzled the boy's cheek.

Jesse opened his mouth but Dean silenced him. "Don't try to talk... not now. Let me get you out of here, before it's too late. We'll talk later. There'll be plenty of time later." He looked up at the top of the crater, searching for Jackie.

A flash of movement drew his eye to an area just below the rim. Two figures appeared in combat. He heard the gun, once, twice and then a third time.

His blood ran cold.

There was no way he could reach her in time.

He watch in disbelief as a third figure appeared on the rim.

**

Jackie felt the pressure on her throat, saw the monster's teeth approach and felt the blackness begin to overcome her.

She fought the sensation.

The pressure was unbearable, reinjuring her bruised throat and she twisted her head, feeling slight relief. The creature was hit, she was sure of it, could see his blood running freely on the ground. If she could just hold out a little longer, maybe he would weaken from loss of blood.

No such luck. He was already increasing the pressure, aware she'd gained a fraction of an inch by turning her head.

But she could see his leg now, a disgusting stocky leg with ape-like feet. She saw the wound and twisted sharply, bringing her left foot in contact with the raw flesh.

The creature groaned in agony but held fast. She kicked again, harder, then again. He howled, enraged.

But his grip was weakening. She brought her right hand up and slammed it into his face, aiming for the eyes.

He let go entirely and she lurched away, gasping, searching for a weapon.

The gun was gone. She'd heard it drop earlier, knew it was out of her reach forever, but still she searched.

The creature was reaching for her and Jackie looked back, appalled. His appearance was alarming, not just because of its hideous shape. She recognized those features, had seen them before. He reminded her of... no... It couldn't be.

But it was. This... aberration, for it couldn't be called animal and certainly wasn't human, bore a distinct resemblance to Don Blume.

And he was reaching for her again.

Jackie's fingers closed around a rock and she hurled it at him, hitting him squarely on the forehead. He howled again, but it didn't deter him. He was gaining....

She reached for another, groping, not finding anything useful. Scrambling madly, fingernails raking the dirt in an attempt for traction.

He had her by the ankle now, and she kicked back, striking him once more, but still he held fast. Then he stopped suddenly and she shook herself free, looking forward as the ground before her grew dark with shadow.

Jackie looked up with dread.

There, standing above her, his dark skin gleaming nakedly in the afternoon sun, was Samuel Hudson. He smiled widely, his large teeth dazzling in a huge, demonic smile, and he reached forward and picked Jackie up.

**

"No," cried Ben Hoight, finally, unable to take anymore. "Stop this insanity!" He stood, frantically. The ringed wall of faces parted. The thumping noise abated. He went forward to take his rightful place.

**

Dean cradled the sobbing child tightly against his chest. He started to climb, tried to go quickly, knowing he was too far to do anything but watch as the drama above him unfolded. All the while, at his back, he felt the magnetic pull of the crater beckon him.

**

"No," Jackie screamed, beating against Samuel's glistening chest. He tossed her aside and she scrambled up the edge, reaching the rim in a desperate attempt at escape.

She heard the beast-thing howl in rage, then in pain, and it came to her that Samuel hadn't been after her at all. It was Don he wanted, the beast-thing.

She paused, scarcely taking her eyes off the two combatants for the moment it took her to ascertain Dean was alright, that he was more than alright, that he was fantastic and held Jesse safely in his arms.

Her eyes flickered back to Samuel and the beast-thing. Samuel held it around its throat, just as the beast had done to her, and he carried it high, so the creature's feet were off the ground. The creature squirmed but Samuel held fast. Jackie watched in disbelief as Samuel made his way down the crater, dragging the beast-thing with him.

She held her breath as they neared Dean and Jesse. Saw Dean drawback, holding the child protectively, saw Samuel nod and the Don-thing growl, watched as the foursome passed each other, and shook her head in disbelief as Samuel continued toward the center of the crater.

There would be no further confrontation.

She hurried down the crater, ignoring Dean's motions to stay put. She couldn't remain apart from him any longer; felt a desperate need to be at his side.

When she reached him, finally, hugging and reigning kisses over his dirt encrusted face, and kissing the boy, they stood and took a final look at Samuel and Don, now approaching the center.

"Look away," Dean said after a moment. "Don't watch."

"But the colors..." She tore her gaze away, magnetised by the brilliance. "What is Samuel doing?"

Dean shrugged. "It appears he's going to the center."

Jackie shuddered violently. Dean shifted Jesse slightly, tucking him under one arm, and reached for Jackie. "Shhhh. It's over now. At least for us."

"And for them too." Jackie cautioned one last quick glance as she heard the Noisy Thing start again as Samuel dragged the screaming creature into the center. As the two figures disappeared, the thumping stopped abruptly, almost like a giant burp. The color that wafted up was black, then it dissipated entirely, surrounded once again by vibrant, opalescent hues.

When they reached the rim, they turned around for one last look. There was no sign of movement. All color had dissolved. Dean watched for a moment, and then said, "Well, that's it."

Jackie nodded. They began the long climb down the outside of the crater.

No one noticed the old Indian standing solemnly on the opposing edge, watching them with ancient eyes.

No one, except for Jesse.

His eyes were wide open, his mouth determined. Across the crater, he met the eyes of the ancient Indian and he tipped his chin slightly. This was not over.

It was only the beginning.

-The End-

The journey continues:

THE MANITOU: BOOK TWO

The Manitou, Book Two

'A vision came to him, and he gasped again. A vision so gruesome he couldn't face it. He fought the urge to bury his face under the bedcovers, to hide. He moved his tongue around his dry, chalky mouth, trying to force moisture into the cracks and crevices as he began to admit to himself that he'd made a terrible, horrible mistake.'

Escaping the Stein is only the beginning. Dean and Jackie's desperate quest to save Jesse Littlefoot takes the fugitives from perilous wilderness to bustling city, but there is no safe place to hide. Wanted for murders they did not commit, they are forced to elude the law and the long reach of a wealthy man who will stop at nothing to stop them.

Reginald K. Bloodsworth believes he has learned the ancient secret of the Stein. Sure, the exclusive logging rights to the valley are worth billions, but that's not what he's really after. Jesse Littlefoot is the key and he must find the child to keep his end of the unholy bargain with the ancient Spirits, The Manitou.

Dean and Jackie are forced to return to the Stein Valley to save Jesse. This time the stakes are higher: not only their own destinies linked to the Stein, but also that of mankind. The Manitou will fight to protect what is theirs, even if means the destruction of the human race.

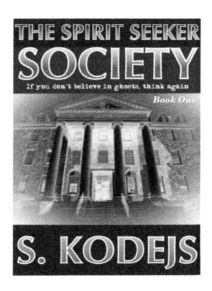

The Spirit Seeker Society

"Why not search for ghosts?" Maggie Bench suggests, almost as a joke. First year students at King's College were given the task of creating a campus society. With its rich historical background, Nova Scotia has its share of haunted sites. Surely the assignment will be a breeze. No one expects to find anything – it's not like ghosts are real, right?

The Spirit Seeker Society is born, as five students band together in a quest that will alter their lives. They'll learn that the dearly departed don't always stay buried. That corpses have horrifying secrets. And, that danger doesn't always come from the dead. Sometimes, it's the living who are the most terrifying of all.

The Spirit Seeker Society is a scary, tightly-woven tale that blends fiction with reality and brings historical events into the present.

If you don't believe in ghosts, think again.

Better Off Dead

Welcome to King's College, the bloody scene of multiple deaths. But that was so last season. It's a fresh school year and students are eager to begin.

Ben Bontel knew frosh week was a mistake. Others gaped at his tattoos, facial piercings and imposing frame like he was the most dangerous thing on campus. Little did they know how wrong they were. Pulled into a forbidden, secret society, Ben learns that the deceased rarely play fair and neither do the living.

Ti Ducasse has his own problems. How is he supposed to act like a normal student while fighting off the amorous advances of one pesky ghost? Sure, she was beautiful, even with the gruesome stab wound to her neck, but the last thing he needed to complicate his life was a girl. Especially a dead one. It was bad enough that she followed him everywhere, but was her dark baggage threatening his home and family?

From the barren, rocky shores of historic McNabs Island to the depravity of the Haitian *Tonton Macoutes*, the remnants of the previous Spirit Seeker Society join forces with the new recruits. This time, the stakes are higher. This time, demons have come to play. This time, no one is safe.

Buckle up and prepare for a wild, paranormal ride. BETTER OFF DEAD, Book Two of the SPIRIT SEEKER SERIES

Dance For The Devil

When offered his dream job, Jake Montclaire agrees to move across the country. And why not? His wife has left him, his teenage daughter Amy is taking rebellion to a whole new level and his twelve-year-old son Skeeter started wetting the bed, which he hasn't done since he was three. Maybe a fresh start is just what the Montclaire family needs.

It seems almost too perfect: a gorgeous house on the beach and a readymade social life offered up by his enigmatic boss, Gil Vandercamp. Jake is finally getting his life under control. Or is he? Amy comes home with a pentagram carved into her arm and Jake is alarmed: isn't that the sign of the Devil? "Just a fad," Gil assures him. "All the kids are doing it."

Amy disappears, and Jake finds evidence to suggest that cult activity is involved. And now the cult is targeting him, intent on ruining every facet of his life. As his life systematically unravels, Jake enlists the help of a neo-pagan witch to search the shadowy underworld of Satanism. What they learn terrifies them: Devil worshippers can be anyone: your boss, your friend, your next door neighbor. Their search leads them to a shocking discovery of ritual abuse and sex slaves, a world where nothing is what it seems and the players will stop at nothing to feed their obsession with serving Satan.

Eternity

Eternity. If you could live forever, would you? No matter what the cost?

When Gillian Leigh returns home to Cedar Island she finds the idyllic hamlet is not what it seems. Not only are her husband and baby acting strangely, so is everyone else. Toddlers able to perform unthinkable physical acts, schoolchildren with disturbing intellectual abilities, robotic adults studying her with an intensity that is frightening. It's as if all of Cedar Island has gone mad... or maybe it's just her. With a mental breakdown in the past, Gillian recognizes the symptoms.

10-year-old Stacy Kennedy has plenty of experience evading difficult situations, but what's happening on Cedar Island is beyond her capabilities. Not only is her drunken mother and current live-in boyfriend acting weirder than normal, so are her classmates. They want something from Stacy – but she's too afraid to find out what.

As the few uninfected residents of Cedar Island try to escape, their only avenue is abruptly cut off. Hunted by their families and friends, they must band together to uncover what horrors really lie at the center of Cedar Island. They must choose if the path to eternity is evil or simply another technological breakthrough.

About the Author:
S. Kodejs was born in Vancouver, British Columbia and currently lives in Halifax, Nova Scotia. She loves writing scary fiction with a socially conscious edge. "My best compliment is when my readers say they need to keep the light on after reading my work. I practise reading my material on my husband and three sons. It's hard to creep them out, so when I do, I know the material is working. My goal is to craft stories that give goosebumps while making the reader think, 'Hmm... What if that really happened?'" Hobbies include a love for travel, cheering on St Mary's University soccer and football teams, and hiking with her dog, Bru.

S. Kodejs Author page:
http://amzn.to/17MraLO

Facebook Page: Scary Reads:
http://on.fb.me/17WtyQb

The Spirit Seeker Society:
(The Spirit Seeker Series, Book One)
http://amzn.to/15pgLZY

Better Off Dead:
(The Spirit Seeker Series, Book Two)
http://amzn.to/14YsSsx

The Manitou, Book One:
http://amzn.to/ZY7kbI

The Manitou, Book Two:
http://amzn.to/13boOt0

Dance For The Devil:
http://amzn.to/ZxOKqR

Eternity:
http://amzn.to/13gJCvh

Printed in Great Britain
by Amazon

40767213R00152

How do you fight what no longer exists?

When Jaclyn Hart's brother mysteriously disappears while working for a logging company, she joins a seven-day guided tour to learn what really happened. Strange things start occurring in this northern rainforest: group members disappear while others exhibit alarming personality changes. Worse, an ominous thumping noise emanates throughout the forest, growing more forceful as the group gets closer to its spiritual center.

Dean Stockton is on his own quest. Although he'd sworn never again to set foot in the Stein, he is fulfilling a deathbed promise to teach a young orphan, Jesse Littlefoot, his Native heritage, and the two embark on a journey that pits them against an eddy of outside forces: governmental and corporate, the desecration of the rainforest, and a primal spirit that threatens to claim Jesse as its own.

As Dean and Jackie team up to save Jesse, they find themselves fighting for their own survival, and uncover some long ancient secrets that lay in the center of the Stein.

ISBN 9781492897033